THE PACKAGE INCLUDED MURDER

THE PACKAGE

Also by Joyce Porter

IT'S MURDER WITH DOVER
A MEDDLER AND HER MURDER
ONLY WITH A BARGE POLE
DOVER STRIKES AGAIN
THE CHINKS IN THE CURTAIN
DOVER AND THE UNKINDEST CUT OF ALL
SOUR CREAM WITH EVERYTHING
DOVER THREE
DOVER TWO
DOVER ONE

INCLUDED MURDER

A Novel of Suspense featuring
the Honourable Constance Morrison-Burke

by *Joyce Porter*

THE BOBBS-MERRILL COMPANY, INC.
Indianapolis / New York

Copyright © 1976 by Joyce Porter

All rights reserved, including the right of reproduction
in whole or in part in any form
Published by the Bobbs-Merrill Company, Inc.
Indianapolis   New York
Originally published in Great Britain by Weidenfeld & Nicolson
(London)
Designed by Jacques Chazaud
Manufactured in the United States of America

First U.S. printing

Library of Congress Cataloging in Publication Data

Porter, Joyce.
    The package included murder.

    I. Title.
PZ4.P8464Pac3   [PR6066.072]   823'.9'14   75-30854
ISBN 0-672-52171-7

THE PACKAGE INCLUDED MURDER

ONE

"Somebody is trying to murder me!"

Penelope Clough-Cooper mopped at her eyes with the edge of the sheet and risked a tearful glance at the circle of faces surrounding her bed. There wasn't much comfort there. The faces expressed dismay, horror, fear, curiosity, annoyance, disbelief—but she searched in vain for even a flicker of sympathy. When the English are on holiday (especially on a package tour for which they have paid in advance) the last thing they wish to encounter is trouble. And there is no getting away from it—the attempted murder of one of their number spelt trouble all right.

It was young Roger Frossell who found his tongue first. A long-haired, spotty-faced, eighteen-year-old man of the world and misogynist, his reaction was predictable. "Bloody women!"

"Oh, Roger dear, I do wish you wouldn't use that word!" His mother, standing next to him, softened the rebuke with an indulgent smile.

Ella Beamish made her observation without fear or favour, and, as usual, she spoke for herself and her husband. "The girl's delirious!"

Mr. and Mrs. Smith were still, even at that ungodly hour in the morning, chewing away like a couple of contented cows. They wrapped their arms tighter round each other and giggled. This, for the Smiths, was about par for the course.

It was left to the Lewcock brothers to come up with something more practical. Jim Lewcock, the elder of the two, shifted his weight unhappily from one bare foot to the other and thrust his hands deep into the pockets of his shabby raincoat. "Well, I suppose we'd better get 'em to send for the police, eh?"

I

"Judas Priest, Jim!" mumbled his brother. "You taken leave of your senses or something? Send for the bloody cops?" He appealed direct to Miss Clough-Cooper. "You just had a bit of a nightmare, didn't you, love?"

Penelope Clough-Cooper's chin rose, damp but defiant. "No, Mr. Lewcock, I did not! I have never had a nightmare in my life. I know exactly what happened. I woke up and sensed that there was somebody else in the room. I was therefore quite wide awake when I felt a hand pull the pillow from under my head. I began to scream, and then the pillow came pressing down on my face, covering my face and mouth. I couldn't breathe!" Penelope Clough-Cooper's voice broke as the distressing memories came flooding back.

And it is at this point that that well-known personality, the Honourable Constance Morrison-Burke, steps forward with an easy grace into her rightful place in the centre of our story. The Hon. Con, as she is known to admirers (and detractors) throughout the civilised world, was strikingly arrayed in a scarlet silk dressing gown liberally embellished with black frogging. She was much the most memorable figure in that rather plebeian hotel bedroom and now attracted every eye as she cleared her throat, loudly and awkwardly. Damn it all, if there was one thing the Hon. Con couldn't stand, it was seeing a woman cry! She bent forward and gave Miss Clough-Cooper a rough sort of thump on the shoulder. "Pecker up, old fish!" she advised in a gruff voice.

By the Hon. Con's side and slightly behind her stood her alter ego and maid-of-all-work, Miss Jones. Miss Jones had been dead against this package-holiday idea from the very start, but, as the Hon. Con was naturally footing the bill for both of them, her opposition had had to be more subtle than effective. Miss Jones was a passionate advocate of Budleigh Salterton, and nothing that had happened since the Hon. Con had first received those horrible travel brochures had tempted her to change her mind. Quite apart from the fact that anybody contemplating a holiday in the Soviet Union must, ipso facto, be courting disaster, there were other disturbing omens which Miss Jones had been overquick to point out. The holiday firm, for example, whose sheer cheapness had seduced the Hon. Con's bargain-loving heart, was called Albatross

Travel (Glencoe) Ltd., and, as Miss Jones would keep saying, if that didn't send cold shivers down your spine, nothing would. The final straw, though, had been reached in Moscow when Miss Jones had first discovered that there were exactly thirteen of them in their group. There had been quite a dust-up about this, and the Hon. Con had been reduced to telling Miss Jones quite bluntly that she reckoned such silly, superstitious fears came jolly ill from the daughter of a Church of England clergyman. Since then, Miss Jones had kept her lips huffily sealed.

Such Christian restraint didn't stop Miss Jones from thinking, though, or from keeping her eyes and ears open for more disasters. She noted the Hon. Con's kindly gesture now and pursed her lips. Instinctively distrusting the Clough-Cooper girl (if you could call a woman of at least thirty a girl), Miss Jones could only hope that dear Constance wasn't going to let herself get involved. Miss Jones just couldn't help recalling all those other occasions when . . .

Desmond Withenshaw took the floor. Even art teachers tend to like the sound of their own voices, and Desmond Withenshaw was no exception. "Frankly, I think we ought to make up our minds what we're going to do. And pretty damned quick!"

"What's the bloody hurry?" Tony, the younger Lewcock brother, had been reacting badly to Desmond Withenshaw ever since they had first come in contact with each other on the aircraft which had swept them through the Iron Curtain. It was a matter of chalk and cheese, except that neither of these commodities could strike the sparks off each other that the two men achieved without the slightest effort.

Desmond Withenshaw's lip curled. "Simply that time's running out, old chap!" He spoke in the kind of voice that he probably used when addressing educationally subnormal children. "The dezhurnaya po ploshshadke heard Miss Clough-Cooper's screams just as clearly as we did, and you can bet your boots that she's shot off to report what's happened to her superiors. As far as I'm concerned, the only surprise so far is that they haven't descended on us in force already."

A ripple of annoyance passed through the assembled company. Dezhurnaya po ploshshadke, indeed! Desmond Withenshaw spoke a few words of Russian, and, in the three short days they had been together, this feeble achievement had not endeared him to his fellow travellers. Why the blazes couldn't he say "floor maid" like everybody else?

The scrape of Norman Beamish's match as he lit yet another cigarette stoked more fires of irritation. The chap smoked like a blessed chimney!

Desmond Withenshaw grasped hold of the helm once more. "We've simply got to make up our minds about what we're going to do," he said again, scowling at the vacant faces that were turned towards him and sighing impatiently. "Look, if Miss Clough-Cooper persists with this story about somebody trying to kill her, the matter will have to be reported to the Russian police." He paused to allow this unpalatable fact to sink in. "Well, is that what you want?"

"Why not?" enquired his wife through a huge yawn. "If there's some maniac loose in the town, the sooner he's caught and sent to Siberia or whatever, the better."

Mrs. Frossell clutched at her son for support. "But they'll be *communist* policemen, won't they?"

Roger Frossell pulled away. "For Christ's sake, Mother," he said wearily, "what's that got to do with it? They'll be the criminal police, not the KGB."

"And I'll lay odds that won't make much bloody difference," growled Jim Lewcock. "Me, I'm not keen on getting mixed up with Red cops of any sort."

There were approving murmurs for this point of view, and it was left to Zoë Withenshaw, stifling her yawns and shaking herself into wakefulness, to take a less selfish line. "Oh, come on!" she said. "We can't just ignore the fact that somebody's tried to kill Miss Clough-Cooper. You can't hush up a thing like that."

"Why not?" demanded a voice deliberately made anonymous.

Zoë Withenshaw shrugged her shoulders. "Personally, I think it's our public duty to report what's happened to the appropriate authorities. I mean, suppose he tries again or attacks someone else? I don't want a murder on my conscience, even if you do."

"Hear, hear!" approved Norman Beamish loudly, and then fell silent under his wife's basilisk glare.

The Hon. Con ranged herself staunchly on Mr. Beamish's side. "Think Mrs. Withenshaw's got something there!" she boomed.

"After all, we are representatives of England in a foreign country, and we shouldn't shirk our duty just because we've got to deal with a bunch of lousy commies. Besides, if we let this alien brute get away with it, there's no telling how many defenceless women he'll desecrate with his lascivious hands."

Penelope Clough-Cooper wriggled impatiently. "I don't know why you're all assuming that the man who attacked me is a Russian," she said crossly. "I never said he was."

"Well, I hope you're not suggesting it was one of us, love!" Jim Lewcock chuckled patronisingly. "I know our Tone here's an oversexed young devil, but he's got his hands full with this new Intourist guide they've given us. Well, you've seen her, haven't you? Talk about . . ."

The Hon. Con. blew her nose in a loud and resounding clarion call. It was one way of putting a stop to Lewcock Senior's disgusting innuendoes. She had already pigeonholed both the Lewcock brothers as a couple of foul-mouthed oafs as soon as she'd laid eyes on them, but she had another reason for butting in and putting a sock in Jim Lewcock's wheel. The Hon. Con.'s finely chiselled nostrils had caught an intriguing whiff of mystery in Penelope Clough-Cooper's remarks—a whiff that other, less sensitive noses might have missed.

Ella Beamish shivered. "I'm getting quite cold," she complained. "Norman, go and get my white cardigan, will you? It's in the blue suitcase. *Norman!*"

"Just a minute, dear!" Norman Beamish was looking at the Hon. Con. "Were you going to say something, Miss Morrison-Burke?"

"Have got a couple of questions I'd like answered," admitted the Hon. Con with a quasi-embarrassed laugh. She could behave quite tolerantly towards the male sex if only they showed a bit of respect. She turned to the young woman on the bed. "You believe that an attempt was made to murder you tonight, eh?"

"I *know* an attempt was made to murder me!" snapped Penelope Clough-Cooper. "How many more times? Look"—she held up the murder weapon—"this is the very pillow he tried to smother me with. If I hadn't all but screamed the . . ."

"And you suspect that this somebody—let's call him Mr. X—is not a Russian?"

"Yes."

The Hon. Con narrowed her eyes shrewdly. "Because this is not the first attempt that's been made on your life, eh?"

Penelope Clough-Cooper's face suddenly crumpled. "They've tried to kill me twice before!" she wailed, her voice cutting through the murmurs of consternation that arose round her bed. "That's how I know it must be one of us."

All hell broke loose. Those who weren't heatedly disputing the logic of Miss Clough-Cooper's deduction were loudly objecting to having the finger of suspicion pointed at them. One or two even found time and breath to label Miss Clough-Cooper a stupid bitch of a troublemaker who should go get her head examined. Such were the passions aroused that the honeymooning Smiths actually stopped mauling each other for a full thirty seconds.

The Hon. Con was experiencing difficulty in making herself heard. "Hey, steady on, chaps!" she bawled in a voice that was probably audible in Outer Mongolia. "Quiet, please! Oh, come on, you rotters, put a sock in it!"

Her appeals eventually produced the desired effect, and gradually the howls toned down to sullen mutterings.

Mrs. Beamish was still very bitter. "I do think the least she could do is apologise," she said angrily before transferring her wrath to her husband. "And if you were anything of a man, Norman, you'd see to it that she did! Most husbands would be ashamed to stand idly by while their wives were being insulted."

Norman Beamish was too sensible to answer back, and let Desmond Withenshaw take the centre of the stage again. "I'm afraid this changes the whole complexion of the problem," he announced loudly, "and I, personally, don't go much on our chances if we ourselves are going to be the object of the Soviet police's investigations. They will almost certainly insist on detaining us all until they have discovered the guilty party, and God only knows how long that might take. We could be held on suspicion for months. Now, I don't know about the rest of you, but my time happens to be extremely valuable. I work to a very tight schedule, and I've got commitments back in England that I simply can't afford to miss. The last thing I can contemplate is sitting locked up in some god-forsaken prison while some Russian bobby decides which one of us to pin the crime on."

Desmond Withenshaw's mode of expression might have verged on the pompous, but his sentiments found an echo in many hearts. It seemed that all of them had pressing engagements back home in England, and it was imperative that their sojourn in the Soviet Union should not last one second longer than the prescribed fourteen fabulous days. This consensus emerged with quite remarkable clarity and speed. Hard luck on Penelope Clough-Cooper and all that sort of thing, but nobody—but *nobody!*—had any intention of tangling with the Russian police on her behalf. No, thank you very much! If somebody was trying to murder Miss Clough-Cooper, Miss Clough-Cooper was just going to have to grin and bear it.

A gleam came into the Hon. Con's eye. She leaned forward to give the disconsolate-looking Miss Clough-Cooper another encouraging pat. Miss Clough-Cooper, taken by surprise, no doubt, jerked her arm away as though she had been stung, but the Hon. Con didn't appear to notice. "You're in luck, m'dear," she said with a grin. "It just so happens that I am not inexperienced when it comes to the successful investigation of murders. You ask old Bones, here! She'll tell you how many times the police have come round, hammering at my door and begging me to . . ."

We shall never know to what extent the Hon. Con was prepared to imperil her immortal soul (to say nothing of Miss Jones's), because it was at this precise moment that the hotel floor maid chose to fulfil Desmond Withenshaw's predictions.

The floor maid had been fast asleep, curled up on an old chaise longue behind a screen, when Penelope Clough-Cooper's bloodcurdling screams had rent the night air of Alma Ata. The poor woman had exploded into wakefulness with all her worst fears about foreign tourists confirmed. As she fought her way out of the sheet in which she had been enfolded, she heard doors opening and voices raised in querulous complaint. Before she could get free, she'd one of those accursed capitalist bloodsuckers actually standing over her and shouting. She didn't know what he was saying and she didn't much care. She could recognise danger when she saw it. The man went away, and the floor maid realised that the hotel corridor had emptied. It would appear that they had found the room of the screamer and entered it. Gradually the screams died down into heavy sobs.

7

The floor maid seized her chance and made her getaway. There was only one thing to do with an emergency like this, and that was shove it onto somebody else's shoulders as soon as possible. The Siberian prison camp, the floor maid reminded herself grimly as she headed for the stairs, was never nearer than when you'd got your quota of bedrooms full of double-crossing, double-dealing enemy agents from the accursed West.

Unfortunately, this was an attitude of mind that others shared, and none of the hotel's administrative staff (including the statutory KGB man) seemed at all willing to help out, and there was much metaphorical washing of hands and passing on of the baby. Eventually the hotel director's wife came up with the solution. "Why don't you let Ludmilla Stepanovna deal with it?" she had asked, and the entire Kazakhstan Hotel collective had sagged with relief. Of course! Why hadn't they thought of Ludmilla Stepanovna before? Who better than the Intourist guide herself to deal with these bloody foreigners? They were all so delighted with the hotel director's wife's brilliant idea that they overlooked the fact that it was half past one in the morning and that Ludmilla Stepanovna lived right on the other side of the town. With the best will in the world, Ludmilla Stepanovna couldn't get to the hotel in under three quarters of an hour—and who said Ludmilla Stepanovna would have the best will in the world, anyhow?

The hotel director resolutely put these quibbles right out of his mind and reached for the telephone. Provided he could raise the night operator, they were home and dry!

TWO

"What happens, huh?" Ludmilla Stepanovna, who in spite of a certain florid charm looked as though she could spit nails, was a great one for asking questions. She was notably less able, though, when it came to listening to the answers, but she recognised that this was no time to change one's spots. She made a quick head count. Thirteen! That meant—slava borgu!—that nobody had escaped. She looked round the room. No signs of drinking or gambling. They must be having a protest meeting. Of all the cheek! The sooner Ludmilla Stepanovna put a stop to that kind of subversive nonsense, the better!

Now, what was all this they were babbling about? Nightmare? Nightmare? What in the name of all the Supreme Soviet was a nightmare? Ludmilla Stepanovna scowled. Even the best linguists have their off days, and for the moment she couldn't for the life of her remember what a nightmare was. Not that she was going to let a little thing like that throw her.

"To your beds!" she barked, and then, recollecting that she was addressing her country's honoured and paying guests, added in a slightly modified tone, "Tomorrow is a hard day."

The windows stopped rattling.

"Er—yes," said Desmond Withenshaw, avoiding everybody's eyes. "Well, I don't think there's anything else we can do here, is there?" He pushed his wife ahead of him. "Well"—he smiled ingratiatingly at Ludmilla Stepanovna—"spakoyni nochi!"

If he had addressed her in Swahili she couldn't have displayed less comprehension, and Desmond Withenshaw took his departure in an embarrassed silence. The other Albatrossers didn't linger. They trooped out of Penelope Clough-Cooper's bedroom and tried to look as though the word *police* had never quivered on anybody's lips. Only the Hon. Con stood her ground.

Ludmilla Stepanovna glanced at the distressed woman on the bed and summed up the situation in one shrewd, experienced, and probably actionable sniff. She also curled her lip.

It was lucky that these subtleties went clean over the top of the Hon. Con's Eton-cropped head. "Think I'll just hang on for a couple of secs," she explained blandly. "Miss Clough-Cooper's nerves are shot to pieces, don't you know? I'll stay and do a bit of the old hand-holding."

Ludmilla Stepanovna nodded all too understandingly. The one in the bed was quite pretty, she supposed, but far too thin for her taste. Anyhow—Ludmilla Stepanovna stiffened her backbone—this was no time for dalliance. She had bigger fish to fry and—chestnoye slovo!—those uncultured hotel imbeciles were going to rue the day they were born. By the time Ludmilla Stepanovna had finished with them they'd think twice before rousting a full colonel in the Secret Police out of her bed in the small hours of the morning for nothing.

She opened the door. "I wish you a good night!" she proclaimed formally before closing the door with a bang behind her on a widely grinning Hon. Con and a somewhat apprehensive Penelope Clough-Cooper.

Down the corridor in the double room which for reasons of economy she shared with the Hon. Con, Miss Jones struggled to stay awake. On the face of it she shouldn't have had much difficulty, motivated as she was not only by jealousy and loyalty but by abject terror as well. Miss Jones had not had one carefree moment since she had set foot in the Soviet Union. The Hon. Con might laugh (indeed, the Hon. Con *had* laughed) but Miss Jones stuck to her guns. Nobody was safe in that dreadful country, and, as a clergyman's daughter, Miss Jones was doubly at risk. Everybody knew what the communists had done to the Church since the Revolution, and it was not the kind of record that permitted an unmarried lady of nervous disposition to rest easy in her bed at night.

In these circumstances, and taking one thing with another, Miss Jones should have had no trouble in tossing and turning until she was satisfied that the Hon. Con was safely tucked up in the other twin bed. The flesh, however, is weak, and the flesh of reluctant tourists is perhaps weaker than most. After a mere two and a half days of relentless sightseeing, Miss Jones was frankly worn out. Mentally, physically, and emotionally. She fought a gallant rear-guard action, but gradually sleep overcame her. She'd just, she told herself, rest her eyes for a couple of minutes, and . . .

Russian plumbing is pretty noisy at the best of times.

The Hon. Con emerged from the bathroom and gave a startled Miss Jones a friendly nod. "That ball-cock thing's gone for a Burton again," she announced. "Hope I didn't wake you, Bones!"

Miss Jones gradually relaxed her grip on her heart. No doubt the beating would steady down to something approaching normal. Eventually. "What time is it, dear?"

The Hon. Con consulted Big Ben—her jocular and not entirely inappropriate nickname for her wristwatch. "Twenty-five past three."

Miss Jones stifled her groan. "Have you been with Miss Clough-Cooper all this time, dear?"

The Hon. Con stripped off her dressing gown and stood revealed in all the glory of blue-striped army-surplus pyjamas. She did a couple of perfunctory physical jerks and then dived into bed. "Had to get all the gen, old fruit. And Penny had quite a tale to tell!"

"Miss Clough-Cooper struck me as a rather excitable young woman," observed Miss Jones sourly, noting the familiarity of that "Penny" but forbearing to comment on it. She plumped up her pillows with some vigour.

"Can you blame her?" asked the Hon. Con reasonably. "I had the dickens of a time gaining her confidence, I can tell you. Had to tell her all about my experience in the investigating of murders. Must say, she seemed quite impressed." The Hon. Con smirked a sort of deprecating smirk. "Said she hadn't realised I was a kind of unofficial advisor to our local CID."

"You're not, dear!" Miss Jones's affection for the Hon. Con was not allowed to blind her entirely to the latter's faults.

"Near as damn it!" protested the Hon. Con. "Is it my fault that the police force is so hide-bound and pigheaded? And I did solve two murders, Bones! Even you've got to admit that."

Miss Jones wasn't, actually, prepared to admit anything of the sort, which was a wee bit naughty of her, as the Hon. Con's claim was not without some justification. Instead, she tried to change the subject slightly. "Why don't you just concentrate on writing your book, dear?"

"Book?" The Hon. Con looked genuinely bewildered. "What book?"

Miss Jones could have willingly shaken her until the teeth rattled in her head. "The book you were going to write about life and society behind the Iron Curtain, dear," she said through tightening jaws. "That's why we came to Russia in the first place. After you'd decided to become a writer and when you'd reached the conclusion that novels weren't your cup of tea. Don't you remember, dear, how you said that you couldn't write a white-hot exposé of the Soviet system unless you'd seen for yourself how they mismanaged things? Your point was that . . ."

"All right, Bones, all right! No need to go on all night about it!" The Hon. Con sat hugging her knees while she thought up some face-saving way out of this one. "Being an author's all right," she said at last, "but crime's my real métier." She made the whole thing sound rather pathetic.

Miss Jones sighed and reflected that knowing a problem didn't solve it. And the Honourable Constance Morrison-Burke certainly had problems.

The Hon. Con had been born not only into the purple but into considerable wealth as well. It would be naïve to claim that these two blessings had ruined her life, though they were certainly far from having enhanced it. The Hon. Con was a positive powerhouse of energy, inventiveness, and intelligence, and if she could have found an outlet for these qualities, she would have been an asset in any society. If she had married, for example, some of the verve and dash might have been soaked up in bossing a husband and kids around. If she had been an impoverished nobody, she could have worked off some of the surplus by carving out a career for herself. But what do you do when you're an unplucked rose and already have an annual income many a county borough council would envy?

Not that the Hon. Con took all this lying down. On the contrary, she tackled her problems with such enthusiasm and violence that the pieces hadn't yet been put together. Plunging into voluntary work, the Hon. Con joined all the right societies and wrecked them in days rather than weeks. Looking for a hobby, she became a member of clubs which almost immediately sank without trace and with all hands. Unfortunately, Totterbridge, where she lived, was only a small provincial town, and its resources were limited. In a distressingly short space of time the Hon. Con had gone through the lot, and there was no cultural, educational, recreational, sporting, or charitable organisation which wasn't left licking its wounds. The Hon. Con, on the other hand, hadn't changed at all and was still frantically searching for something worthwhile to do. It was during this quest—and really quite fortuitously—that the Hon. Con had found herself involved, on two separate occasions, in the investigation of a murder. The police hadn't liked what they referred to as the Hon. Con's unwarranted interference, but she didn't let little things like that stand in her way. She had learned in the hard school of personal experience that hardly anybody accepted her cooperation except under duress, and the realisation that it was her vocation in life to be a private detective lent power to her elbow. A neo-Lord Peter Wimsey— that's really how the Hon. Con saw herself. An aristocrat of the deductive process, wealthy, courageous, intelligent, and completely unhindered by all those mundane considerations which prevent the rest of us from living out our fantasies.

There was one snag in this scheme which will not have escaped the discerning reader. Small country towns (even including the outlying villages) don't have all that many murders. Almost before she knew what had happened, the Hon. Con found herself back with her perennial problem of underemployment, and, after her last murder case (for the solution of which she received not one jot of credit from the local police), she was forced to turn back to sport again and for a time had tried to organise a ladies' Rugby football league. She had not succeeded, and from sport she had finally descended to rock bottom and announced her decision to become a writer.

With this sort of background, it was fairly obvious that the Hon. Con wasn't going to let Penelope Clough-Cooper slip through her fingers.

"Can't just pass by on the other side, Bones," she said in a quasi-religious appeal deliberately calculated to wring Miss Jones's tender withers. "That girl's in deadly danger."

"Is she?"

"I made her tell me all about these two previous attempts on her life." The Hon. Con's eyes sparkled. "Jolly fascinating!"

Miss Jones sighed and wrapped her mohair bed-jacket tightly round her shoulders. "Are you sure it's not all her imagination, dear?"

It was the opening the Hon. Con had been angling for. "Well, now, it just might be, Bones," she lied easily. "Listen, I'll tell you just what she told me, and see what you think, eh?"

Miss Jones acknowledged, with a martyred smile, that it was a fair cop.

The Hon. Con came and sat on the foot of Miss Jones's bed. She had already searched the room for hidden microphones, without success, but she didn't believe in taking needless risks. "Both the earlier attempts," she began, "took place in Moscow. The first one was the very day after our arrival, and it happened in that GUM department store place. Remember GUM, Bones?"

"Of course I do, dear! It was that huge place on the Red Square opposite the Kremlin. Like a bazaar. Oh, it was horrible! All those dreadful crowds, pushing and shouting. It wasn't a bit like Harrod's."

"Penny Clough-Cooper claims that somebody tried to shove her over the railings on the first floor. Funny way to try and bump somebody off, don't you think? Well, what with all those milling crowds and everything, she naturally didn't see who it was. Just felt somebody trying to push her over. She struggled a bit, seemingly, and whoever it was sort of got the wind up and cleared off. Anyhow, there didn't seem to be anybody looking guilty when she finally managed to turn round. Well, she got out of the place as soon as she could, and when she'd cooled down a bit she began to think that her imagination was running away with her. Basically she's a deuced levelheaded lass, you know."

In spite of several good resolutions to the contrary, Miss Jones found herself getting involved. "But not everybody in our holiday group went to the GUM stores, did they, dear? It was after we came out of Lenin's mausoleum. Now, somebody—Mr. Beamish, was it?—said he wanted to go and see the History Museum and—"

"All right, all right!" interrupted the Hon. Con rudely. "Already worked that out for myself, old girl—thank you very much! Still"—the Hon. Con didn't overlook the chance to improve the shining hour—"glad to have you on my side, eh? Now, if you really want to lend a helping paw, how about taking down a few notes for me?"

"Oh, Constance dear, must I?" Miss Jones shied fretfully at the thought of moving out of her warm and comfortable bed.

The Hon. Con placed one foot on the floor. "Not if you don't want to," she said, taking care not to move too swiftly. "Just tell me where I can find a pencil and a bit of paper and I'll manage for myself."

Miss Jones was naturally across the room and opening a suitcase before the Hon. Con had finished speaking. The thought of having all her careful packing tossed to the four quarters of the globe lent wings to Miss Jones's feet. "Go on with your story, dear!" she called back across her shoulder.

The Hon. Con sank back contentedly, confident that the day had not yet dawned when she wasn't at least a couple of jumps ahead of poor old Bones. "The next attempt on Penny Clough-Cooper's life took place yesterday."

"Our second day in Moscow?" Miss Jones looked up. She had been carefully removing a number of packages from the suitcase and laying them equally carefully on a chair. Every package was neatly wrapped either in tissue paper or in a transparent plastic bag. "Fancy!"

"Our second day in Moscow," agreed the Hon. Con. "Though, if you remember, we spent most of our time out at that flipping old monastery place."

"Zagorsk!" sighed Miss Jones, whose mind, being totally uncluttered with the problems of social-survey authorship, was free to retain things like the names of what they'd seen. "The Trinity-Sergius Monastery!" She sank back on her heels, still lost in wonder. "Wasn't it simply marvellous?"

The Hon. Con couldn't see anything marvellous about a collection of mouldy old churches, but she wasn't going to be outdone by Miss Jones in aesthetic appreciation. "Smashing!" she said. "However, it was when we got back to Moscow that the trouble started."

"Oh, you mean that argument at the railway station, dear?" Miss Jones stared in bemusement at an oddly shaped bundle. What on earth . . . ? Her face cleared. Spare bedsocks! Of course! "When the guide told us we'd got to find our own way back to the hotel by Underground? I must say, I thought it was a bit of a cheek, but I didn't think there was any call for Mrs. Beamish to fly off the handle like that. After all, the Underground system is supposed to be one of the sights of Moscow."

"Hm, she did get a bit aerated, didn't she?" The Hon. Con had a quiet snigger to herself as she recalled Mrs. Beamish's outburst. "Mind you, Bones, we are supposed to be on a conducted tour. I mean, you don't expect to be abandoned in the middle of a hostile city while the blooming guide slopes off home for an early evening, do you? And old Ma Beamish really was worn out. All she wanted was to get back to the Metropole as soon as poss and get her shoes off. That's why she made her husband take that taxi. I don't know why she bothered coming out here," the Hon. Con added righteously, "if she doesn't want to see things."

"Oh, it was her husband's idea," said Miss Jones, who attracted gossip like a magnet attracts iron. "He was very keen, she said. Ah!" She pounced triumphantly and seized one of the bundles. What a silly old thing she was! Fancy forgetting that she'd packed the writing pad with the box of Auld Tam's Homemade Scotch Oat Cakes! It was a good thing that her head was fastened on! Now—a pencil! Oh, yes—in her handbag, of course! She began to replace the things she'd taken out of the suitcase. "Miss Clough-Cooper didn't return by taxi though, did she, dear?"

"She jolly well didn't!" said the Hon. Con, waxing somewhat indignant at this slur on Penny Clough-Cooper's character. "She's like us—dead keen to see every aspect of Soviet life."

Or too mean to pay for a taxi, thought Miss Jones—and then blushed fiercely at her disloyalty. To cover her confusion she relocked the suitcase and scuttled back to bed. "Was Miss Clough-Cooper attacked on the Underground, dear?"

"She certainly was, Bones! Makes you wonder what the world's coming to, doesn't it? I mean, in England you'd expect it. Any woman who ventures onto the Tube in London takes her honour in her hands, so I'm told. The whole network's positively riddled with those disgusting men in dirty raincoats who . . ." The Hon. Con remembered Miss Jones's susceptibilities in time. "Well," she concluded lamely, "you'd think things'd be different in Russia."

"The Underground was very crowded," remembered Miss Jones unhappily. She had not enjoyed her first and abrasive contact with the ordinary people of the Soviet Union. Not that anybody, she acknowledged rather sadly, had actually tried to . . . "Er— what happened, dear?"

"To Penny Clough-Cooper?" The Hon. Con was doing a few push-ups to while away the time. "Well, you know how we all got split up even before we'd gone through those stupid turnstiles where you have to drop your money in. It was worse than a blooming Rugby scrum," added the Hon. Con—and she spoke as an expert.

"You and I didn't get separated, dear," said Miss Jones fondly. "I hung on to the belt of your raincoat. My word, it would take more than the might of the Muscovy rush hour to part us!"

"Poor old Penny Clough-Cooper wasn't so lucky," grunted the Hon. Con, and decided that bicycling on her back was more trouble than it was worth. She came up for air. "By the time she got down on the platform, she said she couldn't see hide or hair of any of us. Couldn't see much of those famous chunks of marble they're so blooming proud of, either," added the Hon. Con with a snigger. "Packed like sardines in a tin, was how she expressed it. Deep in the bowels of the earth and surrounded by a mob of screaming peasants. And she was in much the same boat as us, Bones. No idea where the flipping heck she was going. You would think"—the Hon. Con interrupted her secondhand story to voice a complaint that many a tourist in the Soviet Union had voiced before her—"you would think they'd use the same blooming alphabet as us, wouldn't you?"

"They're a very difficult people," sighed Miss Jones. "Everybody says so. Well, Miss Clough-Cooper reached the platform, dear. Then what happened?"

"She stood there, surrounded by the plebs, until a train came roaring in. Everybody surged forward, like they do, but Penny Clough-Cooper felt something more. Somebody was deliberately shoving her, hand in the small of her back, as hard as he could towards the edge of the platform. Gruesome, eh? If the poor lass hadn't grabbed hold of a nearby soldier and hung on for dear life, she'd have been forced right in the path of the incoming train. Makes the blood run cold to think of it."

Miss Jones busied herself opening the writing pad and taking the blue plastic top off her ball-point pen. "Clung on to a *soldier*, did you say, dear? Fancy!"

The Hon. Con scowled. "You've got a mind like a cesspool, Bones!" She climbed back into her own bed. "Anyhow, are you ready to take a few notes?"

Miss Jones held her writing pad aloft.

"Right! Well, I propose to work on a simple process of elimination," announced the Hon. Con grandly. "Don't doubt but that'll drop the murderer into our laps as easy as shelling peas. Now, we can forget this suffocation lark tonight, because any one of our group could have done that. But the two previous attempts—well, they're a horse of a different colour, because we split up on both occasions. Not everybody visited that GUM shop and not everybody travelled by Underground. You following all this, Bones?"

Miss Jones wished that, just once in a while, the Hon. Con would refrain from treating her as though she were the village idiot. "Yes, dear, I'm following you."

"Whacko! Well, I suggest you make a start by writing everybody's name down in a list."

Miss Jones's lips grew thin. "I've already done that, dear."

"Have you? Good show! Well, let's deal with this GUM incident first. Stick a G after everybody who went to the shop and an M after those who preferred that crummy old museum. Now, who went where?"

"You and I, dear," said Miss Jones, wielding her ball-point pen with a flourish, "both went to GUM, so we're G's."

The Hon. Con let loose a guffaw of approval. "That's the stuff, Bones! No fear or favour, eh? Now, who else?"

"The Withenshaws went to the museum," said Miss Jones crisply.

"And so did the Beamish couple." The Hon. Con grinned. "Easier than falling off a chair! Who else?"

Miss Jones crimped her lips distastefully. "The Lewcock men?"

"Museum, too."

"The Frossell boy and his mother came with us, didn't they? I remember thinking how sulky he looked. What about the Smiths?"

"God knows!" said the Hon. Con, who disapproved of the Smiths. "I don't remember seeing that soppy pair at all after lunch."

"Oh, they were definitely ahead of us in the queue when we went to see Lenin's tomb, and I really did think that their behaviour was quite deplorable. I know it isn't exactly a church, but . . ."

"Stick 'em down as GUM!" ordered the Hon. Con. "I can't see 'em bothering with a museum, myself. In fact, I'll lay odds they shot back to the hotel and into bed. Nauseating!"

"They are married, dear."

"Says who? You can buy wedding rings in Woolworth's, you know. Anyhow"—the Hon. Con dismissed the obnoxious subject from her mind—"is that the lot?"

"Yes, dear. The Smiths, the Frossells, you and me, and Miss Clough-Cooper to the GUM department store."

"Okay!" The Hon. Con nodded with great satisfaction. "Now let's do the Underground. That's you and me again, of course, and Penny Clough-Cooper."

Miss Jones forced her eyelids up. It really was very late and she really was very tired. "The Smiths returned by taxi," she said, stifling a yawn. "That I do remember. And so did the Beamishes, because it was Mrs. Beamish who broached the idea of going back by taxi in the first place." There was a certain wistful note in Miss Jones's voice. She'd been pretty weary herself after their strenuous expedition to Zagorsk and would have been grateful to have been spared the rigours of the Moscow Underground in the rush hour.

"The Withenshaws came with us," said the Hon. Con. "And so did those ghastly Lewcock men. I remember them specially because that oldest one kept on talking about finding a gents' loo at the station. They are a foul-mouthed couple, aren't they? What about the Frossells?"

"Oh, taxi," said Miss Jones without hesitation. "The boy'd got a touch of traveller's tummie—or said he had. I overheard them talking about it on the train, so I wasn't surprised when they decided to take the quickest possible means back to the hotel. I believe they shared a cab with the young Smith couple."

"And that's the whole bang shoot of 'em!" The Hon. Con beamed across the narrow strip of floor which separated the two beds. Silly old Bones, frowning away there over her bits of paper! Bless her old cotton socks but she did like to make a flipping meal out of everything! "Well, come on, old fruit! Spit it out! Who does the old computer say was trying to croak Penny Clough-Cooper?"

Miss Jones's frown deepened, and she had the grace to look slightly embarrassed. "You and me, I'm afraid, dear," she said with a placatory smile. "Everybody else has got an alibi for one attempt or the other."

THREE

This revelation knocked even the Hon. Con back on her heels, and she stumped downstairs to breakfast the following morning looking antisocial and bleary-eyed. So much for your flipping old scientific methods!

She found the rest of her party huddled dejectedly round a table upon which a small Union Jack hung limply and upside down on its little flagstaff. Polite good-mornings were meticulously exchanged, but nobody made any reference to the fracas of the night before. For the third time they set about ordering their breakfast, with great difficulty and little hope. Only Miss Clough-Cooper, pale but composed, ventured into the unknown. She ordered blini and, when they arrived, ate them quietly, with her eyes fixed modestly on her plate.

The Hon. Con struggled against a feeling of total anticlimax and was indeed so low that she was practically reconciled to going back to being a best-selling author again. Funnily enough, it was the elder Lewcock brother who put the starch back into her backbone. It was when, after breakfast, they were getting into the minibus which was to take them on a conducted tour of the town. The Hon. Con was immediately ahead of Jim Lewcock in the queue, and the steps of the minibus were steep and awkward.

"Whoops-a-daisy, Sherlock!" quipped Jim Lewcock, giving the Hon. Con a helpful shove.

In normal circumstances, of course, the Hon. Con would have felled any man who placed his hand where Lewcock Senior had had the temerity to place his, but the circumstances were not normal, and in return for the affectionate sobriquet that he had bestowed upon her, the Hon. Con was prepared to forgive and forget this harmless little liberty.

Her cheek was red but her heart was light as she squeezed into the seat by the window that Miss Jones had been guarding for her. "I say, everybody," she called loudly, "do you think we could have a bit of a chat before that guide woman turns up?"

The rest of the group were busily settling themselves and their belongings, loading cameras and swallowing travel-sickness pills according to their wont, and for one dreadful moment it looked as though nobody were going to answer.

Then Mr. Beamish spoke up. "A bit of a chat about what, Miss—er—Morrison-Burke?"

The Hon. Con squinted cautiously round. No sign of the guide yet, and even the driver had disappeared. "About these dastardly attempts to murder Miss Clough-Cooper, of course!"

There were audible groans all round.

"Dear God, we're not going through all that again, are we?" Mrs. Beamish fanned herself with her Intourist brochure. "Oh, do open that window, Norman! It's so stuffy in here." She glared across at the Hon. Con. "If Miss Clough-Cooper's life really is in danger, we must inform the police. If it isn't—well, the least said about last night's little episode, the better, don't you think?"

Penelope Clough-Cooper beat the Hon. Con to it. "Are you calling me a liar?" she demanded furiously from her seat next to the driver.

Ella Beamish smiled the smile of one who knows she can keep her temper when all around are losing theirs. "We can all make mistakes, my dear."

"Too true!" agreed the Hon. Con quickly. "And, if it was only a matter of last night, I wouldn't be taking things as seriously as I am. However"—the Hon. Con kept on talking as several other incorrigible exhibitionists gathered themselves prior to putting their two-pennyworth in—"Miss Clough-Cooper claims that there have been other attacks, and she has accused one of us of being responsible."

"She wants suing for slander!" That was the Frossell boy, tossing his contribution lazily and insolently from the back seat.

"Oh, *Roger!*" wailed his mother.

But the Hon. Con didn't believe in wasting good breath on

pimply adolescents and paid him no attention. "Look," she said, "we can't just ignore this problem and hope it'll go away. We ought to come to some decision here and now, before that blooming guide woman turns up."

"She should be here now by rights," the Smith girl complained in an accent that would, in happier times, have set the Hon. Con's teeth on edge. "I don't know why everything's always so late here."

The Hon. Con merely pretended that this lower-middle-class interruption had simply never happened. "I just want to know if I can count on your wholehearted cooperation."

Jim Lewcock tried to speed things up. "Here, have I got this straight, love? You want to investigate these attacks on Miss Clough-Cooper so that we don't have to get ourselves in a tangle with the Russian police?"

"The Honourable Constance is not motivated by vulgar curiosity," said Miss Jones, leaning forward in her seat so that she could get the message across to everybody. "As a matter of fact, the Honourable Constance is a highly experienced criminal investigator." Under the cover of her folded mackintosh, Miss Jones carefully crossed her fingers. Not that it was exactly lying to call the Hon. Con a highly experienced criminal investigator, but . . . "Surely you don't intend just to sit back and let Miss Clough-Cooper get killed?"

Desmond Withenshaw stirred uneasily. He had managed to appropriate the best seat in the minibus, and the last thing he wanted was trouble. "I don't know that I feel entirely happy about letting an amateur detective loose in our midst. Er—couldn't we sort of work out a guard roster for Miss Clough-Cooper until the end of the holiday?"

The suggestion fell on noticeably stony ground. "Bugger that for a lark!" said Jim Lewcock, his memories of his time as a National Serviceman flooding painfully back.

Young Mr. Smith tightened his grip on his wife. "Well, you can count me out for a start, mate! I haven't paid all this money to turn into a blooming watchdog. Look, if the judy's life really is in danger, call the cops in and let them deal with it. It's what they're paid for—see?"

"Oh, no!" Penelope Clough-Cooper broke in, her eyes round with apprehension. "Not the police! I couldn't bear having the

Russian police questioning me and . . . Oh, no!" She buried her head in her hands.

Everybody, being English, looked highly embarrassed.

"If we bring the Russian police into this, we'll be held here forever." Roger Frossell, very pink in the face, returned the stares and stuck resolutely to his somewhat surprising guns. "I vote we give Miss Morrison-Burke a free hand to make enquiries into this matter in any way she thinks fit."

Mrs. Frossell knew where her maternal duty lay. "I second that!" She raised her hand as though at the weekly meeting of her W.I.

"And so do I!" Miss Jones, overeager, perhaps, to get the bandwagon rolling, raised her hand too and basked happily in the warmth of the Hon. Con's smile. "What about the rest of you?"

Now that it had come to making a firm and public decision, the Lewcock brothers exchanged worried glances. "Well, we don't want no trouble, do we, Tone?" Jim Lewcock tried to keep a light, bantering note in his voice.

"No, we bleeding well don't!" agreed his brother. He nodded at the Hon. Con. "We're on your side, love!"

Norman Beamish stuck his hand up, and after a moment's hesitation his wife followed suit. "Oh, all right!" she said ungraciously. "But only because we simply can't afford to be detained out here after the fifteenth. We must be back for Daddy's birthday, mustn't we, Norman?" She smiled proudly. "He'll be seventy-five, you know."

Norman Beamish looked less besotted. "I have got one or two fairly important engagements myself," he pointed out.

His wife dismissed this contemptuously. "Oh, we can safely leave Daddy to deal with all that side of things!"

The Smiths had been whispering frantically together. Trevor Smith looked up and transferred his chewing gum to the other cheek. "You can count us in," he said. "We've got nothing to hide, one way or the other, but . . ." He shrugged his shoulders.

The Hon. Con swung round on the Withenshaws. "Looks as though the ball's in your court!" she informed them curtly. She glanced out the window. "And you'd better hurry up and play it. Madam Bossy-Boots is coming!"

Zoë Withenshaw opened her guidebook. "Frankly, I find the

whole situation quite farcical, but I'm quite prepared to abide by the decision of the majority. Okay, Desmond?"

"No skin off my nose," said her husband sulkily.

The Hon. Con snapped up this unanimous vote of confidence with gratitude, but her thanks, promises, and resounding resolutions were mercifully cut short as the redoubtable Ludmilla Stepanovna was piped aboard.

She greeted her flock brusquely and then counted them. Only when she was sure nobody was missing did she turn her mind to other matters. "Where," she demanded in a voice of thunder, "is your chauffeur?"

Tony Lewcock had a ready, if crude, wit. "I reckon he's having a leak, love!" he chuckled, and Miss Jones spent the next ten minutes wondering if their driver could, perhaps, be a vegetarian. But even if he was—how did Mr. Lewcock know? She would have referred the problem to dear Constance if it hadn't been only too obvious that dear Constance was deep in planning her forthcoming campaign. Miss Jones naturally knew better than to disturb her.

Before too long the minibus driver appeared and took his place. Ludmilla Stepanovna unhooked the microphone from the dashboard and blew into it to see if it was working. The Albatrossers perked up and began to pay attention. They were off!

Alma Ata is a pleasant enough town, though somewhat undistinguished. There is not a great deal to be said about it, but, whatever there was, Ludmilla Stepanovna duly said it. The microphone was somewhat de trop in the restricted confines of the minibus, and it lisped rather badly. This, coupled with Ludmilla Stepanovna's thick Russian accent, made listening a little less than pleasurable, but luckily most of the Albatrossers knew they weren't there to enjoy themselves.

The Hon. Con fought hard to keep Ludmilla Stepanovna's commentary out, but her voice was hard and unrelenting. Snatches of useless information kept breaking through in spite of the Hon. Con's fierce determination not to know.

Alma Ata, Ludmilla Stepanovna informed her group (and, beyond them, the world), was the capital of the Soviet Republic of Kazakhstan. Before the Revolution it had been an unimportant garrison town called Verny, and on the left was the bus station—a product of the present glorious regime. The current population was five hundred and seventy-six thousand and the main nationalities were Kazakhs and Russians. On the right was the . . .

The faces of the tourists were beginning to look blank. Desmond Withenshaw tried to dam the battering of Ludmilla Stepanovna's voice and inexhaustible supply of facts. "Er—excuse me, but isn't that a mosque?"

Ludmilla Stepanovna's eyes narrowed. *Bozhi moi*, but there was one in every group! "Is Mussulman temple," she agreed indifferently. "Is not important."

"Is it open for worship?"

Ludmilla Stepanovna bared her teeth. "I do not know. On left is town market. Very picturesque."

Desmond Withenshaw slumped back in his seat. "Isn't it funny," he remarked to his wife in a loud voice, "how very uptight they always get when you ask them anything even remotely connected with religion. Guilty conscience, do you suppose?"

"Yonder is house of former military governors," said Ludmilla Stepanovna, trying hard to think how best she might wreak vengeance on this revolting and bearded hooligan. "Nowadays, is town hall." The driver pulled the minibus to the side of the road and stopped. "I now tell you amusing anecdote. In czarist times was governor of town called Kolpakovsky. He was very fond of trees and—"

"Oh, well," sniggered Tony Lewcock, "it takes all sorts!"

"—and paid everybody who planted a tree in the town ten copecks." Ludmilla Stepanovna paused dramatically before delivering the punch line. "And ordered all who cut one down to be flogged in public by soldiers!"

It is a well-known fact that the English are a reserved and humourless lot, but Ludmilla Stepanovna was still bitterly disappointed by the lack of response. The faces that were raised to hers were insultingly uncomprehending. She took it out on the driver, ordering him to drive on by means of a grammatical construction which is normally used only to address one's intimate acquaintance and dogs.

The driver retaliated by letting in his clutch so fiercely that half the Albatrossers found themselves rolling in the aisle. Before they had time to collect themselves, the brakes were slammed on.

Ludmilla Stepanovna explored her bruises grimly and then

continued with her commentary to an audience that was now totally indifferent. This time she exhorted them to admire a church—the Cathedral church. Mr. Withenshaw was still scrabbling round on the floor for the contents of his wife's handbag and offered no comment. The church, Ludmilla Stepanovna said, was built of wood and had been constructed at the beginning of the twentieth century, without the use of a single iron nail.

The Albatrossers received this intelligence stoically.

"Is now principal museum of Kazakhstan Republic. We visit. All will now descend. Hurry, please!"

In the confusion and turmoil that inevitably accompanies any move made by any bunch of tourists, the Hon. Con managed to catch hold of Miss Clough-Cooper and draw her to one side. "You and me must have a little talk."

Miss Clough-Cooper tried unobtrusively to pull away from the Hon. Con's unyielding grasp. "Yes, yes . . . of course. Er—this evening, perhaps?"

"Speed," observed the Hon. Con, looking owlish, "is of the essence. How about now? You're not really interested in trailing round this soppy old museum, are you?"

"Well . . ."

"Oh, blimey!" The Hon. Con unconsciously tightened her grip on Miss Clough-Cooper's arm. "What's happening now?"

The little group of Albatrossers, which had struggled just about as far as the church door, milled about aimlessly for a few seconds and then began to straggle back crossly down the path. Ludmilla Stepanovna snapped apologetically at their heels.

Miss Jones trotted up to report, happy to drive a wedge between the Hon. Con and Miss Clough-Cooper. "The museum's closed, dear. Nobody seems to know why. Mrs. Beamish is absolutely furious!"

"Oh, damn and blast!" said the Hon. Con. "Best laid plans of mice and men, eh? Never mind"—she gave Miss Clough-Cooper's shrinking arm an encouraging squeeze—"we'll perhaps get another chance later on. Keep an eye out for me, will you?"

Miss Clough-Cooper's face and voice were quite expressionless. "Yes," she promised, "I certainly will."

Ludmilla Stepanovna was in a bad temper. She had been counting on snatching half an hour's peace and quiet while somebody else conducted her flock round the museum. The minibus driver, extracted prematurely from his favourite boozer, wasn't too pleased either. However, the Cathedral museum frequently closed without rhyme, reason, or prior notice, and Ludmilla Stepanovna had her contingency plans ready.

"We'll go to the Agricultural Exhibition," she told the driver as they stood watching the tourists clamber back into the bus.

"Sofia Ivanovna won't like it," the driver pointed out gloomily. "She said last time that she wanted at least twenty-four hours' notice."

Ludmilla Stepanovna was luckily able to bear other people's misfortunes philosophically. "What can't be cured must be endured," she said. "I'll handle Sofia Ivanovna!"

The Agricultural Exhibition was located in a park on the outskirts of the town, and, in her eagerness to avoid trouble, Ludmilla Stepanovna tended to oversell its attractions. The Albatrossers examined the huge two-storied wooden building with something short of rapture.

"I go to get director of exhibition," Ludmilla Stepanovna told them, grasping her handbag belligerently. "You will wait here and admire our world-famous mountains." She indicated a row of distant snow-covered peaks.

"Oh, aren't they simply lovely!" cooed Mrs. Frossell.

Zoë Withenshaw turned her back on them. "Frankly, I don't think they're a patch on the Alps. Do you, Mrs. Beamish?"

Mrs. Beamish purred at this flattering appeal. "Well, I hardly think you can compare this place with Davos, can you?" She laughed gaily. "And I really think Davos is my favourite, you know. The après ski is always so *good* at Davos."

"Better than St. Moritz?" queried Miss Clough-Cooper, slipping easily into this jet-set conversation. "Well, I suppose it's all a matter of taste, but I . . ." She didn't get a chance to expand her theme. The Hon. Con had work to do, and Miss Clough-Cooper found herself being dragged away into the bushes.

"Have a pew!" invited the Hon. Con, pointing to a rustic bench which stood mouldering in the sun.

Miss Clough-Cooper, mindful of her summer frock, declined. "Tell you the story of my life?" she echoed fretfully. "What on earth for?"

The Hon. Con reckoned it was a bit too early in the game to inform the girl that anything connected with her was bound to be fascinating, and produced a more acceptable explanation. "It's all connected with the theory I've been working out—about this joker who's trying to kill you. Now, it's highly unlikely that a sweet-natured kid like you could possibly have made a mortal enemy in the few short days we've been together on this trip. So, if the chappie really is a member of our little party, the motive must go back to your life at home in England. Mustn't it?"

"It could be a maniac," Miss Clough-Cooper pointed out unhappily.

The Hon. Con grinned indulgently at her. " 'Fraid we tend to regard homicidal maniacs as pretty much a last resort," she explained. "They're considered a mite—well, unprofessional, don't you know. No, I think we'll find in the end that this blighter's as sane as you or me. Now, then"—she sat down on the bench and, in spite of Miss Clough-Cooper's previous refusal, patted the space next to her invitingly—"why don't you take some of the weight off your feet and tell me all about what a nice girl like you is doing in a lousy dump like this?"

FOUR

"There's no need to push!" The Hon. Con was quite pleased with the way she kept her cool and refused to be provoked by that dratted Intourist guide woman. She just hoped that young Penny Clough-Cooper appreciated the sacrifice.

Ludmilla Stepanovna was nursing a few grievances on her own behalf. Her confrontation with the dreaded Sofia Ivanovna had been nasty, brutish, and short, and, though she had eventually emerged victorious, it had been a traumatic experience. Her shattered nerves had taken another hammering when she found that her flock, in spite of clear and forceful instructions to stay where they were, had scattered. You couldn't, she told herself in a paroxysm of rage, trust these bloody capitalists out of your sight for two seconds!

The Hon. Con and Miss Clough-Cooper had been the last ones to be rounded up, and Ludmilla's meagre supply of tact had long since been exhausted. She herded them as fast as she could into the Agricultural Exhibition, where that arch-hypocrite Sofia Ivanovna, all smiles and girlish charm, was waiting to receive them. Even a dictatorship of the proletariat, reflected Ludmilla Stepanovna bitterly, doesn't ensure perfect justice.

Sofia Ivanovna, still looking as though butter wouldn't melt in her mouth, launched herself into her little speech of welcome. The Hon. Con wasn't the only one whose attention began wandering, though she was probably the first. She looked round her gloomily. The place was full of display cabinets full of unlikely-looking fruit and stands covered with photographs of animals. Mostly sheep. Big deal!

Sofia Ivanovna was telling her captive audience at some length

30

that Alma Ata meant "Father of Apples." One or two people made a faint effort to appear interested, while the Hon. Con scowled at a basket of plastic oranges that weren't even trying to look real. She peered round to see where Penny Clough-Cooper had got to. Right on the other side of the group. The Hon. Con sighed. Sometimes you'd almost think that that girl didn't want her problems sorted out for her.

Sofia Ivanovna had reached the sticky part. Still smiling through, she asked her visitors which particular aspects of Kazakhstan agriculture especially interested them. This innocent, even kindly question produced a blank and embarrassed silence during which the Albatrossers severally and despairingly examined their boots. It was the beastly unfairness of the query, they told themselves, that really got up their noses. Blimey, you could write what they knew about any kind of agriculture on a one-copeck piece and still have room left for the Lord's Prayer.

Sofia Ivanovna was still waiting. Loudly.

"The Honourable Constance is very interested in horses!" Miss Jones became the blushing cynosure of all eyes, but she stood her ground like a trooper. The Hon. Con was not, in actual fact, all that keen on horses, but Miss Jones conceived it as her duty to promote the Hon. Con's "county" image where and when she could. Considering that the Hon. Con had never done any huntin', shootin', or fishin' in her entire life, Miss Jones's self-imposed task was uphill work.

"Horses?" Sofia Ivanovna's deep, dark eyes flashed with excitement. "But of course! As you know, Kazakhstan is famous throughout the world for the excellence of its horses. This way, please!"

Secretly relieved and very impressed with Miss Jones's astonishing savoir-faire, the rest of the party followed obediently as she was conducted with some ceremony up a shallow flight of wooden stairs to the first floor. Here were even more improbable samples of local produce and more photographs of sheep.

"Oh, I do wish we could read the language!" lamented Mrs. Beamish prettily as she gazed at a brightly coloured poster emphasizing the importance of manure in modern farming practice. "I'm sure it would make everything much more interesting."

Sofia Ivanovna elbowed her out of the way and hauled out of

the shadows a little nut-brown gnome of a man, who smiled shyly at nobody in particular. "Here is our expert!" She gave the little man a shake and addressed him in a machine-gun burst of Russian. The little man continued to smile. "His name is Alexander Nikolaievitch Chichibabin!" said Sofia Ivanovna proudly. "He will tell you everything about our universally renowned horses."

Miss Jones insisted that the Hon. Con should be removed from the back row and brought to stand beside her, right at the front. There wasn't, unfortunately, room for Miss Clough-Cooper as well, a disappointment that Miss Jones bore with fortitude. Alexander Nikolaievitch waited politely until everybody was settled before embarking on his dissertation. In Russian.

It wasn't long before the Hon. Con was huffing and puffing with frustration. Alexander Nikolaievitch got into his stride and, gesticulating enthusiastically, soon forgot all about the desirability of having a translation. The Hon. Con sighed noisily and, for want of anything better, began glaring at the display of photographs in front of which they were all standing like a lot of lemons. Miss Jones, equally at loose ends, followed suit.

The Hon. Con got it fractionally ahead of Miss Jones. "Great steaming Jehoshaphat!" she gasped. "The lousy, rotten swine!"

Miss Jones turned eyes watery with dismay on the Hon. Con. "Oh, Constance, it can't be"—she swallowed hard—"can it?"

Credit where credit's due—the Hon. Con didn't hesitate. "Don't look, Bones!" she hissed, and, ignoring the tiny Alexander Nikolaievitch, who was still talking, though less confidently than before, she grabbed hold of Desmond Withenshaw. "You'd better get the women out of here!" she whispered fiercely, squeezing the last ounce of drama out of the situation. "Pronto!"

"I beg your pardon?"

The Hon. Con shook the art teacher vigorously. Oh, for those halcyon days when you told somebody to do something and they did it—without arguing! "Are you blind or something?" She indicated the display of photographs with a quivering finger. "The horses, man!"

"What about them?"

Everybody was looking anxiously at the Hon. Con.

She took a firm grip on herself. "They eat them," she said, as clearly and calmly as she could.

Mr. Withenshaw recoiled. "Oh, surely not!"

The Hon. Con looked round for an illustration which would clinch the argument. She pointed. "Then what," she demanded, struggling to keep her gorge in its place, "is that photograph of a plateful of *sausages* doing there?"

The Albatrossers were back at their hotel nearly two hours early for lunch, though not many of them felt very hungry. Some of the weaker sisters had already declared that they weren't going to touch another mouthful for the rest of their holiday, and the maternal Mrs. Frossell was in tears.

"I'll never eat another sausage as long as I live!" she declared, holding a lavender-perfumed handkerchief to her ashen lips. "Never!"

Her son clutched at his head. "Oh, *Mother!*" he groaned.

"Them poor bloody horses!" Even young Mrs. Smith had been touched by the startling gastronomic revelations. "Fancy breeding 'em for meat! Bloody disgusting, I call it."

"They milk 'em, too," her husband pointed out, wrapping his arms affectionately round his wife's neck.

Mrs. Frossell gulped. "And I shall drink my coffee *black* in the future!"

The question of how they were to spend the rest of the morning arose, and Ludmilla Stepanovna, grim-faced and washing her hands of the whole stupid business, was unhelpful. They could, she supposed scornfully, go look at the shops.

The Hon. Con caught Miss Clough-Cooper just in time. "It's an ill wind," she observed cheerfully. "Now we can have our little confab, eh? Your room or mine?"

Penelope Clough-Cooper didn't put up much of a fight. Some people know when they're beaten. She did suggest that, perhaps, the Hon. Con's room might be more convenient, and when they had repaired there, she settled herself rather deliberately on the stool in front of the dressing table.

The Hon. Con sprawled blissfully across the nearer of the two beds. "Shoot!" she invited with a boyish grin. "Tell me all about yourself! Er—live alone, do you?"

"No, I live with my father, actually. He's a doctor. Well, an orthopaedic surgeon, really."

"You housekeep for him, eh?" The Hon. Con beamed encouragingly, approving as she did of womanly women.

"Well, yes, I suppose so. But I have a job of my own as well. Part time. Secretarial work. In a solicitor's office. Bensons and Jowett. Er—do you know Wattington at all?"

"Been there," said the Hon. Con, "once or twice. Nice sort of little town. It's not too far from us, you know. I live in Totterbridge."

"Oh, yes." Miss Clough-Cooper smiled politely. "That's quite a nice little town, too. I was just thinking that, if you knew Wattington, you'd probably know Bensons and Jowett. They're the leading solicitors in the town. They have their offices in that lovely old Regency house at the top of Market Street."

"You don't say." The Hon. Con's love of architecture was not very highly developed. "Any romantic involvements?"

"I beg your pardon?"

"Well, are you engaged to be married or"—the Hon. Con looked stern—"mixed up with a married man or anything like that?"

"No."

The Hon. Con relaxed. "You mean that nobody's any reason to be jealous of you?"

Miss Clough-Cooper shook her head. "Not as far as I know."

The Hon. Con sat up and scratched her scalp so vigorously that her hair stood out like a golliwog's. "Must be money, then," she grunted.

"Money?"

For one fleeting moment the Hon. Con wondered if she could have been making a mistake about Penny Clough-Cooper. The girl looked bright enough, but she did seem more than a trifle slow on the uptake. "The motive for your murder," she explained briefly. "If it isn't some form of emotional entanglement, it must be money. What else is there?"

Miss Clough-Cooper didn't know. "But it can't be money." She managed a rather disgruntled laugh. "I mean, I haven't got any. Well, not much. We're quite comfortably off, I suppose, but there's no question of any sort of fortune."

"You've got expectations, though?"

"Well"—Miss Clough-Cooper was obviously finding this line of investigation rather distasteful—"only from my father. I imagine I shall inherit whatever he leaves. I'm an only child."

"And who stands to benefit when you pass through the pearly gates?"

Miss Clough-Cooper frowned. "I don't exactly know," she admitted reluctantly. "There isn't anybody, I suppose. I haven't any near relations at all."

"Made your will?"

"No, not yet."

The Hon. Con rolled over onto her back. "I do hope," she said grumpily, "it isn't going to be one of *those* cases!"

Miss Clough-Cooper smiled vaguely.

"What about the rest of the party?"

"The rest of the party?"

The Hon. Con propped herself up on one elbow. Talk about Little Sir Echo! "Look, ducks," she said, muffling her impatience, "you were the one who said your attacker was a member of our group. Remember? Mind you, considering that attempts were made on your life both here in Alma Ata and in Moscow, I'm somewhat inclined to agree with you—as a working hypothesis, of course. So, let's have a look at our dear chums, eh? Did you know any of 'em back home in the UK?"

"Not really. The Smiths come from Wattington, I understand, though of course"—Miss Clough-Cooper smiled at her reflection in the looking glass and fluffed up her hair—"I don't know them socially. Wattington is quite a big town."

"Interesting!" mused the Hon. Con, endeavouring to look enigmatic. "The Smiths, eh? Well, there may be a connection." She flexed her shoulders. "I shall have to do some digging. Anybody else?"

Miss Clough-Cooper shook her head. "Well, I did meet Mr. Withenshaw once. It must have been—oh, about three years ago. I went on one of these weekend courses for amateur painters. You know the sort of thing. This one was held in a converted castle and it rained the whole time. Mr. Withenshaw was one of the instructors. He didn't actually teach me, of course. He was running the life classes and I was studying flower painting."

"Withenshaw, eh?" The significance of the life classes was not lost upon the Hon. Con. At an earlier stage in her career she had been deeply involved in a campaign to achieve sexual equality for artists' models, and there was little about la vie bohème with which she was not pretty familiar. "Yes, I can see him as a potential murderer. We'll have to see how he stands up to a touch of the old third degree." She managed to crack her knuckles in a rather sickening way.

Miss Clough-Cooper glanced up in alarm. "Good heavens, you can't accuse Mr. Withenshaw! I mean, we just happened to be on this weekend course together, that's all. As a matter of fact, I don't even think I spoke to him—and he certainly didn't know me when we met at the airport."

"You mentioned your previous meeting to him?"

"Why shouldn't I? I recognised him—well, he is rather striking-looking with that touch of grey hair at the temples—but he'd obviously no idea who on earth I was. I felt a complete fool. However, when I explained where it was I thought we'd met, he sort of smiled and pretended that he remembered."

There was a tap on the door, and in response to the Hon. Con's bellow, Miss Jones came in.

"I'm so sorry to interrupt you, dear, but it's nearly time for luncheon, and Ludmilla What's-her-name was most insistent that we shouldn't be late for our afternoon outing. We're going to see the computer at the university."

Miss Clough-Cooper must have had a secret passion for Russian computers, because she got to her feet with alacrity. "How marvellous!" she gushed. "Well, we certainly mustn't be late for that!" Miss Jones stepped smartly to one side so as not to be trampled in the rush. "I'll see you both in the dining room . . . I expect."

Miss Jones shut the door on the departing guest with the merest touch of smugness. "And how are your investigations going, dear?"

The Hon. Con rolled off the bed and did a few quick chest-expanding exercises. "Not bad," she opined, puffing a little. "Making progress."

"That's nice, dear."

"Enjoy your shopping expedition, old fruit?"

"It was hardly a shopping expedition, dear. We were only looking." Miss Jones got a clean handkerchief out of the special sachet in which she kept them and tucked it neatly into the breast pocket of the Hon. Con's hacking jacket. "I walked round with the Beamishes. They seem quite a nice couple, really, though she is a wee bit overbearing at times. They had quite an argument while we were looking at some gramophone records."

"You don't say." The Hon. Con was examining her tongue in the dressing-table mirror. You can't hope to be a successful detective if your health's bad, and though she was feeling perfectly chirpy, the Hon. Con wasn't going to take any chances. She decided to take a dose of that stomach powder stuff before she went to bed. Probably nothing but powdered chalk, of course, but old Bones swore by it. She let her tongue slide back into her mouth. "What about?"

Miss Jones was used to the Hon. Con's conversational style. "About which opera it is we're going to see tonight, dear. Mr. Beamish said it was called *Ivan Susanin* and Mrs. Beamish said it was called *A Life for the Tsar*. They were almost shouting at each other at one time."

"Funny thing to argue about." The Hon. Con toddled off to the bathroom. Being tone deaf, she didn't reckon on working herself up into a muck sweat over some crummy old Russian opera, but she thought it was only fair to take a polite interest in Miss Jones's little adventure. "Who's right, then?"

Miss Jones giggled. "They both are, dear! They finished up by dragging that poor Ludmilla girl out of the kitchen, right in the middle of her lunch. You should have seen her face! However, she sorted things out."

The Hon. Con paused in the doorway. "And?"

"It's the same opera, dear. By a man called Glinka. It seems they called it *A Life for the Tsar* before the Revolution and *Ivan Susanin* after the Revolution. Isn't that interesting?"

"Very." The Hon. Con disappeared into the bathroom, secure in the knowledge that she was going to be able to catch up on last night's lost sleep. She just hoped that the blooming music wasn't going to be too loud.

FIVE

Tashkent! A name to conjure with! The hearts of even the more prosaic members of the group began to beat a little faster, and the extremely unsocial hour of their departure from Alma Ata provoked only a muted storm of protest. The Hon. Con had fully intended to get on with her detecting during the short flight, but six o'clock in the morning was one of those bleak facts of life which took the bounce out of even her.

She clamped the safety belt across her stomach and sank back in her seat. "Wake me up when we get there!" she grunted, secure in the knowledge that a cowardy-custard like old Bones would remain on the qui vive until they were all back on terra firma again.

Miss Jones dutifully took time off from her anxieties to admire dear Constance's quite incredible coolness. To be able to drop off to sleep in an aeroplane—and a Russian aeroplane at that! Ah, that's what breeding did for you!

When they landed at Tashkent Airport, the Albatrossers found themselves slipping easily into a routine with which they were already becoming familiar. As they trooped off the plane, they were speedily and skilfully separated from the rest of the passengers and conducted to a waiting room situated, in this case, on the first floor of the main airport building. There was hardly any delay at all before somebody found the key and got the room unlocked. The Albatrossers were herded inside.

"Wait here, please!"

The supercilious young woman who had escorted them across the tarmac disappeared before the questions and objections could start and was never seen again. Thus balked of their legitimate prey, the Albatrossers gloomily spread themselves and their hand luggage over the acres and acres of space which had been placed at their disposal.

"They've probably not finished wiring our rooms for sound!" Tony Lewcock's feeble attempt at a joke fell on stony ground.

The chairs, the Albatrossers soon discovered, were modern and uncomfortable. Whenever you stretched your legs, you knocked against occasional tables groaning under their burden of unread and unreadable literature in several languages. At the far end of the waiting room a souvenir counter temptingly displayed its colourful wares and goodies. It was shut, of course.

Bored and sleepy, the Albatrossers settled down to wait. And wait they did. For an hour and twenty minutes. The only thing of note that happened during the whole of this time was the clanking arrival of a cleaning operative. Politically reliable and looking neither to her right nor to her left, she began slowly to mop the floor.

Eventually, however, their Intourist guide turned up. He was a young, studious-looking man who probably wouldn't have known what an apology was if one had jumped up and bitten him. He informed them that his name was Oleg, and, under his somewhat Olympian guidance, the party collected their heavy luggage from the pile in the corridor and took their places in the bus which was to convey them to their hotel.

Oleg clearly intended to start as he meant to go on. Norman Beamish lit yet another cigarette. Oleg tapped him on the shoulder and pointed officiously at a notice written in Russian. "No smoking!" he said.

We all have our breaking point, and Norman Beamish had been on edge all morning. He pushed Oleg's hand away. "Oh, drop dead!"

"Good for you, mate!" The Lewcock brothers were delighted with this spirited display of sturdy independence in the face of foreign tyranny. "You tell the bossy little bastard where he bloody well gets off!" Jim Lewcock, going berserk on national solidarity, produced his own packet of duty-free, and both brothers lit up with a flourish.

Oleg's face darkened. He didn't say anything at the time, but he had his own methods of dealing with obstreperous tourists. He made a start by allowing this bunch a bare ten minutes before dragging them off on their conducted tour of the town. He turned a magnificently deaf ear to all protests and could hardly wait to hear what they would say when they got back and found that they'd missed lunch.

The Hon. Con galloped off to the private bathroom, which is an expensive and unavoidable luxury for Western visitors to the Soviet Union, to have a quick cat lick and inspect the plumbing. "Oh, lord," she groaned, emerging at a hand canter, "another wonky ball cock! And watch your feet when you go in, Bones! There's something jolly unpleasant leaking all over the floor."

Miss Jones blenched.

"I'll try and fix it when we get back," promised the Hon. Con, plying her silver-backed military hairbrushes. "Meantime," she appealed to Miss Jones's fastidiously retreating back, "try not to make it any worse, eh?"

Tashkent, it soon emerged, was a town excessively addicted to earthquakes, and it had been virtually rebuilt after the last one. Oleg, from his perch at the front of the bus, spoke of little else. The earthquakes were, after all, extremely useful. They forestalled any criticism of Tashkent as a tourist attraction, and they provided eloquent sermons in stones for those who wished to illustrate the fraternal compassion of Soviet man.

"All these new blocks of workers' flats," said Oleg, waving a limp hand, "were built for the people of Tashkent by the various towns and cities of the Soviet Union. These various towns and cities provided everything—builders, materials, transport. It was a gesture of friendship." His tone implied that this was a sentiment that he didn't expect his listeners either to appreciate or to understand. "On your left are three blocks built by the city of Leningrad. On your right, two blocks built by the city of Novgorod. Straight ahead, four blocks . . ."

It was Mrs. Frossell who eventually, and through clenched teeth, gave expression to a sentiment which others, less articulate, shared. "If," she told her nearest neighbours, "I have to look at any more of these *hideous* buildings, I shall scream! And"—she turned furiously on her son—"don't you dare 'oh, Mother' me, Roger! I'm tired, I'm hot, I'm bored, and I'm hungry! And if this"—she indicated the dusty scene outside the bus window—"if this is a sample of the brave new world we're all supposed to be heading for, you can keep it!"

Oleg's amplified voice rode roughshod over Mrs. Frossell's tetchy whine. "You will now descend from our bus and go to look at Tashkent's famous football stadium, of which you have all heard. It has been the scene of countless international football matches."

"My God!" swore Desmond Withenshaw, speaking from the heart. He didn't offer any further protest, though, and eventually followed the rest of the party as they trailed slowly and reluctantly out of the bus.

It had gone two o'clock when their ordeal came to an end and they were allowed to abandon their sightseeing and set off back to the hotel. The Hon. Con's stomach wasn't the only one that was protesting loudly. "I could eat a horse!" she confided hungrily to Miss Jones—and then realised that she might have said the wrong thing. She changed the subject quickly. "What's on the programme for this afternoon, Bones?"

"It's free, dear. We've been left to our own devices. I was thinking that it might be a good idea if we had a little nap after lunch."

"A little nap?" queried the Hon. Con, who thought siestas weakened you.

"We did have a very early start, dear, and we want to be fresh for the opera this evening."

"The opera?" The Hon. Con's face expressed the horror of the tone deaf. "Not again, surely?"

"Mussorgsky's *Khovanshchina*," said Miss Jones, justifiably proud at having cleared that particular linguistic hurdle. Not that she was given much time to bask in the glory. Hardly had she finished speaking when the air was torn asunder by the most awful, ear-splitting roar. The driver reacted quickly and dragged on his hand brake. The Albatrossers, regrettably behaving like a flock of panic-stricken chickens, clutched one another, grabbed frantically at their belongings, and shrieked at the tops of their voices.

The driver switched off his engine and the roar subsided. He muttered something to Oleg and clambered out of his seat.

Oleg, visibly shaken by the row his passengers were kicking up and forgetting all about his microphone in the heat of the moment, tried to restore order. "Comrades!" he screamed. "Comrades, *please!* There is no danger. Only some minor mechanical failure which our chauffeur will rectify immediately."

Tony Lewcock was the first to recover his savoir-faire. "It's only the bloody silencer that's gone for a Burton," he said. "All you need is a bit of bloody string." He turned to his brother. "Come on, Jim, let's go and give the poor bugger a hand."

The Lewcocks scrambled out, and the remaining tourists gradually settled down into a despondent apathy. Outside, the traffic, mostly bottle-green trucks, swirled noisily round them, and the tropical midday heat built up with surprising speed. The Albatrossers wound down the windows and the dust came swirling in. Oleg took a swift look and calculated by the number and variety of tools that had been laid out in the road that they were going to be stuck there for at least the next half hour. It was clearly up to him to take his charges' minds off their predicament. He smiled all round and, being a KGB agent of many years' standing, naturally thought of interrogation as being the best way of passing the time. The Beamishes were nearest to hand and looking sufficiently apprehensive.

"In which town do you reside in Great Britain?"

"Eh? Oh—er—Carding." Mr. Beamish provided the answer after a preliminary glance at his wife. "That's a town in—"

"I know precisely where Carding is located!" Oleg interrupted rudely. "In fact, I know all about Carding. It is a town with a population of approximately thirty thousand inhabitants, is it not?"

"More or less," agreed Mr. Beamish sullenly.

"Carding is noted for industries connected with light engineering and the manufacture of agricultural products."

"That's right," muttered Mr. Beamish. "And the mayor's Christian name is Harry!"

Oleg's chin jerked up. "I beg your pardon?"

Mr. Beamish shook his head. "Nothing."

Oleg thought about it for a minute or two and then graciously decided to let it go. He turned to Mrs. Beamish. "You have a profession?"

"I certainly do not! I am a housewife, a married woman."

Oleg feigned astonishment. "You spend the whole of your time looking after *him?*" The nod aimed in Mr. Beamish's direction was not flattering.

Mrs. Beamish's jaw, always a little on the firm side, set in a hard line. "I do a great deal of unpaid, charitable work," she said stiffly. "I also have my father to look after. He lives with us."

Oleg was very understanding. "The housing problem in England is very acute," he informed the rest of the bus and then grinned nastily. "Your father, Mrs. Beamish, is of course an extremely *old* man."

"He's nothing of the sort! He's extraordinarily active and fit." Mrs. Beamish drew herself up so as to deliver her broadside with more effect. "Believe me, my father puts in a day's work that is harder and longer than that of many a man half his age." The implication was so obvious that her glance at her cringing spouse was almost superfluous. "I do assure you, my dear Mr. . . . er . . . Oleg, that we would be in Queer Street if it weren't for my father."

Oleg was a little puzzled as to why homosexuality had been introduced into the conversation, but it didn't lessen his interest. The Albatrossers, too, were taking it all in with flapping ears, and there was tacit agreement that this was the best entertainment the Soviet Union had so far provided.

"What is your honoured father's profession?" asked Oleg silkily.

"He is the senior partner in Lindsay-Smith, Fowler, Collins and Beamish." Mrs. Beamish forestalled the question that was hovering on Oleg's lips. "Lindsay-Smith, Fowler, Collins and Beamish are estate agents. I think I can say without fear of contradiction that, under my father's guidance, they have become the leading firm of estate agents, not only for Carding but for all the surrounding district."

Somewhat surprisingly, Oleg picked up a point which had escaped most of Mrs. Beamish's eagerly eavesdropping compatriots. "Beamish?" he repeated. "One of these—er—estate agents is named Beamish?"

Mrs. Beamish nodded and Mr. Beamish gazed miserably out the window. "My husband," explained Mrs. Beamish without enthusiasm. "Daddy gave him a junior partnership as a wedding present. Just as well, in my opinion," she added, quite unforgivably. "I simply can't imagine how we would ever have made ends meet if we'd had to rely on Norman's unaided efforts."

Oleg's close-set eyes sparkled. "Is that indeed so?"

"My husband," confided Mrs. Beamish, leaning towards the Intourist guide and speaking in a slightly lowered voice, "is by nature a playboy. I am always telling him that it's one thing to have the tastes and habits of a lounge lizard or a member of the jet set, and quite another to have the income to maintain such a state." Mrs. Beamish bared a fine set of predatory teeth—just to show that she was having her little joke. "Over a hundred pounds last month for a new set of golf clubs and nothing at all wrong with his old ones, as far as either Daddy or I could see. Do you know what Daddy calls him? The Lothario of the Links! Don't you think that's simply marvellous? The Gay Lothario of the Golf Links!"

"For God's sake, Ella!" Norman Beamish's anguished protest had the virtue of, at least, interrupting his wife's shrill discourse and making her realise that she was embarrassing others besides her natural whipping boy. She stared round the bus. Some of her audience were registering emotions even stronger than embarrassment. Desmond Withenshaw and young Roger Frossell looked frankly disgusted.

"What an evil-minded old cow!" said Roger, making sure his comment was just loud enough to be heard.

Desmond Withenshaw offered an even coarser comparison, and the Smiths sniggered in muted and mutual delight.

Oleg stepped in smoothly again before the situation got out of hand. "The English," he announced, "are a very sporting race. They play many games—football, tennis, hockey, rowing"—he smiled as he reached the pièce de résistance—"*cricket.*"

Desmond Withenshaw threw himself back irritably in his seat. "Don't you think it's about time you stopped trotting out all these tired old clichés about the English?" he drawled. "That one about our being a nation of sportsmen is about on a par with fog-bound London and little boys sweeping chimneys."

This criticism caught Oleg unawares, and for a couple of seconds he stared in open-mouthed silence. He soon recovered, though. Miss Clough-Cooper didn't look the sort to answer back.

"And you, miss, do you play sport? Are you perhaps a player of golf?"

Miss Penelope Clough-Cooper's hand flew, somewhat dramatically, to her throat. "I beg your pardon?" she whispered.

Oleg raised a pair of moth-eaten eyebrows. "I am asking if you play the game of golf, miss."

"Golf?" Miss Clough-Cooper was shooting distraught glances all round her like a hunted animal. Even the Hon. Con, unlikely to err on the overcritical side where Penny Clough-Cooper was concerned, reckoned that she was coming on a bit strong. "No, I don't play golf! I never have! *Never!* Why should you think I'm a golfer? Who suggested that . . ."

There is no knowing how far the hysteria would have mounted, but luckily it wasn't given the chance. The driver's door opened and a motley collection of tools in a canvas bag were slung onto the floor of the bus. A hot and sweating driver followed them and, somewhat incongruously, gave Oleg the thumbs-up sign. The Lewcock brothers, equally sticky and dirty, swung aboard, and the bus set off through the busy streets back to the Tashkent Hotel. Oleg, assisted by the driver and Fate, had timed it beautifully, and the dining-room doors were slammed shut right in the faces of the ravenous Albatrossers.

Tashkent, it will be seen, wasn't proving much of a success, and things didn't improve as the afternoon wore on. Some of the party, including Miss Jones, retired to bed and awoke in time for an early dinner feeling cross and muzzy. Others, headed by that well-known student of human nature—the Hon. Con—plodded dejectedly round the town, observing the passing scene and even, at one low point, actually paying to go into a museum of Uzbek art so as to get out of the sun.

An evening at the opera did nothing to raise anybody's spirits, and as far as the Hon. Con was concerned, it merely provided a fittingly crummy end to an extraordinarily crummy day. Sleep, she soon found, was completely out of the question, thanks to all that caterwauling coming from the stage and the orchestra pit. The Hon. Con sat in the box in which all the Albatrossers had been penned and stared miserably at the gesticulating and squawking figures on the stage. Was it for this that she'd put on a skirt and drenched herself in Old Spice aftershave? For a brief and craven instant she thought wistfully of how nice it would have been in that hotel at Budleigh Salterton, cosily watching the telly with old Bones.

The Hon. Con sighed, folded her arms across her chest, and closed her eyes. Only four more acts to go. Perhaps, if she put her mind to it, she could snatch a well-earned forty winks or . . .

" 'Scuse me, ducks!"

The Hon. Con opened her eyes to find Jim Lewcock bending over her. His stupidly grinning face shone obscenely in the light coming from the stage. She scowled up at him. "What is it?"

"Sorry to bother you, love"—Jim Lewcock's whisper rang through the auditorium, and the heads of one or two music lovers began to turn—"but I've just got to go and shake hands with the wife's best friend."

The Hon. Con blinked and reluctantly tucked up her feet so that Jim Lewcock could push past.

Sitting next to the Hon. Con, Miss Jones momentarily abandoned the passionate but unintelligible duet on the stage and turned to watch Jim Lewcock leave the box. She seemed puzzled.

The Hon. Con, eager to occupy her mind with anything other than the glories of nineteenth-century Russian music, gave her a nudge. "What's up?"

Miss Jones shook her head. She knew, of course, that it was terribly wrong to talk during artistic performances of any kind, but the temptation was too strong to resist. After all, the Hon. Con was always saying that the essence of detection was the spotting of discrepancies—or something like that. "It's Mr. Lewcock, dear!" she murmured from behind a white-gloved hand.

"What about him?"

"I'd no idea he was married. Had you?"

SIX

Actually, in the end, Tashkent didn't prove to be a total disaster—at least not from the detection point of view. The credit for the way things bucked up in that direction was really due to Miss Jones, but the Hon. Con didn't bother much about that. Gratitude to the doormats of this world (however well beloved) was not one of her strong points.

The Hon. Con had gobbled through her breakfast the following day at her usual indigestion-producing speed and had returned to the bedroom for a touch of the old bicarb. The flight to Bukhara, their next port of call, wasn't until eleven o'clock, a timing which effectively (and certainly deliberately) ruined the whole morning. The Hon. Con waited moodily for the fizzing to stop and stared at the suitcases, which, apart from one, were all packed and locked. Miss Jones didn't like to be all at the last minute.

Having taken the bicarb, the Hon. Con had nothing much else to do. She ambled into the bathroom and, watching very carefully where she put her feet, began to clean her teeth. She heard someone come into the bedroom and spat out a mouthful of minty foam. "That you, Bones?"

"Yes, dear."

The Hon. Con examined her tongue dubiously. Either she was sickening for something or that mirror had got the damp. "You've been a long time."

"Have I, dear?" Miss Jones came over to the open bathroom door to account for the odd five minutes that she had been out of the Hon. Con's ken. "I was with Oleg."

"Oleg?" The Hon. Con sprayed a generous mouthful of water round the bathroom. "That rat!"

47

"He wanted me to hand the passports out, dear. He said he was very busy this morning and simply couldn't spare the time to . . ."

"Passports?" The Hon. Con granted Miss Jones the courtesy of her undivided attention.

It is the custom in the Soviet Union for tourists to surrender their passports when they book into their hotel, rarely getting them back again until just before they leave. The authorities like to give the police as long a time as possible with them.

"*Passports!*" The Hon. Con came out of the bathroom like a champagne cork out of the bottle. She stretched out a toothpaste-besmattered hand. "Gimme!"

Miss Jones had some scruples and demurred.

"Oh, don't be so blooming pi, Bones!" snapped the Hon. Con, grabbing successfully. "Passports are what we call primary sources of evidence."

Miss Jones blinked. "Are they, dear?"

"Cross my heart!" The Hon. Con shuffled eagerly through the pack. She quickly discarded her own passport and Miss Jones's and sat down on the bed with the one she was really after—Penelope Clough-Cooper's.

Miss Jones hovered unhappily.

"Jolly nice photograph!" said the Hon. Con, lost in admiration.

"She's changed her hair style." Miss Jones sniffed. "I wonder why. She looked much better with it long. Made her look younger."

"Either way," said the Hon. Con, "she's a dashed pretty girl!"

"Girl?" Miss Jones got really nasty. "How old is she, by the way?"

"Eh? Oh"—the Hon. Con did her arithmetic and frowned—"er —well—thirty-one."

Miss Jones, peeping over the Hon. Con's shoulder, was nippier with the numbers. "Thirty-two," she corrected.

"Same thing!" grunted the Hon. Con crossly and snapped the passport shut. The next one she opened was the Withenshaws'. Very dull. Seems they lived in Bishop's Thorpe and shared their passport with three small kids. The Hon. Con offered up a silent prayer of thanks that she had been spared the young Withenshaws. Desmond Withenshaw had given his profession as artist, but, apart from this harmless vanity, there was nothing of interest. The Hon. Con tossed the passport on the bed.

48

Miss Jones gathered it up anxiously. "People will be wondering where their passports are, dear."

"Fiddlesticks!" The Hon. Con's eyes were busy dissecting the Smiths' passport. It was very dull, too. "Hm," she growled as she slung it over to Miss Jones, "seems they are married after all. But only just! Looks as though they're on their flipping honeymoon."

The Hon. Con's curiosity was catching, and Miss Jones ventured a peep into the private life of the Smiths on her own account. "Isn't it funny how we all seem to come from the same part of the country, dear?"

"Nothing funny about it at all," said the Hon. Con, who frequently had an answer for everything. "Albatross is a pretty third-rate concern, run on a shoestring. I imagine they tried to keep their costs down by restricting their advertising to one area. After all, it was in our local rag that I spotted their advertisement, wasn't it?"

"Yes, dear," agreed Miss Jones, remembering and rueing the day. "It's just that with its being a Scottish company—Glencoe, you know—I thought it would have—well, a sort of international flavour. Oh—er—thank you, dear!" She caught the next passport in midair.

"Roger Frossell!" snorted the Hon. Con in explanation. "Student! Aren't they all? He lives in Mapperly."

"That's quite near us, too, isn't it, dear?"

"Mrs. Mary Frossell," read the Hon. Con. "Housewife." She looked up. "Funny there's never any mention of Mr. Frossell, isn't it? Suspicious, that."

"They're separated, dear," said Miss Jones in a discreet whisper. "The marriage broke up over ten years ago. He went off with another woman. Isn't it sad?"

The Hon. Con was highly indignant. "Who told you that?" she demanded. Damn it all, the way old Bones picked up the tittle-tattle was positively disgusting.

Miss Jones grovelled apologetically. "Mrs. Frossell told me herself, dear. I had quite a long chat with her one day. In Moscow. We were waiting for our luncheon. You," she added quickly, "were discussing the reform of the laws of Rugby football with Mr. Beamish, I think."

The Hon. Con got busy with the passports of the Lewcock

brothers. Both documents were, she noted with the shrewdness of your case-hardened detective, brand new. She wasn't surprised that a couple of plebs like the Lewcock brothers should choose the Soviet Union for their first holiday abroad. "What," she asked, "is a lathe operator, exactly?"

"I'm afraid I don't know, dear. I suppose it's some sort of factory worker."

The Hon. Con sighed heavily. "I'd guessed that much for myself, old girl!"

Miss Jones added the Lewcock passports to her growing pile. "Will you be long, dear?"

"Eh?" The Hon. Con was deep in the Beamishes' passport. She chuckled. "Well, well! Fancy that!"

"What is it, dear?"

"Did you know that Mrs. Beamish—the elegant Ella—is eight years older than her husband?"

"No, I didn't."

The Hon. Con sniggered maliciously. "Can't say I'm surprised. I mean, she's fighting a gallant rear-guard action and all that sort of thing, but the years are beginning to show. Have a guess—how old do you think she is?"

Miss Jones felt herself going pink. She did so hate it when the Hon. Con got catty. It was so out of character. "I really don't know, dear," she said. "Middle thirties, perhaps?" She saw the expression on the Hon. Con's face and tried again. "Or maybe the late thirties?"

"Forty-three!" trumpeted the Hon. Con, highly delighted at being able to drop this bombshell. She slapped the last passport into Miss Jones's hands. "And he's only thirty-five! How's that for cradle-snatching?"

"Some marriages where the wife is older than the husband can be very happy, dear."

"Well," said the Hon. Con, blowing unpleasantly down her nose, "theirs certainly isn't! Anybody can see that with half an eye." She changed the subject. "On your way, Bones!"

"Yes." Miss Jones emerged reluctantly from a rather delightful reverie in which . . . "I'd better distribute these passports, I suppose." She got as far as the door before—oh, so casually—she asked her innocent little question. She could have looked for herself, of course, but when one has been strictly brought up . . . "Er—did you say that the two Lewcock gentlemen were both unmarried, dear?"

"I didn't," said the Hon. Con, giving Miss Jones a sharp glance, "but, since you mention it, they are."

"Oh," said Miss Jones.

"One's forty-nine," said the Hon. Con, rubbing it in, "and the other's fifty. They're not exactly chickens."

"They look," ventured Miss Jones, "younger."

The Hon. Con curled an aristocratic lip. "Doubt if working in a blooming factory takes much out of you," she sneered. "They're always on strike."

Miss Jones returned to the harsh realities of the world as it really is. She opened the bedroom door. "I won't be more than a couple of minutes, dear."

It may have been Miss Jones's unsavoury interest in the Lewcock brothers that inspired the Hon. Con to interrogate them in depth on the flight from Tashkent to Bukhara. The brothers, sporting the little embroidered Uzbek skull caps which they had bought as souvenirs in Tashkent, and a mite the worse for Armenian brandy, were surprised and a little alarmed to find the Hon. Con inserting her ample behind in the seat which they had carefully left vacant between them. They realised that the sobering sleep to which they had been looking forward was now out of the question.

Whatever the advertisements say, you can't really hold an intimate conversation in an aeroplane, especially not in the type of plane used on flights within the Soviet Union. Luckily the Hon. Con possessed a fog-siren voice and a pair of leather lungs.

"Tell me all about yourselves!" she bellowed, accompanying her invitation with a leer that would have unnerved a man-eating crocodile.

The Lewcock brothers, unable to communicate with or even see each other, suddenly felt naked and alone.

Jim Lewcock, being the elder, took the initiative and tried to stall for time. What did Miss Morrison-Burke mean, exactly? He and his kid brother were just a couple of ordinary blokes about whom there was really nothing much of interest to be said.

"Got something to hide, have you?" asked the Hon. Con in a

would-be joky voice. She licked the writing end of her pencil as though to ensure that anything taken down was going to be of the blackest.

Jim Lewcock couldn't wait to reassure the Hon. Con on this point. Neither he nor his brother knew a thing about these strange attacks on poor Miss Clough-Cooper. They had absolutely nothing to hide, never had had in the past, and never would have in the future. See this wet, see this dry . . .

"Methinks," said the Hon. Con, who was never at a loss for an apt misquotation, "methinks the fellow doth protest too much!"

Jim Lewcock wiped the sweat off the palms of his hands. "Where would you like us to begin, miss?"

The Hon. Con was never at a loss for a cliché, either. "Begin at the beginning," she instructed grandly, "and go on until you come to the end!"

Hesitantly at first, and then with growing confidence, the Lewcock brothers complied.

Dad, it appeared, had been a cowman, and Mum—a horny-handed, golden-hearted old trooper—had done a bit of charring when she could get the work. There were eight Lewcock children altogether (not counting the one who had died)—six girls and two boys. They'd all done quite well at school, but there was, of course, no question of going on to the grammar for the likes of them. The girls had taken up a variety of jobs. Lucy . . .

"Skip the girls!" The Hon. Con let a huge yawn split her face. "In fact"—she blinked furiously in an effort to keep herself awake—"you can skip all this rubbish about your early life and hard times. We've all had to rough it, you know, and you're not the only ones who've pulled themselves up by their boot laces. Maybe if I ask you a few questions it'll speed things up."

"I think that would help," agreed Jim Lewcock humbly. He and his brother had had some rather unkind things to say about the Hon. Con in the privacy of their bedroom, but now, face to face with the daunting reality, they were very subdued.

"All right," grunted the Hon. Con. She donned her thinking cap. "Did either of you know Miss Clough-Cooper before you came on this trip?"

"No."

The Hon. Con didn't let a flat denial like that put her off. "You sure?"

"Of course we're sure!"

"But you live in Pear's Hill. That's only a couple of miles from Wattington."

Jim Lewcock never questioned from where the Hon. Con had got this snippet of information. He shrugged his shoulders. "I can't help that, love. We still don't know her."

"When did you decide to come on this particular package holiday?"

"About a bloody week ago." Tony Lewcock's voice was almost as surly as his face. "We was all set to go to your Costa Bravo, but there was some sort of bloody mix-up over the bookings. By the time they'd got things sorted out, this trip was all they could give us that fitted. Believe you me, missus, this isn't *our* idea of your dolce vita!"

The Hon. Con scratched her head. It certainly didn't sound as though these two yobboes had come to the Soviet Union with the deliberate intention of murdering Penny Clough-Cooper. Still, the attacks might have been triggered off by some accidental and unexpected encounter, though the Hon. Con couldn't quite see Penny Clough-Cooper as a grisly spectre from somebody's past. "Miss Clough-Cooper works for a solicitor in Wattington, you know. Either of you ever had any dealings with him?"

"No!" The answer came sharply and independently from either side.

The Hon. Con was floundering. "You sure?" she asked again.

"Jesus!" Tony Lewcock got out his cigarettes and lit one defiantly. It was only when he'd finished coughing up his guts that he continued. "Our trade union sees to all that sort of thing for us, lady. The Southern Lathe Operators Brotherhood and Society. They've got their own solicitor and everything. He's a right sharp laddie up in London—so why should we start messing round on our own, hiring some bloody country yokel in the next bloody town?"

Trade union, eh? Well, the Hon. Con was not surprised. She'd always thought that the Lewcock brothers looked like a couple of anarchists. She remembered the passports again. "Ah, yes," she said, "I meant to ask you. What exactly is it that you do for a living?"

"I'm off sick at the moment," said Tony.

"We own a garage," said Jim.

Somebody far more dense than the Hon. Con would have noticed that the Lewcock brothers immediately regretted their simultaneous and disparate answers. There was a moment or two of confusion, and the Hon. Con felt instinctively that there was a guilty secret lurking round somewhere.

"I thought you were supposed to work in a factory," she said.

The Lewcock brothers did it again.

"That's right!" said one.

"We used to," said the other.

The Hon. Con grinned. Better and better!

Jim Lewcock tried to sort things out. "I was just doing a bit of swanking," he explained lamely. "About the garage, I mean."

The Hon. Con didn't yield an inch. "Oh, yes?"

"It's only a matter of time," said Tony Lewcock, plunging disastrously to the rescue.

"What is?"

"Well . . ." Tony Lewcock gazed hopelessly out the window and sighed. "It's a long story, miss."

The Hon. Con consulted Big Ben. "It had better not be, laddie!" Her jocular manner struck a gruesome note. "We're due to land in this Bukhara place in ten minutes, and I want this whole business settled before then."

The Lewcock brothers nervously lit more cigarettes and, after an abortive attempt to swear the Hon. Con to eternal secrecy, came out with their pathetic little story.

"We did work in a factory," began Jim Lewcock. "Bromberg and Sons. Making specialised components for the mining industry. As jobs go it wasn't bad, and the money was fairish. With overtime. But—well—you know how it is. I suppose everybody wants to be their own master when you get right down to it."

The Hon. Con nodded her agreement. "That's what's wrong with the world these days," she pointed out sourly. "Too many chiefs and not enough Indians." As one of nature's chiefs, she spoke with feeling.

"We tried to save," explained Tony Lewcock, examining the tip of his cigarette with apparent interest, "but it was bloody uphill work. It's one thing earning good money at the bench, but you need bloody thousands to put down on the smallest sort of business. Before long you find yourself beginning to think again, don't you? And the prospect of having a dirty great mortgage tied round our necks for the next ninety years didn't help, either."

The Hon. Con rolled her eyes in exasperation. Really, how the poor went on about money!

"Then," Jim Lewcock broke in wistfully, "we had ourselves a bit of luck."

"Yes," agreed his brother, without bitterness, "I crooked my bloody back at work."

The Hon. Con's eyes popped. "You call that luck?"

In the heat of the moment Jim Lewcock forgot the precariousness of his situation and patted the Hon. Con on the knee. "The compensation, love!" he explained. "Prove it's the firm's fault and you're sitting bloody pretty! And our solicitor—the trade-union one I was telling you about—he's no doubts at all. Tone's accident, he says, was definitely due to negligence on the part of Bromberg and Sons, and he personally was going to see to it that they paid through the nose. And I'm talking in thousands, you know. Well, why not? Our Tone here'll never be fit for a proper day's work again."

"He looks perfectly healthy to me," said the Hon. Con firmly.

"Not on your life!" objected Jim Lewcock. "He'll never be able to do the sort of job he did before he ricked himself. Besides"—he couldn't repress a triumphant grin—"there's no bloody law that says you've got to rupture yourself for the bosses, is there?"

This kind of revolutionary talk was usually like a red flag to the Hon. Con, but she couldn't be bothered with questions of industrial loyalty just at the moment. "Here," she demanded, "have I got this straight, or do my ears deceive me? You"—she jabbed an accusing finger at Tony—"have allegedly damaged your back in some kind of sordid industrial accident. As a result, you and your blooming trade-union lawyer are claiming some vast sum in compensation. And it is with the money thus fraudulently extracted from your employers that you intend to set yourselves up in the garage business. Right?"

"I don't go much on calling it fraudulent," objected Tony Lewcock. "My back plays me up something cruel some days."

"But not badly enough," the Hon. Con pointed out, licking her lips as she delivered the coup de grâce, "to stop you from enjoying a pretty strenuous holiday."

"We told you—we was intending to be sunning ourselves on a bloody Spanish beach," objected Jim Lewcock. "Casting a friendly eye over the birds. It'd have done poor Tone's back a power of good. It's not our fault that we've got lumbered with this bloody endurance test."

"What," said the Hon. Con, "would your employers, or the compensation tribunal, say if they knew that he"—she jerked a thumb at Tony—"was hopping round Russia like a two-year-old?"

"They wouldn't say nothing!" snarled Jim Lewcock. "Nothing! Why should they? Even the bloody labouring classes are entitled to a bloody holiday once in a bloody blue moon."

"They're not entitled to swindle people by claiming to be sicker than they actually are!" retorted the Hon. Con. "That's dishonest! No wonder you didn't want the Russian police enquiring into our affairs."

Jim Lewcock sucked in a sharp intake of breath and lowered his voice as much as he could while still remaining audible. "Listen, love," he growled, "don't you start getting any clever ideas! What compensation assessors don't know won't hurt 'em, will it? We're not asking for nothing that isn't our bloody rights."

"That," interrupted the Hon. Con with a smugness of which only the very rich are capable, "is a matter of opinion, my good man!"

"What's likely to happen to you won't be a bloody matter of opinion, love!" Jim Lewcock's face was black. "Look, I'm giving you a friendly warning, see? Don't stick your nose in where it's not wanted. That way you won't come round to find it smashed flat in your stupid face, will you?"

There was nothing wrong with the Hon. Con's courage—mental or physical. Indeed, some admirers considered her at times brave to the point of foolhardiness. On this occasion, however, there was an undercurrent of such viciousness in Jim Lewcock's voice that even our lion-hearted one held her fire. The Hon. Con wasn't frightened, of course. In her book, being frightened was a luxury to be indulged in only by women and children, and, in any case, it would take more than a peasant like Jim Lewcock to put the wind up her. Still, she was in a strange country a thousand miles from home and . . . She was jolly pleased when the flashing of illuminated signs and a general air of bustle indicated that they were getting near to landing. The arrival of a bossy young air hostess saved her the trouble of finding a suitably defiant piece of repartee for Jim Lewcock.

The Hon. Con clipped her seat belt into place as the plane banked sharply. Poor old Bones, she thought as she braced herself against the centrifugal force, she'll be dying a thousand deaths back there all alone. The plane levelled out.

"And I'll tell you something else, missus!" Jim Lewcock leaned over so that he could bawl straight down the Hon. Con's ear. "I'll admit that Tone and me aren't too keen on having the Russian police sniffing round, but Tone's back isn't the only bloody reason. That Clough-Cooper bird! She's having you on! I've met her sort a million times. She's just one of these tarts that'll do anything as long as she's the centre of attention. Anything! Listen"—he gave the Hon. Con a nudge to make sure she hadn't fallen asleep on him—"I don't reckon as how anybody's trying to bloody murder her at all!"

SEVEN

"Well, dear"—Miss Jones tried to sound tactful—"perhaps Mr. Lewcock has got a point."

The Hon. Con thumped her fist into a handy pillow. "Et tu, brute?" she demanded bitterly.

Although Miss Jones suffered from the benefits of a sound classical education, she didn't allow herself to be diverted. She went on placidly unpacking the suitcases.

"Dunno why you're bothering," grumbled the Hon. Con, still sulking. "We're only spending one flipping night here."

Miss Jones ignored this red herring, too. "Miss Clough-Cooper," she went on, stretching the truth a little more than she liked but comforting herself that it was a good cause, "is a very nice young woman, and I'm sure she doesn't actually mean to tell fibs. I think she's probably deceiving herself just as much as she's trying to deceive us. My guess is that something or other happened to frighten her, and she's built up a whole persecution mania on the basis of that. She strikes me as being very highly strung, dear."

"Fiddlesticks!" muttered the Hon. Con. She propped her feet in their heavy shoes on the counterpane of the other bed and waited to see if this would divert Miss Jones into a homily on the need for respect for other people's property.

It didn't.

"And something of an exhibitionist," added Miss Jones, putting away the Hon. Con's shirts in one of the dressing-table drawers.

"An exhibitionist?" howled the Hon. Con.

Miss Jones steeled herself. "Can't you see, dear, that she's simply trying to draw attention to herself? She's trying to make herself appear interesting. That's why she's making up all these silly stories about somebody—one of us, no less!—attempting to kill her. I mean, what proof have you got, dear?"

"Holy cats, Bones!" exploded the Hon. Con, well and truly stung into defending herself. "I know when somebody's trying to pull the old wool over my eyes, for goodness' sake!"

"All you've got is what she says," continued Miss Jones, being cruel to be kind. "I mean—all that business in Alma Ata about somebody trying to smother her—well, she never did get round to explaining how this 'somebody' got into her room, did she?"

"She probably forgot to lock the door."

"After two attempts on her life?" asked Miss Jones incredulously. "A single woman travelling by herself? I don't think that sounds very likely, dear. And what about that Russian floor maid who slept outside all night on the landing? Wouldn't she have noticed somebody breaking into one of the guests' rooms?"

The Hon. Con ripped off a few isometric exercises that were supposed to strengthen the thigh muscles. "The window was open!" she recalled triumphantly.

"Miss Clough-Cooper's bedroom was like ours, dear—on the second floor."

"There was a balcony."

"That still doesn't explain how this attacker reached it—or how he got away again without anybody spotting him."

The Hon. Con bounced off the bed and strode over to the window. "An agile chappie could have nipped across from one balcony to another as easy as anything. Bet I could have done it myself if I'd put my mind to it. And it's not my fault I didn't get a chance to give Penny Clough-Cooper's bedroom a real forensic going over, is it?"

But Miss Jones, who lived in a constant fear of being murdered in her bed, had as a matter of routine examined all the possibilities of forcible entry into the hotel at Alma Ata. In her considered opinion, the defences had been impregnable, and she had subsequently slept the sleep of the just until Miss Clough-Cooper had raised the roof with her screams. However, she saw no sense in antagonising the Hon. Con by challenging her in the field of detection, a field which the Hon. Con jealousy regarded as her own. Faute de mieux, Miss Jones returned to personal attacks on Miss Clough-Cooper.

"She's sly, too."

The Hon. Con turned away from the window as comprehension dawned. "Bones, you don't like her!"

"That has absolutely nothing to do with it, dear." Miss Jones bustled off into the bathroom with the sponge bags and continued the conversation from there. "You just can't believe a word she says, that's all. The woman's a congenital liar."

"Here, steady on, Bones!" exclaimed the Hon. Con miserably. "You've no cause to go round uttering calumnies like that."

"Oh, haven't I?" Miss Jones emerged from the bathroom. "And what about her smoking?"

"Smoking?" echoed the Hon. Con, only too painfully aware that she was on a hiding to nothing.

"Oh, and while I think about it, that toilet needs looking at, dear. It's just like all the others we've had—leaking. Do you think they're made that way especially for foreign tourists?"

The Hon. Con screwed up her face. "Never mind the blooming toilet, Bones! What about the *smoking?*"

"The . . . ? Oh, well, only that I've heard her say two or three times that she doesn't."

"Well?"

"Well, dear"—Miss Jones smoothed the Hon. Con's best cavalry twill slacks over a hanger—"when I popped in to give her her passport back in Tashkent, her room smelled very strongly of stale tobacco smoke. Somebody had quite definitely been smoking in there."

"Could have been the chamber maid."

"Even Russian chamber maids don't go round puffing out smoke like factory chimneys, dear. Besides, the room hadn't been done."

The Hon. Con forced herself to think, even though she felt more in need of the skills of a defending counsel than those of a detective. "What about the ashtrays?"

Miss Jones hesitated. "The ashtrays?"

The Hon. Con pressed home her advantage. "If Penny Clough-Cooper had been smoking all that much," she pointed out triumphantly, "she must have used an ashtray. Blimey, the way you tell it, every blooming ashtray in the room must have been full to overflowing—and the wastepaper basket too, I shouldn't wonder."

Miss Jones went on brushing the collar of the Hon. Con's best hacking jacket, but you could see that her heart wasn't in it. "I don't really remember noticing the ashtrays, dear."

"Exactly!" The Hon. Con gripped the lapels of her second-best hacking jacket like a lawyer clasping his gown and rested her case.

Miss Jones might, somehow, have lost round one, but she had more shots in her locker. "But I did notice, dear, that she'd bought her carton of duty-free cigarettes, because I saw them lying in her suitcase. I must say that that strikes me as a rather funny thing for a supposedly nonsmoker to do."

"Maybe she bought 'em for tips or little presents," said the Hon. Con, scraping the bottom of the barrel.

"Oh, anything's possible, dear," agreed Miss Jones with infuriating restraint.

"But why should she lie about smoking? Crumbs, it's not a crime to smoke, is it?"

Miss Jones had an answer for that one. "Men don't like it, dear," she said in a suitably hushed voice. "They can—er—taste it. I've heard before that it's not a good thing for ladies to advertise that they are addicted to nicotine."

The Hon. Con was obliged to bow to Miss Jones's judgement in these matters. "It all sounds pretty feeble to me," she grumbled.

"Well, what about her father?"

"Her father?"

"Well"—Miss Jones was ashamed of herself, but she couldn't stop—"all this rot about him being a Harley Street specialist or whatever it is."

"He's an orthopaedic surgeon," said the Hon. Con.

"Precisely! Just having an ordinary doctor for a father isn't good enough for her."

The Hon. Con stared at Miss Jones in dismay. "Draw it mild, old fruit!" she begged.

Miss Jones tossed her head. "Well, you can think what you like, dear, but I'll bet you anything that her father is a perfectly everyday, run-of-the-mill general practitioner like everybody else. And now"—Miss Jones looked at her watch—"we've got five minutes before we're due to set off on our tour of the town. Don't you think you'd better pay a visit to the bathroom first, dear?"

Bukhara is one of those jewel towns where exotic Eastern wonders catch the eye on every side. It is a magical treasure trove of ancient mosques and minarets, of mausoleums and medersas. There were citadels and summer palaces and narrow, labyrinthine streets lined with blind, whitewashed walls. Even the hardbitten Albatrossers felt their hearts touched by the wonder of it all.

They had an excellent guide in the person of a girl art student called Masha. She was something of a slave driver, but she knew her stuff and even managed to impart some of her own enthusiasm. As the afternoon drew on, though, even the keenest sightseers showed signs of flagging. The town was hot and dusty, the pavements were hard. And, after a bit, one old mosque begins to look remarkably like another. Still, it wasn't all dreary old culture, and even the Hon. Con managed to forget her poor old feet for a couple of minutes when they came to the Kalian minaret.

"In the bad old days," said Masha, smiling prettily and using the phrase as a synonym for "before the glorious Russian Revolution," "prisoners of the emir were executed by being taken to the top of the tower and thrown down from it. Their bodies landed here on the pavement where we stand."

Miss Jones wasn't the only one to take an involuntary step backwards.

Later on, the citadel—once the town residence of the emirs of Bukhara—proved good for a few laughs, too. As the Albatrossers panted up to this fortress set high on a rock, Masha cheerfully regaled them with tales of stinking prisons and unspeakable tortures. More than one stiff-necked, foolhardy Victorian Englishman, it appeared, had met his death in the emir's dungeons, and Masha didn't resist the temptation to imply that it was mostly their own fault. It was when she led them through into the small museum that she really got the bit between her teeth. The last emir's sexual proclivities (little boys) were prudishly revealed, and then Masha paused dramatically before a glass case containing a long, narrow-bladed knife with a crudely serrated edge. "What," she demanded, "do you imagine that was used for?"

Jim Lewcock had long ago appointed himself tour comedian. He raised his hand like a child in the classroom. "Cutting bread, miss?"

Masha stared at him for a second or two in complete disbelief and then turned to the others, who were behaving decently and disclaiming all knowledge. "It is the knife of the executioner!" she announced with gusto. "I will explain how it was used."

"Must you?" murmured Mrs. Beamish, getting out her handkerchief in readiness.

"The condemned criminal," said Masha, who had clearly learned this bit by heart as her party piece, "was forced to kneel on the ground and his head was pulled back with the hair. The point of this knife was then inserted into the side of his neck, with the jagged edge pointing towards the back. Do you understand?"

"Only too well!" moaned an ashen-faced Mrs. Beamish. She shook her husband by the sleeve. "Why don't you stop her, Norman?"

It would have taken more than Norman Beamish to stop Masha now. "The knife," she went on, "having been thrust right through the criminal's neck, was then twisted round until the jagged edge was pointing to the front . . . so!" She mimed most realistically what she meant. "Then"—the miming continued—"the throat was cut from the *middle* to the *front!* Uncultured, huh?"

Even the Hon. Con thought this was going a bit too far, but she wasn't given the chance to make a protest. Masha was off again, describing more and more horrors, and it seemed ages before they found themselves outside again, back on the tourist trail.

It was a weary and foot-sore bunch that Masha eventually marched back to the hotel as the early tropical night fell with startling speed. Miss Jones and the Hon. Con were stickily arm-in-arm, each affectionately insisting that she had only assumed this posture in order to support and assist the other. Everybody thought that he was tireder and hotter than everybody else, but such is the resilience of the human spirit and frame that the whole caboodle of them was raring to be on the go again even before they'd finished dinner.

"It's not having any opera," decided Mr. Withenshaw, draining his wine glass and refusing coffee. "It leaves the evening strangely empty."

Mrs. Frossell thought this was a most profound analysis of their situation. "And, of course," she added fatuously, "we can't watch the television here, can we?"

Her son went bright red. "Don't be so *bourgeois*, Mother!" he begged in an agonising mutter.

"Why," asked Mr. Beamish, looking almost boyish in his enthusiasm, "don't we all go out for a walk? Just a gentle stroll round the town and maybe a cup of tea in one of those tea houses—*chaynayas*, they call them, don't they?"

"Something like that, old chap!" said Desmond Withenshaw patronisingly.

"Would it be safe, though?" queried Miss Jones nervously. "Some of the native men we saw today . . ."

Mr. Beamish was now thoroughly sold on the idea. "It's only eight o'clock," he pointed out. "And if we all stick together . . ." He pushed his chair back. "Oh, come on, everybody! Let's make a night of it!"

In the end, nearly everybody did rally round, and, feeling very daring without a guide to look after them, they ventured out into the warm, scented darkness. The only exceptions were the Smiths, who announced, with perfectly straight faces, that they were feeling rather tired and thought they'd sooner go to bed. The guffaws of the Lewcock brothers could have been (and probably were) heard in Riga.

Once they were outside, the Albatrossers soon found their eyes growing used to the dark. They formed themselves into a sort of untidy crocodile and, with Norman Beamish and his lady wife at their head, set off.

"Isn't the sky a simply *divine* colour!"

Since the remark emanated from Penelope Clough-Cooper, the Hon. Con experienced an instant conversion to the appreciation of natural beauty. "Scrumptious!" she agreed eagerly. "And look at all those smashing little stars twinkling away up there!" She tried to sidle across to join Miss Clough-Cooper, but somehow Miss Jones always seemed to be in the way. Still, on such a glorious night as this, minor disappointments were soon forgotten.

Desmond Withenshaw called from somewhere at the rear, "Anybody know where we are?" He seemed temporarily to have chummed up with the Frossell boy, while his wife was walking with the lad's mother.

From time to time turbanned figures in cotton caftans slipped past on soft, sandalled feet, disappearing into the darkness almost before they had been seen. It seemed strange to find this Eastern mysteriousness in the Soviet Union.

"We're in that big, open square—you know!" shouted Mr. Beamish, obviously confident that he'd got the situation under control. "Look, there's the citadel up there! You can just see that throne thing that old devil of an emir used to sit on. Er . . ."—he was simply brimming over with bright ideas that evening—"how about a short rest, everybody? There are some benches we could sit on."

They sat, chatting desultorily and enjoying the fresh air, for five minutes or so. On two separate occasions little dark-eyed, importunate boys came rushing up, begging for cigarettes. Jim Lewcock good-naturedly doled out a ration of half an English cigarette per child and accompanied it with a lecture on how smoking stunted your growth. Across the square, at a safer distance, older girls—teenagers—stared in shy fascination and giggled melodiously amongst themselves.

It was all very pleasant and relaxed.

Afterwards, of course, nobody could quite remember who had made the first move, but at a given moment, almost as though responding to a signal, they all got up and began drifting aimlessly back towards their hotel and bed. The Hon. Con was deep in conversation with Mrs. Frossell, discussing, of all things, education in the Soviet Union. It was not a topic that either of them knew much about, but a recent television programme proved of great help, and they both had a great deal of fun blinding each other with science.

Mr. Beamish had drawn Miss Jones in the general post, and he was finding the going hard. Miss Jones commented timidly on the apparent scarcity of doggies in Bukhara. "Pet doggies, I mean, of course."

"Of course!" Mr. Beamish searched round for something else to say, preferably something less banal, and eventually proffered the opinion that the shortage might somehow be due to the heat. No sooner was the word out than he deeply regretted it. Would Miss Jones think he was making some kind of indelicate . . . Oh, hell! He tried again. "Er—has anybody seen Miss Clough-Cooper, by the way?"

"Not to worry!" The Hon. Con's voice boomed comfortingly

out of the darkness. "She's up in front with Mrs. Withenshaw. I'm keeping an eye on her."

"With Mrs. Withenshaw?" Mr. Beamish shoved Miss Jones out of the way. "Are you sure? No, no"—he shook his head angrily—"that's my wife! She's the one walking with Mrs. Withenshaw."

"Your wife?" The Hon. Con squinted through the gloom. "Are you sure?" For one who frequently claimed to have the eyesight of an eagle, it was jolly galling to . . .

"I can recognise my own wife when I see her!" snapped Mr. Beamish.

Miss Jones saw which way the wind was blowing and rushed in to pour oil on the troubled waters. "Actually, they look extraordinarily similar—from a distance. I've mistaken one for the other several times." She twittered on. "It's the dark hair, you know, and the way they wear it. And their stature. Then, of course, they are both of them wearing pink cardigans tonight . . . such a sweetly pretty pink, too! A mistake in identity is all too . . ."

"Oh, stop blethering, Bones!" The Hon. Con was busy counting heads as the other Albatrossers, attracted by the noise of battle, came rushing back to see what was going on. The Hon. Con counted again. It was still one short, and nobody remembered seeing Miss Clough-Cooper for simply ages.

"I'm sure she was with us in the square by the citadel," said Zoë Withenshaw, producing one of those totally useless remarks that people are prone to in a crisis.

The Hon. Con was keeping both feet firmly on the ground. "We must organise a search party!"

The proposal didn't go down at all well. There were murmurs of discontent.

"Organise a search party?" whined Jim Lewcock. "In all these bloody pokey little streets?" They had left the comparatively bustling city centre and were now in the residential area. "We wouldn't find her in a month of bloody Sundays. Jesus, she could be anywhere."

"She'll have gone back to the hotel," asserted his brother. "And I can't say as how I blame her. I dunno about you lot, but my dogs are killing me!"

Desmond Withenshaw was equally restrained in his enthusiasm. "We can't send out a search party for Miss Clough-Cooper," he objected, attempting to laugh the whole thing off. "It's dark and we don't know the town well enough. Look, why don't we go straight back to the hotel and see if she's there. If she isn't—well, we'll tell the Intourist people and let them handle it."

The Hon. Con began to doubt the evidence of her own ears. "Have you forgotten that there have already been three attempts on Penny Clough-Cooper's life?" she demanded furiously. "Good grief, she may be lying dead in a pool of her own blood at this very moment!"

"In which case we'd be too late anyhow," muttered some unidentifiable rotter.

The Hon. Con pressed pigheadedly on. "I propose we divide ourselves into four groups of—well—three or whatever it is. Then we'll set off in different directions—north, south, east, and west—calling Miss Clough-Cooper's name, and . . ."

"And that'll bring the cops down on our bloody necks quicker than anything!" This time there was no mistaking Tony Lewcock's uncultured tones. "I thought that was what the Honourable Miss Bossie-Boots was trying to spare us."

"Now, look here, you!" It was a well-known fact that the Hon. Con had the patience of a saint, but enough was enough. She squared up to Lewcock minor in an attitude strongly reminiscent of bare-fist pugilism. Tony Lewcock sportingly prepared to defend himself, and with no holds barred. There might have been a classic encounter if Miss Jones, ever inclined to overdramatise, had not flung herself between the two heavily breathing protagonists. The rest of the party, having unconsciously formed themselves into a ring, were hard put to restrain their disappointment.

However, the dust-up did serve to clear the air, and the Albatrossers sullenly agreed to undertake a search for the missing Miss Clough-Cooper. The Hon. Con once more attempted to get things organised, but nobody's cooperation stretched that far. Almost before she realised what was happening, the Hon. Con found herself alone with Miss Jones.

"Where've they all gone?" she howled. "Holy cats, it's no good wandering off like that! We ought to quarter the town and . . ." She ranted on for some time while Miss Jones, as was her wont, stood there meekly and took it.

"Perhaps," she suggested at last, "that's Miss Clough-Cooper coming now, dear."

Don't think that the Hon. Con hadn't heard the approaching footsteps, too. "Don't be silly, Bones!" she retorted automatically, and then fell silent as she caught sight of the pathetic and exhausted figure which came limping through the gloaming towards them. "Oh, blimey!"

When Miss Clough-Cooper was sure she had been spotted, she sagged weakly against the nearest wall.

The Hon. Con charged over. "What's happened? Are you all right? Oh, you poor girl! Where on earth did you get to? Why didn't you . . . Bones, don't just stand there, you chump!"

The search party hadn't gone very far. Attracted by the Hon. Con's bellows, it seized the opportunity to come rushing back and gathered around.

Miss Clough-Cooper sagged dramatically at the knees and was caught—much to his wife's and the Hon. Con's disgust—by Mr. Beamish. Miss Clough-Cooper muttered something unintelligible.

"What did she say?" The Hon. Con crowded nearer and tried to shove everybody else out of the way. "Give her air! I say, you rotters, do stand back and let the poor lass breathe!"

Miss Clough-Cooper rallied her flagging forces, filled her lungs, and, enunciating her words clearly, made the announcement which they had all been dreading. "Somebody tried to kill me again!"

This was greeted by a general groan.

The Hon. Con glared angrily at her companions. "When?" she demanded.

"I don't know," whispered Miss Clough-Cooper, and raised a languid hand vaguely to her head.

"Where?"

Miss Clough-Cooper gesticulated even more vaguely behind her. "Somewhere over there, I think. In one of those narrow little alleys with the whitewashed walls." She choked back some sobs. "My tummy's been a bit upset all day, with the strange food and everything, and I thought I'd better get back to the hotel as soon as possible. Naturally"—she cast her eyes down modestly—"I didn't want to disturb the rest of you or have to answer a lot of embarrassing questions."

"Quite, quite," rumbled the Hon. Con, pleasurably surprised to find such modesty. She had somehow got hold of Penelope Clough-Cooper's hand and now patted it encouragingly. "Still, you could have confided in me, you know."

Miss Clough-Cooper shyly acknowledged the reproach. "I'm sorry," she murmured.

"Well, chin up, old fruit!" The Hon. Con was never one to bear a grudge where a pretty girl was concerned. "It doesn't matter. Now, try and tell me exactly what happened. Somebody"—she frowned hideously—"try to—er—grab you?"

Miss Clough-Cooper shook her head. "They threw a knife at me!" she gasped, and, to the Hon. Con's dismay, began to blub in good earnest.

"A *knife?*" queried nearly everybody else.

Miss Clough-Cooper raised a puffy, tear-stained face which shone in the moonlight. "This one!" she said, and held up her hand. Across her palm lay a large pocket knife, its broad, heavy blade open. "I pulled it out of the wall where it had stuck, quivering, after just missing my head." Those with really keen night vision could actually see a flake of white powder on the tip of the blade.

"Bloody hell!" Jim Lewcock reacted predictably to this new crisis. "Here, is that a Russian knife?" He leaned forward and stretched out his hand.

"Don't touch it!" howled the Hon. Con, who'd probably read more detective stories than the rest of them put together. "Fingerprints," she explained in a more reasonable tone.

Any tendency to explore the problem of how the Hon. Con was going to cope with fingerprints, if any, was abandoned in the face of yet another sensation. Mrs. Frossell, well to the fore, was staring in fascination at the knife. It is debatable how much of the earlier proceedings had actually sunk in, but her contribution now was loud and clear. It was also unambiguous. "Why," she said, even smiling a little, "that's Roger's knife!" She turned to her son. "Isn't it, dear?"

Roger Frossell raised both hands in the air and excelled himself. "Oh, *Mother!*" he wailed.

EIGHT

"I," said the Hon. Con with that passionate determination which has got England in its present mess, "am prepared to sit up all night, if needs be, as long as we get at the truth."

Young Roger Frossell gulped down a yawn. "Well, I'm not!"

They were sitting in the bathroom. The Hon. Con, cashing in on the privileges of rank, proprietorship, and age, had got the prime position and was reasonably comfortable on the polished wooden seat. Roger Frossell had had to be content with the edge of the bath. When he wasn't fully occupied with yawning his head off, he concentrated on keeping his feet securely resting on the narrow strip of duck boarding.

He yawned again. "Oh, God," he grumbled sleepily. "Look, can't we leave this till morning?"

"You youngsters!" sneered the Hon. Con. "Not an ounce of the old stamina amongst the lot of you. And watch your language, sonnie!"

"When you're my age, you need your sleep!"

The Hon. Con scowled. "Don't be cheeky!"

Roger Frossell tried to ease the ache in his back. "Sorry," he mumbled. "Look, I'm not trying to be obstructive or anything, but I really am tired. I'd be much more use to you in the morning, when we've both had a good night's sleep. And there's my mother, too," he added in a vain appeal to the Hon. Con's maternal instinct. "You know what she's like. She won't go to bed while you've got me penned up in here."

"Your knife!" said the Hon. Con. They were words she'd said several times before.

Roger Frossell let his exasperation show. "For the nine

millionth time," he snarled, "anybody could have got hold of that f . . . flaming knife! I missed it when we were in Moscow and I haven't seen it since. Not until Miss Clough-Cooper produced it this evening."

"So you say!"

"Ask my mother, then! She'll tell you exactly the same thing."

"Ever heard of collusion?" asked the Hon. Con scathingly. "Your mother would swear black was sky-blue pink if she thought it would save your miserable skin."

Roger Frossell acknowledged the truth of this sadly. "Why do women have to be so possessive?"

The Hon. Con spurned so obvious a red herring. "Don't change the subject!" she snapped. "Where did you keep this knife?"

"I didn't keep it anywhere specially. Sometimes I had it in my pocket and sometimes I didn't. I left it in my suitcase or on the dressing table or in the pocket of another jacket."

"Trust you," said the Hon. Con gloomily. "And where had you purportedly left this knife when it disappeared?"

Roger Frossell shrugged his thin shoulders. "Search me. I told you, it could have been lost days before I missed it. Hours, anyway. As a matter of fact, I didn't know until this evening that I'd really lost it. I thought it was still kicking round somewhere and would turn up in due course."

The Hon. Con sighed. It all sounded so plausible. She wished she could be sure that this smooth-tongued young whippersnapper wasn't trying to pull the wool over her eyes. "You don't fool me," she said.

Roger Frossell had a great deal of charm when he wanted to. He turned on a bit of it now. "I wouldn't even try!" he protested, twinkling his eyes. "You'd be more than a match for an idiot like me, Miss Morrison-Burke. That's why," he pointed out slyly, "I was so keen for you to undertake this whole investigation. You may recall that I was one of your most enthusiastic supporters."

"Sez you!" responded the Hon. Con, weakening a little in spite of herself. She tried to live up to the flattering image the young pup had of her. "Has it struck you that our potential murderer must be a blooming boy scout or something?"

"A boy scout? How do you make that out?"

The Hon. Con hitched up her left trouser leg and gave her calf a good scratch. That was the trouble with ankle socks: they left gaps where the creepy-crawlies could sneak in and get you. She rearranged her clothing. "Listen," she said, "suppose our joker fellow knicked your chiv in Moscow." She beamed with satisfaction as she remembered the jargon. "Even if it was after the two attempts to kill poor old Penny Clough-Cooper in Moscow, it was still *before* the attempt to snuff her in Alma Ata." She leaned back. "Hence, the boy scout."

The rim of the bath was biting into young Roger Frossell's buttocks. "I'm afraid I don't quite see . . ."

" 'Be Prepared'!" explained the Hon. Con. "Oh, come on, laddie! Shake the old grey cells! Our putative murderer steals your knife to kill Penny Clough-Cooper with—right? Well, how did he know that the attempt on her life, by suffocating her with a pillow, in Alma Ata was going to fail? That's why I said he must be a boy scout. Prepared for every eventuality."

"Oh." Roger Frossell had always suspected that people's brains started softening at twenty-five, and now he was sure. He gave the Hon. Con his most dazzling smile. "Gosh, aren't you clever!"

"Comes of having a tidy mind," said the Hon. Con modestly. "On the other hand, though, maybe our laddie isn't really trying to kill Penny Clough-Cooper. Perhaps he just wants to scare the living daylights out of her."

Roger Frossell looked up in surprise. "Why on earth should he want to do that?"

"I dunno," said the Hon. Con, and glared hard at the boy. "Sort of silly prank kids of your age get up to, though, isn't it?"

"Oh, come on! I'm eighteen, not eight."

"You could just be trying to take the mickey out of your elders and betters." The Hon. Con was beginning to wonder if she'd stumbled on the answer to her problem at last. "And that might explain why you're so keen to keep the Russian police out of it. And why you were so keen on me taking charge of the investigation." Her face darkened ominously. "You thought I'd never discover the truth, you little rat!"

Roger Frossell looked alarmed. "It wasn't like that at all!" he protested with considerably more vehemence than he'd shown for some time. "Honestly it wasn't!" He seemed on the point of saying something more but caught himself in time and clamped his mouth shut. It was so obvious that he was trying to hide something that even the Hon. Con noticed it. Instead of pursuing the matter there and then, though, she decided to box clever and spring it on the cheeky young monkey at some later date, when he was least expecting it.

"Eighteen, eh?" she said, hoping to confuse him by this abrupt change of subject. "Why aren't you at school?"

Roger Frossell sighed. "Well, I am, really."

"It looks like it!" sneered the Hon. Con.

"Well, I don't leave officially till the end of term, of course, but I'm not going on to university, so I don't really have to bother all that much about exams. My uncle's a publisher, and I'm going to join him after the summer vac. He's footing the bill for this little jolly, actually."

"Is he?" The Hon. Con's eyes bulged enviously.

"Yes"—Roger Frossell dismissed his uncle's extremely generous gesture with a careless wave of the hand—"he wanted to give my mother a bit of a break, and choosing Russia was his way of bribing me to go with her. I am not," he added loftily, "in the habit of holidaying with my mother."

"Young prig!" The Hon. Con might have expressed herself at greater length if she hadn't leaned back and accidentally rested her elbow on the handle which jutted out of the cistern. Roger Frossell experienced a moment of sheer joy as he anticipated the upheaval . . . but, no! Soviet loos aren't built to flush as easily as that. There was a great deal of clanking and gurgling, but that was all. The Hon. Con, still doggedly chewing over her problems, remained undisturbed on her throne. "Ungrateful, too," she commented, just as though nothing had happened. Which, when you came to think about it, hadn't.

Roger Frossell realised that the Hon. Con was still regarding him with a jaundiced eye and, being quite a bright boy, hunted round for something with which to divert the old girl's attention. Another suspect, perhaps? "What do you think about Desmond Withenshaw, Miss Morrison-Burke?"

The Hon. Con squinted at her interrogator cautiously. To admit that she hadn't really thought about him at all looked like slacking. "Got my eye on him," she growled. Curiosity overcame pride. "Why?"

"I just thought he was acting in a rather odd way, that's all."
Roger Frossell glanced speculatively at the Hon. Con and wondered just how much guff she would swallow.

"Oh?"

Roger Frossell was very naughty. "Haven't you noticed the way
he tries to keep his wife and Miss Clough-Cooper apart? It stands
out a mile. I thought everybody would have spotted it."

The Hon. Con's eyes were like saucers. "Some people can't see
further than the ends of their noses."

"Good thing you're not like that."

"Well, that's my job—keeping the old jeepers-peepers sharp!"
The Hon. Con grinned. "Still, let's not bother our heads about Mr.
Withenshaw. It's you we've got to deal with at the moment. I still
think you're hiding something."

Roger Frossell stood up. "Look," he said, "I've simply got to be
shoving off now." The Hon. Con's conversational style was
catching. "Dashed sorry and all that, but my dear old mater will be
raising Cain if I'm absent without leave much longer."

"Tell me what you're hiding first!"

Roger Frossell grimaced. The Hon. Con's resemblance to a
bulldog was not merely facial, it seemed. "I am not hiding
anything, Miss Morrison-Burke."

"Oh, yes, you are!"

"Oh, no, I'm not!"

"You are!"

"No!"

"Yes!"

There is no knowing how long this intellectual debate might
have lasted if Roger Frossell hadn't picked on the only way he
could think of to take the wind out of the Hon. Con's sails and shut
her up. He suppressed another yawn and placed his finger on his
lips.

The Hon. Con frowned. "What's up?"

Roger Frossell rolled his eyes.

The Hon. Con's frown deepened. "You sickening for something, laddie?"

Roger Frossell cupped his hands round his mouth. "Walls," he
hissed, "have ears!"

"Eh?" The Hon. Con caught on quite quickly. It was, perhaps, an occupational hazard for visitors to the Soviet Union which she should have thought of for herself. "In here?" she asked uncertainly.

Roger Frossell's face expressed acute horror. "Haven't you checked? Look, I think we'd better postpone our conversation until tomorrow, don't you? When we can talk *out in the open air!*" He didn't wait for an argument but shot out of the bathroom, leaving the Hon. Con to make her exit at a more sedate speed.

Miss Jones, sitting bolt upright on the only uneasy chair in the room, winced pathetically as Roger Frossell slammed the bedroom door behind him. She was, of course, fully dressed and had, as a matter of fact, been listening at the keyhole until just before the twosome broke up.

"Think we may be on to something, Bones," said the Hon. Con, beginning untantalisingly to undo the buttons of her shirt.

Miss Jones leaned back in her chair and closed her eyes. "Really, dear?"

The Hon. Con peered through the folds of her shirt. "Where's Penny Clough-Cooper?"

"Oh, she went back to her own room hours ago, dear."

"Damn it all, Bones"—the Hon. Con dragged the shirt back on again—"you were supposed to be standing guard over her!"

The shrug of Miss Jones's shoulders was barely visible. "I couldn't stop her, dear. I offered to go and sit with her in her room, but she wouldn't have that, either. She said she'd lock her door and that she'd be perfectly all right."

"Like she was in Alma Ata, I suppose?" retorted the Hon. Con crossly. "You should have come and told me, Bones!"

"You said you weren't to be disturbed, dear."

The Hon. Con thought about this for a minute or two and then sat down and began unlacing her chukka boots. "I don't mind people being brave," she pointed out, "but I do object to 'em being foolhardy."

Miss Jones contented herself with compressing her lips into an even thinner straight line.

"I'd go and tell her so, too," boasted the Hon. Con, "if I didn't think the poor lass would probably already be in the arms of Morpheus. Not much point in trying to get her to spend the night in here now."

75

The Hon. Con had uttered this last remark in a sort of growling aside, but it proved clear enough to bring tears to Miss Jones's eyes. "Spend the night in here?" she repeated stupidly.

"Hm," said the Hon. Con, chucking her rolled-up socks to land on the dressing table, and missing. "Thought you wouldn't mind kipping in her room for a night or two, just while I sort things out." She hurried to point out the undoubted advantage of this arrangement. "Means you'd be able to have a single room without paying the supplement."

"And you thought I wouldn't mind?" queried Miss Jones bitterly, forgetting all about the headache she was going to have. "Well, why on earth should I mind, dear?" She jumped to her feet and plucked distractedly at her lamb's wool cardigan. "Even if the murderer struck again and killed me by mistake, at least Miss Clough-Cooper would be safe and sound, wouldn't she? And that appears to be all that matters!" Miss Jones snatched up her nightdress from the bed, and the sudden gesture had the Hon. Con ducking instinctively.

"Steady on, old trout!" implored the Hon. Con.

Miss Jones's trembling lip curled scornfully and she flounced off towards the bathroom.

The Hon. Con realised what was about to happen and hunched her shoulders up round her ears.

Miss Jones obliged and closed the bathroom door with a firmness that shook the entire hotel to its foundations.

Luckily, a good night's sleep did wonders for everybody's temper, and when the new day dawned, the Hon. Con was relieved to open her eyes on the view of Miss Jones, happily slaving away at the packing.

The Hon. Con sank back to wallow in the luxury of another ten minutes in bed. "We seem to be living in suitcases these days," she remarked chattily, well aware of how a few kind words can maintain the morale of the troops. "We no sooner arrive somewhere than we have to pack up and move on somewhere else."

Miss Jones continued with her smoothing and folding. "I'm afraid that's the price we have to pay for sightseeing, dear."

"True, true," agreed the Hon. Con, fearful that Budleigh

Salterton was about to raise its ugly head again. "Where's our next port of call?"

"Somewhere called Sukhumi, dear."

The Hon. Con had long since got over her surprise at the places Albatross Travel took them to. "And what's Sukhumi, when it's at home?"

It was one of Miss Jones's duties to read the guidebooks. "It's a seaside town, dear. The Black Sea, of course. The itinerary promises us a couple of days lazing on the beach in the sun."

The Hon. Con began her early-morning loosening-up exercises. "Don't suppose there'll be much rest for *me!*" she grunted.

Miss Jones got to her feet. "I suppose we ought to be going down to breakfast, dear. We've got to be ready to leave in less than three quarters of an hour, and you know it isn't good for you to bolt your food."

It was a longish flight from Bukhara to Sukhumi, right across the Caspian Sea and the whole of Transcaucasia. The Hon. Con had been fully determined not to waste the time, but she had reckoned without her fellow travellers. To a man they slept the sleep of the just and the utterly exhausted. As the Aeroflot plane roared through the blue sky, the Hon. Con stared round at the somnolent forms. Even Miss Jones was snuggled down in the seat beside her. Oh, well, thought the Hon. Con with noteworthy equanimity, if you can't beat 'em, join 'em. She closed her eyes and let her mouth drop open.

The treadmill started again as soon as they landed. It was oppressively hot in Sukhumi, and the Albatrossers filed wearily across the soggy tarmac into the waiting room, which, once again, was specially unlocked for them. This time, though, there was no waiting round. They had barely flopped down before they were rousted out again and herded back into that shimmering furnace. Their guide, seemingly unaffected by the heat, was young, enthusiastic, and energetic. She wasn't a bad looker, either, in spite of a rather pronounced Georgian nose, but even those well-known lechers, the Lewcock brothers, were too bushed to raise so much as a wolf whistle between them.

The Albatrossers' confident expectation of a couple of days' peace and quiet in Sukhumi was soon shattered. Their Intourist guide wanted to get her free English lessons as much as anybody else. She was called Tatiana and gleefully outlined their programme over the minibus loudspeaker system. There wasn't going to be a dull moment. The Sukhumi Intourist Bureau wasn't completely heartless, though. The Albatrossers could have a whole hour for unpacking and settling in their hotel.

"If," observed the Hon. Con, staring bleary-eyed at the sparkling waters of the Black Sea, "somebody was writing a flipping book about this investigation of mine, they'd jolly well have to call it 'Detection under Difficulties.' " She'd been thinking this out for some time and was disgruntled that she hadn't been able to come up with a snappier title.

Miss Jones came bustling out of the bathroom and generously spared a moment to wonder at the Hon. Con's imaginative powers. Somebody writing a book about her, indeed! Miss Jones brought the conversation back to earth with a bang. "I'm afraid that tap's still dripping, dear. Don't you think we'd better tell them about it when we go downstairs? And what on earth is that that you've got stuck on your face cloth?" She sank on her knees beside yet another suitcase.

"I dunno," muttered the Hon. Con without interest. She wondered whether it was worthwhile getting out her tool kit again and having another go at that blessed tap. "Oh, heck," she grumbled, "I thought it was going to be nice and cool down here by the sea."

Miss Jones seemed unaffected by the heat. "Somebody was saying it would be cool up at this lake we're going to see tomorrow. Mr. Withenshaw, I think. He's usually the one who's read everything up, isn't he? It's up in the mountains, apparently."

The Hon. Con rested her chin on folded hands. "What do you make of this Withenshaw chappie, Bones?"

"In what way, dear?"

The Hon. Con hunched her shoulders. She knew better than to say "as a murder suspect." Miss Jones tended to panic if she was asked to put a noose, more or less, round somebody's neck. "Oh, just as a man, don't you know."

It was fortunate that the Hon. Con was still gazing out the window, because Miss Jones suddenly went a bright pink. All over.

78

She hid her confusion as best she could by burrowing even deeper into the suitcase. "He seems quite nice, dear."

If the Hon. Con hadn't been so cheesed off, she might have taken umbrage at such a wishy-washy, sitting-on-the-blooming-fence type of answer. As it was, she contented herself with a routine moan. "Must you always look on the bright side, Bones?"

Miss Jones sat back on her heels and let herself drift away into the romantic myths of her youth. Black tents, sand, waiting camels, a hot wind blowing off the desert, hairy chests and muscular arms. She sighed. "And passionately jealous!" she said aloud.

The Hon. Con turned away from the window. "Jealous? Withenshaw?"

"No one," throbbed Miss Jones, rocking herself hypnotically to and fro, "would ever be allowed to come between him and the woman of his desires."

"Oh, don't be so wet, Bones!" said the Hon. Con impatiently before returning to her contemplation of the great outdoors. "Tell you why I was asking. Young Roger Frossell reckons Withenshaw is trying to keep his wife and Penny Clough-Cooper apart for some reason."

Miss Jones's dreams of Araby dispersed as the Clough-Cooper woman's name dropped into the conversation yet again. "Well, why shouldn't he?"

The Hon. Con didn't know. "I was just wondering if you'd noticed anything out of the ordinary. I've got to take account of the least little thing that might be suspicious."

Miss Jones took the Hon. Con's other pair of brogues out of their plastic travelling bag (one had to let the leather breathe) and placed them tidily on the floor of the wardrobe. The door squeaked unbearably as she closed it.

"Have to give that a drop of the old oil," said the Hon. Con, who was well equipped to deal with all emergencies.

Miss Jones came over to the window. "If," she said with ill-concealed malice, "you had told me that Mrs. Withenshaw was making every effort to keep her husband and Miss Clough-Cooper apart, I wouldn't have been surprised in the least little bit. That woman, Constance, is a man-eater, if I ever saw one!"

The Hon. Con stared at her aghast. "Penny Clough-Cooper?"

"Sex mad!" exploded Miss Jones, who'd got beyond caring what she said. "Guaranteed to chase after anything in trousers!" Miss Jones wasn't too upset to choose her words with care. She glanced out the window. Down below, in the sunshine, several familiar figures were strolling gently along the paved and tree-lined walk. It was all grist to Miss Jones's mill. "Look at her now!" she exclaimed triumphantly, indicating the small, darked-haired figure some sixty or seventy feet beneath them. "Crawling all over some poor man, as usual. It's disgusting! Much worse than the television. Good heavens"—she leaned forward to take a closer look—"it's poor Mr. Beamish bearing the brunt again, isn't it?"

"Yes, it is!" snarled the Hon. Con, who had also been taking a lively interest in the passing scene. "And that's *Mrs.* Beamish with him, you ninny! Penny Clough-Cooper isn't out there at all." She regarded her chum with naked fury. "It's a pity, Bones, you don't take yourself off to a blooming optician and get yourself some flipping glasses! You're getting as blind as a bat!"

NINE

The sun beat down relentlessly, and although it was only ten o'clock in the morning, the temperature was already soaring into the eighties, and the glare coming off the Black Sea was blinding.

The Albatrossers had been installed in one corner of the Intourist beach, and within five minutes nobody would have taken it for anything other than a British enclave. It was untidy, uncomfortable, and strictly out-of-bounds to foreigners. Mrs. Frossell's Union Jack carrier bag struck a suitably patriotic note, and even little Mrs. Smith's bikini (top half stars and bottom half stripes) at least maintained the national colour scheme. The centre of the outpost was a large beach umbrella under which the tender-skinned speedily established themselves. Those who didn't turn bright pink in the sun or come out in spots took to the sands and spread themselves out on reclining chairs, purloined hotel towels, and some splintery duck boarding that they'd found half buried in the sand.

"This," sighed Mr. Withenshaw luxuriously, and ignoring whatever it was that was sticking in the small of his back, "is the life, eh?" He held his face up to the sun and anticipated the sour grapes of his colleagues at school when he got back home with a Black Sea tan. "In my considered judgement, this place has got your Cornish Riviera knocked into a cocked hat."

His wife spat out a couple of ounces of sand which a sudden breeze had blown into her mouth. "It certainly has!" she agreed loyally.

The Smiths, lying rigidly side by side, were some little way off. Before stretching themselves out they had solemnly and carefully anointed each other with oil.

The Lewcock brothers had moved down nearer to the water's edge and loudly promised each other that they'd go in for a dip when the heat got unbearable. Meantime, they concentrated on ogling such female forms as caught their eyes.

Huddled together under the umbrella were Miss Jones, Mrs. Frossell, and Mrs. Beamish. No bikinis for them, alas! Instead, looking comparatively cool and composed, they lay back in their chairs and sweated gently in long-sleeved frocks and stockings. Roger Frossell had retreated as far as he could from the main group, a retreat which was tactful in view of the brevity of his swimming trunks. The Hon. Con, to name but one, had been so horrified by his appearance that she'd hardly been able to drag her eyes away from the lad.

The Hon. Con had allied herself, of course, to the nature lovers and was even now turning lobster-pink in the full glare of the sun. This was the price you had to pay, she told herself ruefully as she squatted gingerly on the burning sand, for acting as bodyguard to old Penny Clough-Cooper. And old Penny Clough-Cooper was probably going to need a bodyguard! Even to the Hon. Con's indulgent gaze, the young woman did appear to be somewhat overexposed. Not that her bikini was any more outrageous than hundreds that they'd seen on the other beaches they'd walked past. It was simply that her figure made the whole ensemble so much more explosive. The Lewcock brothers had already given expression to their vulgar appreciation, and Norman Beamish looked as though he'd been hypnotised. It was also a fair bet that not all the sweat on Desmond Withenshaw's noble brow was due to the warmth of the day. Roger Frossell, secure in the knowledge that the geriatrics began at twenty-six, had been less impressed, but even he had looked twice.

The Albatrossers were a little uneasy and finding it difficult to settle down. Maybe it was Miss Clough-Cooper's unexpectedly nubile figure that was upsetting them—men and women both—or maybe it was simply that, now that they had some leisure time, they didn't know what to do with it. There they were, lounging in solitary splendour on a private beach specially reserved for foreign tourists and feeling guilty because they weren't using their time more profitably.

Mrs. Beamish attempted a bit of vicarious culture. "Sukhumi is quite a pretty little town, isn't it?"

Miss Jones was constitutionally incapable of rejecting so blatant a conversational gambit. It was the price she had to pay for having been so nicely brought up. "Oh, very pretty," she agreed eagerly. "Much the prettiest town we've seen so far, in my opinion."

Mrs. Beamish introduced a more astringent note. "Of course," she pointed out sternly, "it is not a very historical town."

Miss Jones, sycophantly and simperingly, agreed that it wasn't. That, she suggested, didn't make it any less pretty though, did it?

"It's the trees," said Mrs. Beamish. "The magnolias, the palms, the oleanders. They give the town its special character."

"And the sea," ventured Miss Jones.

"And the sea," allowed Mrs. Beamish graciously.

Several people, unlucky enough to be within earshot, took a firm grip on themselves and tried to believe that tolerance really was a virtue.

"I didn't," Miss Jones went on, lowering her voice and glancing round in the furtive way Western tourists soon develop, "care much for those monkeys."

Mrs. Beamish puckered up her lips and shuddered. "That was disgraceful!" she agreed. "Quite disgraceful! I mean"—she rearranged her handbag on her lap—"if they must keep all those hundreds and hundreds of monkeys for vivisection, there's absolutely no need to show the place as a tourist attraction. There is such a thing as decency—and I told that guide so, too!"

Miss Clough-Cooper was daubing herself with oil.

The Hon. Con scrambled eagerly across the intervening patch of sand. "Here, let me give you a helping paw!" She grinned widely. "I'll do the bits you can't reach, eh?"

Miss Clough-Cooper didn't panic. She quite calmly screwed the top back on the bottle. "It's all right, thanks."

"You go a lovely brown," said the Hon. Con enviously. Miss Clough-Cooper lay back on her towel and closed her eyes. The Hon. Con recognised the signs and knew that if she didn't keep on talking she'd have the blessed girl going to sleep on her. She cleared her throat. "Some people say," she announced loudly, "that it's supposed to be jolly bad for the old skin."

Sheer politeness forced Penny Clough-Cooper to open one eye. "What is?" she asked reluctantly.

"Sunbathing."

"Oh."

The Hon. Con shuffled even nearer. "Er—what does your father think about it?"

"My father?"

The Hon. Con puffed out her cheeks. Jumping Jehoshaphat, but this was uphill work! "He's a doctor, ain't he?"

"Oh, I see what you mean." Miss Clough-Cooper took time off to dispose her limbs more comfortably. "Well, he's an orthopaedic surgeon, actually. I think I told you that, didn't I? I don't suppose he knows much more about skin care than you do."

The Hon. Con had reached the stage of grasping at any straw. "An orthopaedic surgeon, eh? How jolly interesting!"

Miss Clough-Cooper sighed and turned her face to the sea.

The Hon. Con tried again. "Er—what exactly does an orthopaedic surgeon do when he's at home?"

This time Penelope Clough-Cooper's sigh was heavy and pronounced. *"Bad backs!"* she said, slowly, clearly, and finally.

"Bloody hell!" A few yards away across the golden sands Jim Lewcock sat bolt upright. "Oh, sod it!"

His brother grunted sleepily at his side. "What's up?"

Jim Lewcock was scrambling to his feet. "Need you bloody ask?" He stood up and looked round. "Where the hell is it?"

Tony Lewcock sat up too. "Back of the hut we changed in, I should think. Yes, sure to be."

"God damn it!" Jim Lewcock muttered crossly to himself as he set off back up the beach. "Excuse me, ladies!" There was no reason for him to go stepping all over the Hon. Con and Miss Clough-Cooper, but even in moments of dire emergency Jim Lewcock would do anything for a giggle. "Make way there for a man in a hurry!"

The Hon. Con rolled clear of Jim Lewcock's enormous bare feet. "Where the heck do you think you're going?" she demanded angrily.

Jim Lewcock grinned and bent down. He reduced his voice to a whisper that carried from one end of the beach to the other. "I'm just going to point Percy at the porcelain!" he explained. "Back in a minute!"

Foul-mouthed brute! The Hon. Con ignored the barely suppressed sniggers which arose on all sides and flopped down flat on her face. To hell with the lot of 'em! She was going to settle down and have a good old think about her detection problems. Now then—was somebody really trying to do away with Penny Clough-Cooper, or was the poor lass suffering from a too-vivid imagination? Or was somebody simply trying to give her a good scare? The Hon. Con, pleased with the progress she was making, wriggled round until she'd excavated a comfortable hollow in the sand. But why should anyone want to frighten or—even worse—kill Penny Clough-Cooper? She seemed a harmless enough girl—pleasant and intelligent if, perhaps, not very forthcoming. The innocent daughter of an innocent orthopaedic surgeon and the impeccable employee of an impeccable firm of solicitors. Was there—the Hon. Con screwed up her face behind her sunglasses—some emotional tangle somewhere in the background? Penny Clough-Cooper didn't look that kind of girl, but these days you never knew. But, even if she was, why should that make her a murder victim? The Hon. Con drove deeper furrows along her brow. Had she chastely rejected the lascivious advances of some swine of a man? Or—the Hon. Con's face paled—had she perhaps *not* rejected the lascivious advances of some swine of a man and it was his wife who was on the old war path? Oh, blimey!

It was nearly an hour later when a hideous cacophony of raucous shrieks and cries woke the Hon. Con from her slumbers. She sat up, mouth like a parrot's cage and eyes all puffed up, to find that the Intourist beach had been taken over by the hooligan hordes of a latter-day Genghis Khan.

"Good God!"

Miss Jones laid aside her darning. "They're East Germans, apparently, dear. Well"—she dabbed her brow with a handkerchief drenched in eau-de-cologne—"and did you have a nice little nap?"

"Where's Penny Clough-Cooper?"

Miss Jones picked up her darning. "She said she had a bit of a headache, dear, and thought she'd go back to the hotel."

"Oh, no!" roared the Hon. Con, beginning to scramble to her feet. "Not again!"

But Miss Jones didn't have to be told things twice. "Now, there's nothing to worry about, dear! I remembered what you said."

"So why didn't you wake me?" howled the Hon. Con. "You know that girl's in mortal danger and can't be allowed to wander about unprotected and all alone."

"Don't shout, dear!" Miss Jones rarely forgot the proprieties. "Miss Clough-Cooper is not wandering about unprotected and all alone. Mrs. Frossell very kindly offered to go back with her. Mrs. Frossell had developed a headache too, it seems. I can't say I'm surprised. It really is terribly hot."

"Mrs. Frossell?" gasped the Hon. Con.

"Well, I'm sure you don't suspect her of being your murderer, do you, dear?" Miss Jones's silvery laugh tinkled out and was lost in the row the East Germans were making as they indulged themselves in some mass and elaborate calisthenics.

"It always turns out to be the most unlikely person, you chump!" snarled the Hon. Con, making a full-scale production out of the simple actions of gathering up her belongings.

"But, even if it is Mrs. Frossell, she'll hardly dare kill Miss Clough-Cooper this time, will she, dear?"

"Why not?"

"Because that would make her the only suspect, wouldn't it, dear?" Miss Jones's sturdy common sense could be very irksome at times. "All the rest of us are here, aren't we? With cast-iron alibis. Whenever the murderer has struck in the past, you see, he's made very sure that there have been a number of suspects, hasn't he?"

"Hm." The Hon. Con wasn't prepared to surrender her grievances as easily as all that. She shut the screaming East Germans out of her mind and concentrated on her fellow Albatrossers. She couldn't help feeling that she'd done this sort of thing before, and maybe it was this which distracted her. She began the count again.

"Would you like a piece of chocolate, dear?"

The Hon. Con rounded on Miss Jones, clenching her fists and raising them to that blue, cloudless sky. "Drat you, Bones!" she remonstrated. "You've made me get it wrong again! There should be nine here besides you and me, and I only made it eight."

"Oh, it is only eight, dear," said Miss Jones with a touch of embarrassment. "Roger Frossell left some time ago. Long before Miss Clough-Cooper decided she'd had enough, though—so he couldn't be following her, could he?" She saw the look on the Hon. Con's face and interpreted it correctly. "Mrs. Frossell definitely didn't lure Miss Clough-Cooper away, dear. I can give you my word about that. Miss Clough-Cooper made the first move and . . ."

"D'you mind passing over my sandals, Bones?" said the Hon. Con, frightfully distant and cold.

"Are you going after Miss Clough-Cooper, dear?"

On the grounds that a trouble shared is a trouble halved, the Hon. Con decided not to bear a grudge. "*We*'re going after Miss Clough-Cooper, Bones!"

It was something of a disappointment to find Miss Clough-Cooper alive and well behind the locked door of her hotel bedroom. She was rather cross at being disturbed, and the Hon. Con and Miss Jones returned to their own room with ears that were still tingling.

"Poor girl," rumbled the Hon. Con, searching for an excuse. " 'Fraid the strain's beginning to get her down."

Miss Jones was still smarting at the way the Hon. Con had been treated. "She was certainly very brusque," she agreed stiffly. "Well, what are we going to do now, dear? Go back to the beach?"

The Intourist beach at Sukhumi was some considerable way from the hotel and the centre of the town and even involved a short boat journey. Apart from having to negotiate all the normal difficulties of a foreign transport system, visitors to Sukhumi also had to cope with the excessive friendliness of the local population, who were a special breed of Georgians called Abhazians. The Hon. Con and Miss Jones had had to suffer some very unwelcome attentions from swarthy, dark-eyed men who flashed mouthfuls of gold teeth at them and lounged suggestively on the boat rail. It had quite knocked all Miss Jones's soppy ideas of romance on the head and she clung to the Hon. Con for protection. The fact that the propositions which were being made to them were unintelligible didn't make them any less frightening, and—as the Hon. Con was tactless enough to point out—anybody could see with half an eye that they all kept harems, communist state or no communist state.

"It wouldn't be so bad," Miss Jones had wailed, huddling

pathetically up to a padlocked life belt, "if they weren't so foreign-looking."

The Hon. Con kept her mind on the practicalities of the situation. "Good grief, here comes another one! If he takes another step, Bones, kick him where it'll do the most good!"

No, neither of them fancied that boat trip back to the beach.

Besides, the Hon. Con had other fish to fry. For some time now she had been troubled by the realisation that she was not carrying out this investigation with her usual vigour. True, she was operating under extreme difficulties, but, to a private eye of her calibre, that should merely have heightened the challenge. Wasn't—the Hon. Con encouraged herself—the prospect of Penny Clough-Cooper's gratitude enough to put a bit of the old zip, the old get-up-and-go spirit back into one's veins? Yes, by golly—the Hon. Con slapped her thigh—it was!

Miss Jones, frivolously examining her freckles in the mirror, gave a little jump.

The Hon. Con grinned reassuringly. "Steady the buffs!" she advised. " 'Fraid we're going to have to pack in the old sunbathing for today."

Miss Jones began breathing again. "Oh, that'll suit me, dear!" She laughed shyly. "I don't want to finish up with my skin looking like a piece of old leather."

The Hon. Con, whose skin did look like a piece of old leather, failed to appreciate the point. "Listen," she went on, "I want you to pop along and see if Mrs. Frossell and her dratted son are in their rooms. I don't trust that lad as far as I can chuck him."

Miss Jones, well used to being put upon, duly popped. Her report when she returned brought the scowl back to the Hon. Con's face. Mrs. Frossell, Miss Jones stated, was in her room having a rest and—until Miss Jones came hammering at her door—had been asleep. Of young Roger Frossell, on the other hand, there was no sign.

"The mother does not know where the little perisher is?"

Miss Jones shook her head. "She says not, dear." Miss Jones returned to the mirror and her freckles. "Oh, and I even tried asking the chamber maid on the landing, dear. She doesn't speak any English, of course, but I think we managed to communicate. She pointed to her watch, and I rather gather that she hadn't seen young Mr. Frossell since he left for the beach with the rest of us after breakfast."

"He must be somewhere!" insisted the Hon. Con.

"Oh, yes, I should think so, dear."

The Hon. Con picked up Miss Jones's white cotton gloves from the bed and handed them to her chum. "And we're going to find him! Best foot forward, Bones!"

It is unlikely that the natives of Sukhumi had heard the one about mad dogs and Englishmen, but innumerable pairs of large, dark eyes peered unbelievingly out of the shadows as the Hon. Con and Miss Jones slogged unrelentingly through the town. Not that their quest was as untidily random as it looked. The Hon. Con was actually quartering the town in as methodical a manner as she could, given the inadequate tourist map which was all she had at her disposal.

Miss Jones stared, agonised, at the shimmering white road which seemed to go straight up into that mercilessly blue sky. "What about lunch, dear?"

"Faint heart, Bones!" The Hon. Con squared her shoulders. "We'll just do this Trapetsia Mountain place first. Not beyond the bounds of possibility, I suppose, that the wretched lad's gone back to look at those blooming monkeys again."

"He didn't show much interest when we were there yesterday. I heard him telling his mother that he thought the whole place stank."

"Foul-mouthed young lout!" snorted the Hon. Con before the steepness of the ascent deprived her of all further powers of speech.

The Frossell boy was not, however, in the medico-biological section of the U.S.S.R. Academy of Medical Science, though the Hon. Con and Miss Jones had to endure another conducted tour of the monkeys before they could be absolutely sure. It took a full hour to go round all the cages and compounds, and they were eventually seen off the premises by a very puzzled young man in a white coat. They were probably just a couple of lunatic women from the capitalist world, but you never knew. He trotted off to find a telephone. In the KGB you tried to be safe rather than sorry.

Meanwhile, unconscious of all the excitement and trouble they were causing, the Hon. Con and Miss Jones went down the hill considerably faster than they had come up it.

"Where now, dear?" asked Miss Jones bravely.

"Back to the hotel!" The Hon. Con sensed that this answer might give an impression of chickenheartedness. "I've been working it out," she puffed in explanation as she felt the descent dragging mercilessly on the backs of her legs. "Simple deduction, really. It's well on the cards that the Frossell boy will go back to the hotel for his lunch. Because of the coupons."

She really didn't need to say any more because Miss Jones understood perfectly what she meant. All tourists in the Soviet Union are obliged to pay for their meals before they even start their holiday. In return they are given a number of coupons which are accepted instead of money in Intourist establishments. This simple system effectively prevents the tourist from economising and also serves to stop him from mingling too closely with the indigenous personnel who don't normally frequent Intourist restaurants.

Miss Jones forgot all about her aching feet and gazed up at the Hon. Con. "Oh, Constance," she cooed, "aren't you *clever!* Fancy working that out! I'd never have thought of it in a hundred years!"

"Nothing, really," mumbled the Hon. Con modestly. She suddenly felt quite warmly towards old Bones, who mightn't be as handsome as some but whose heart was jolly well in the right place. "Here"—the Hon. Con beamed at her friend—"why don't you take my arm? It'll ease the strain on the old pins a bit."

Virtue, they say, is its own reward, but the Hon. Con, on this occasion, collected a bonus with gratifying speed. She and Miss Jones had barely staggered a dozen yards arm-in-arm when they both caught sight of their quarry at the same moment.

"Don't stop!" hissed the Hon. Con, feeling Miss Jones hesitate.

Miss Jones picked up the step. "It is he, isn't it, dear?"

"It jolly well is!" The Hon. Con whooped her triumph in a whisper. "Now, take a grip on yourself, Bones! We've got to box this one clever."

"Yes, dear!" It was at moments like this that Miss Jones placed herself unreservedly in the Hon. Con's hands.

The Hon. Con shot steely glances in all directions from under lowered brows. "Okay—so this is how we play it! We'll stroll along nonchalantly as far as that bamboo tree thing on the corner—got it? Then we'll turn round—without making a meal of it, Bones!— and amble nonchalantly back in the direction from which we've just come. That way, we'll be *behind* him and thus in a position to follow him."

Miss Jones leaned affectionately towards the Hon. Con. "You mean—*shadow* him, don't you, dear?"

The Hon. Con interrupted her impersonation of your wealthy English tourist out for a leisurely preprandial walk to give Miss Jones a warning scowl. "Don't try to teach your grandfather, Bones!" she growled.

TEN

The Hon. Con and Miss Jones hadn't been tracking young Roger Frossell for more than a few minutes when they made a most remarkable discovery. While they were surreptitiously and unobtrusively following Roger Frossell, he was surreptitiously and unobtrusively following somebody else.

"It's that woman, dear!" Miss Jones barely vocalised the words, so anxious was she not to give the game away. "Can you see her? The one in the flowered frock with the . . ."

"They're all wearing flowered frocks!" the Hon. Con hissed back. It was a slightly unfair comment on the local couture but not without some foundation.

Miss Jones tried to clarify things. "It's the one with her hair drawn back in a bun."

"I know, I know!" snapped the Hon. Con. "Lascivious young pup!" she added.

Miss Jones, a romantic if ever there was one, was inclined to be more charitable. "You can hardly expect a boy of his age not to be interested in girls, dear."

"Girls? If that woman's a girl, I'm a Chinaman! She's old enough to be his grandmother!"

Although the woman in question wasn't even old enough to be Roger Frossell's mother, Miss Jones decided it wasn't worth arguing about. "I believe that some young men prefer more—er—mature women," she said.

The Hon. Con snorted loudly. "I wasn't suggesting that it was a *unique* liaison, Bones," she said. "Merely that it was a disgusting one. *Hey!*"

The Hon. Con's yelp caused several heads to turn, but it merely indicated that the woman with the bun had left the dusty pavement and gone through the gates of a small park. Roger Frossell lost no time in crossing the baking boulevard and following her.

Miss Jones clutched the Hon. Con. "What now, dear?"

The Hon. Con came from a long line of ancestors who had learned to make up their minds quickly. "We must follow them!" she announced as though this were a highly original idea. "Look, there's another gate a bit farther on. See it? We'll walk on and go into the park through that. Savvy? Then we should be able to pick up our quarry without difficulty, and it'll look more natural with us approaching from the other direction."

No sooner said than—in spite of certain misgivings on Miss Jones's part—done. The Hon. Con picked up Roger Frossell again almost immediately. He and his elderly girl friend had joined forces to the extent that they were both now sitting on the same park bench, albeit at opposite ends. Neither was speaking to, looking at, or paying the slightest attention to the other—a fact that the Hon. Con found highly suspicious.

Beady-eyed and with nostrils twitching, she scanned the terrain. "We're deuced short of cover," she complained.

Miss Jones looked at the luxurious growth of tropical trees, flowering shrubs, and riotously multicoloured flowerbeds, and said nothing.

The Hon. Con was extremely sensitive to implied criticism. "We can hardly crawl up behind 'em on our tums across a patch of newly mown grass, can we?"

"No, dear." Miss Jones was examining the statuary with which the park was liberally provided. She was relieved to find that they were all fully clothed. "Er—why do you want to get any closer, dear?"

"To hear what they're talking about, of course! The heat must have addled your brains, Bones!"

Miss Jones tore her mind away from the statues—so natural-looking that one didn't have any doubts at all as to what they were meant to be. "But they haven't said a word to each other, have they, dear? I've been watching their lips ever since we came into the park and they haven't moved. Neither—er—pair of them."

The Hon. Con sought for a ton of bricks, and found it. "Never heard of ventriloquism?" she demanded scathingly. "Of course they're talking to each other! Why else should they both come and sit on the same seat in the same park at the same time?"

"It could just be a coincidence, dear," murmured Miss Jones, and then nerved herself for another observation which might well drive the Hon. Con to physical violence. "But, even if it isn't, well, I don't quite see what it's got to do with us. I mean, Mr. Frossell's private life is—well—his private life, isn't it? I don't see what this"—Miss Jones indicated the distant park bench with a refined gesture—"has to do with these alleged attempts to murder Miss Clough-Cooper."

Don't imagine for one moment, gentle reader, that the Honourable Constance hadn't got an explanation for this, because she had. Several. Cruel fate, however, deprived her of the chance to use them, for at that precise moment the park was invaded. Invaded not by little green men from Mars or even trilby-hatted thugs from the KGB but by something much more sinister. Small children.

The Hon. Con and Miss Jones stood and stared in blank dismay as several million (the Hon. Con's considered estimate) tiny tots swarmed through the park gates in a solid, screaming mass.

"Dear God!" breathed the Hon. Con, trying to brush off the little bodies which were all spotlessly clothed in white. The round, suntanned faces were set and hard as though their owners were intent on taking over the world. "Here," exhorted the Hon. Con, panicking a little, "get away! Shoo! Buzz off!"

A small white boot landed unerringly on one of Miss Jones's most sensitive corns. The first boot was followed by another. . . . Something jabbed the Hon. Con excruciatingly just behind the knees.

If you can't beat 'em, quit!

The Hon. Con and Miss Jones, unable in any case to read the prohibitory notices, took to the grass and left the path to the occupation of the future generation.

"It makes you," observed the Hon. Con when she'd recovered her aplomb, "have a certain amount of sympathy for that Pied Piper chappie. What in heaven's name are they?"

"Children, dear," said Miss Jones, her mind fully occupied with wondering if she had a moral duty to intervene in the case of blatant bullying that was taking place right under her nose. Finally, telling herself that it was because the girl victim was so small and that the two lads tormenting her looked so big, she plumped for the better part of valour.

"I know they're children!" snarled the Hon. Con. "But what sort? Orphans? Test-tube babies? Sunday school outing?"

"Hardly, dear." Miss Jones managed a nervous smile. "I should think they belong to a nursery school or something, wouldn't you? Those two women"—Miss Jones indicated a couple of female warders in white head scarves and overalls who were bringing up the rear—"are probably teachers or minders or whatever they have."

"Well," said the Hon. Con, upon whom the experience had made a profound impression, "it's brought home the meaning of the Red Menace, all right."

Miss Jones stepped back onto the path, which now looked as though a couple of steamrollers had passed that way. "I believe the Russians are very keen on crèches and kindergartens and things. I suppose it enables them to . . ."

"Crikey Moses!" The Hon. Con pointed a trembling finger. "Look!"

Miss Jones duly looked. "Oh, dear!"

"Those bloody kids!" screamed the Hon. Con. "If they hadn't distracted our attention . . ."

Miss Jones liked to look on the bright side. "Well, Roger Frossell is still there all right, dear, and that's the main thing, isn't it? I mean, it's more than likely that the lady with the bun hadn't anything to do with things anyhow, isn't it? She was probably just an ordinary, perfectly innocent . . ."

"Stop wittering, Bones!" begged the Hon. Con. "Another couple of minutes and you'll be telling me that young Frossell's behaviour has been perfectly normal."

"Well, now that you mention it, dear, I do. . . . Oh, look, Constance!" Miss Jones caught the Hon. Con by the arm and, in her excitement, shook her. "*He*'s going, now! Of course"—Miss Jones switched to a rather shamefaced laugh—"it *is* well past our lunch hour, isn't it?"

The Hon. Con sternly suppressed all protests from the inner man and concentrated all her attention on Roger Frossell. With narrowed eyes and furrowed brow, she carefully noted how he brushed the seat of his trousers, glanced at his watch, and pushed his sunglasses farther up his nose. Well, you never knew when this sort of thing might turn out to be significant. Roger Frossell picked up his carrier bag. The casual look he threw round might have been indicative of a guilty conscience, or it might not. The Hon. Con was having some difficulty making up her mind about that.

"Are we going to follow him, dear?"

"Suppose so," said the Hon. Con reluctantly. She was beginning to feel a mite sorry for herself. "I'll lay ten to one he's only going back to the hotel, though."

"Maybe he really did come out just for a walk."

The Hon. Con was too cheesed off to argue. "Maybe," she agreed—and then stopped dead in her tracks. "Good grief!"

Miss Jones glanced back in justifiable alarm.

The Hon. Con struck herself a resounding and overdramatic blow on the forehead. "I need my brains examined!" she chuckled. "Must be going potty in my old age, eh?"

"I don't quite understand, dear."

"Course you don't, Bones!" chortled the Hon. Con. "That's why I'm the detective, and you're not!"

"Yes, dear."

"Now"—the Hon. Con was so bucked with herself that she became quite playful—"how about you giving your old grey cells a bit of a poke round? What makes young Frossell going out of the park different from young Frossell coming into the park? I'll give you thirty seconds!"

Miss Jones was hot, exhausted, and hungry. The last thing she wanted was to start playing silly guessing games. "I'm sure I don't know, dear."

"Oh, come on, Bones! Have a shot!" The Hon. Con could be extraordinarily tiresome at times. "Use your eyes!"

Miss Jones pried thin lips apart with difficulty. "I'm sorry, dear."

"Golly gosh, you're a right *packet*, Bones!" The Hon. Con accompanied this peculiar observation with a broad wink. "I can see that I'll have to take you in hand! You know, you mustn't rely on me to *carry* you the whole time!"

Miss Jones, driven beyond all reasonable endurance, began to look bored.

The Hon. Con was in imminent danger of losing her temper.

She gave the wheel one last spin. "Don't want to have to start calling you an old *bag!*" she rumbled.

Miss Jones masked a tiny yawn with a neatly gloved hand.

Even the Hon. Con couldn't mistake this gesture for enthusiastic participation. "Bones, old fruit," she sighed, "young Frossell is now carrying a plastic bag in his hand. See it?"

"There is no need, Constance," said Miss Jones coldly, "to speak to me in that tone. I may not be as clever as you, of course, but I am not mentally retarded. Yes, I can see the plastic carrier bag which Mr. Frossell is carrying in his hand. What about it?"

"Only that he wasn't carrying it when we followed him into the park," responded the Hon. Con sulkily. "His hands were empty. And stuck in his pockets."

They were out in the street again and, apparently, heading back towards their hotel. Miss Jones stared at the retreating figure of Roger Frossell. He was some way in front and walking quite quickly. "Where do you think he got it from, then, dear?"

The Hon. Con shrugged her shoulders. "In the park, I suppose."

"You mean he just found it lying round?"

The Hon. Con shook her head. "I reckon that woman must have given it to him. She probably left it on the bench and he just picked it up. Who'd notice?"

"Was the woman carrying the bag when she went into the park, dear?"

The Hon. Con frowned. Trust old Bones! "That's what I blooming well can't remember!" she growled. "Anyhow"—she changed the subject before Miss Jones made the obvious comment —"what I want now is a peep into that bag."

Miss Jones turned a pair of apprehensive eyes on the Hon. Con. "You're not proposing to burgle his room, are you, dear?"

From time to time, even the Hon. Con recognised her limitations. "Course not!" she scoffed, and with an effort quickened her pace. "Come on!" she exhorted her companion. "Show a leg there!"

Miss Jones responded as best she could. "Where," she panted, "are we going?"

The Hon. Con was saving her breath to cool her porridge with. The Intourist hotel came into sight, and they could see the sea shimmering and sparkling behind it. Now that they were back in the centre of the town, there were a lot more people about, and, though nobody could call the Hon. Con unobtrusive, she managed to draw level with Roger Frossell without attracting his attention.

Miss Jones trotted gamely in her wake.

The Hon. Con prided herself on never using finesse when a sledgehammer would do. Sucking in a deep breath, she clapped one weighty fist on young Roger Frossell's shoulder. "Got you!" she bellowed.

The results were quite spectacular.

Miss Jones watched in silent dismay as all the colour drained out of Roger Frossell's face and his eyes swivelled upwards in their sockets. The Hon. Con played a more active role and actually made an ineffectual grab at the boy as, knees buckling under him, he sank to the pavement.

The Hon. Con looked questioningly at Miss Jones over the limp and prostrate body.

Miss Jones smiled hesitantly. "I'm afraid he's fainted, dear."

Inevitably and almost instantaneously, a small crowd gathered, motivated partly by compassion and partly by curiosity. The Hon. Con left all the face slapping, the head-between-the-knees routine and Miss Jones's smelling salts to those with a vocation for that kind of thing. She had other fish to fry. She extracted the carrier bag from Roger Frossell's nerveless fingers and, withdrawing quietly from the battlefield, moved into the shade of a huge palm tree.

Miss Jones, on her knees in the dust, was uttering shrill and unheeded appeals for more air for her patient. The surrounding circle, intrigued by the foreign language, pressed closer. A youngish man with a red armband fought his way to the front and administered a particularly enthusiastic slap to Roger Frossell's pallid cheek. Roger Frossell opened his eyes.

"Where am I?" he stammered. "What's happened?"

Miss Jones understandably shrank from the task of explaining to him and let the babble of Russian, Abhazian, and Georgian voices give what comfort they could. The approach of a traffic policeman probably played a major role in inspiring her to reach her decision, and she joined the Hon. Con under the spreading palm tree. "He's coming round, dear."

"Good." The Hon. Con wasn't really listening.

Miss Jones glanced at the carrier bag, which was still in the Hon. Con's hands. "Did you—er—look inside, dear?"

The Hon. Con inclined her head affirmatively. "Dashed odd," she said.

Miss Jones waited.

"Do you know what's in this blooming bag, Bones?"

Miss Jones said that she didn't.

"A dirty great wodge of paper covered with typewriting. Russian typewriting, I fancy. All neatly tied together with string. Do you know what I think, Bones?"

Miss Jones confessed that she didn't.

The Hon. Con wrinkled her nose. "I think it's a blooming *book!*" she said disgustedly.

ELEVEN

"Of course it's a book!" Roger Frossell, almost in tears, clasped the carrier bag to his unmanly bosom. "You interfering old cow, you've probably ruined everything! Poking your bloody nose in where it's not wanted!"

The Hon. Con, seated opposite Roger Frossell on the other twin bed, decided to make allowances. The boy was obviously rattled and didn't quite realise what he was saying—or to whom he was saying it. "But what," she asked, the very personification of reasonableness, "do you want a book for?" The Hon. Con had waded through several books in her time and thought they were, on the whole, somewhat overrated.

"None of your business!"

Miss Jones, relegated to the dressing-table stool, intervened. "The Honourable Constance is only trying to help."

"With help like that, who needs the KGB?" Roger Frossell examined the Hon. Con with all the contempt of modern youth for its elders and betters. "I thought you were supposed to be tied up investigating these attacks on the Clough-Cooper bird?"

"For all I know," snapped the Hon. Con, her good resolutions already beginning to fray, "this may be part and parcel of the same thing."

"It isn't!"

" 'Fraid I can't just take your word for that, laddie!" The Hon. Con chuckled heartily at such naïveté. "There's that business of your pocket knife, too, don't forget. Look, why not be sensible and make a clean breast of the whole business?"

Over by the dressing table, Miss Jones felt her cheeks burn. Really, dear Constance's language could be so *forceful* at times.

"You've a bloody hope!"

"I am not"—the Hon. Con boomed out the warning without malice—"known as the Bulldog of Upper Waxwing Drive for nothing, you know."

Roger Frossell moodily mulled the problem over. At that particular moment the last thing he wanted was the Hon. Con leading a hue and cry after him. The more he thought about it, the more he was driven to the conclusion that the only way to get her off his back was—probably—to tell her the truth. It seemed a pretty feeble solution, but, as things stood, he couldn't think of any other. "Listen," he said at last, yielding that first fatal inch, "if I do tell you, will you swear not to breathe a word to anybody until we're back home in England?"

The Hon. Con shook her head. " 'Fraid I can't agree to have my hands tied like that, old son," she said, "though I will, naturally, do my level best to respect your confidence. Here"—the Hon. Con's eyes bulged as the penny dropped—"you've not got yourself mixed up in anything criminal, have you?"

Roger Frossell was blandly reassuring. "It all depends how you define 'criminal,' " he said. "I've done nothing that would cause anybody to bat an eyelid at home, but you know what they're like over here. Chuck you in the pokey as soon as look at you."

The Hon. Con blenched and Miss Jones clutched her throat.

"These Russians are little better than mindless savages," said young Mr. Frossell airily.

The Hon. Con licked her lips. "You've no right to jolly well endanger the safety of the rest of us," she pointed out. "If the Russkies catch you, we'll all get it in the neck, too."

"If only you'll mind your own business, nobody will be catching anybody! So"—Roger Frossell flung his arms wide in a gesture of exasperation—"what do you want? You can either make like a hoop and roll silently away, or you can give me your word not to go grassing to all and sundry and I'll let you in on what's going on. Who knows"—he grinned maliciously—"you may even be able to help."

This appeal to the Hon. Con's better nature fell on sharp ears. "Help? What do you mean—help?"

"Let's have your decision first."

For someone as unashamedly and blatantly inquisitive as the

Hon. Con, it was Hobson's choice. "Spit it out, laddie!" she urged. "And not to worry about hidden microphones and such like, because there aren't any. I did my wall-to-wall search only this morning."

"My uncle is a publisher."

"You told me that before," interrupted the Hon. Con, just to show the young shaver that she was right on the ball. "You're going to work for him."

"That's right. It's a family business, you see. And my uncle's the one who's footing the bill for me and the mater on this trip."

The Hon. Con nodded impatiently. "So you said. He must be a jolly openhanded sort of chappie," she added enviously.

"Oh, he's got an ulterior motive, don't you worry." Roger Frossell smiled a cynical smile. "Most people of his age have." He sighed. "Have you ever heard of Stepan Michailovitsch Tschitschagov?"

The Hon. Con had no doubts.

"Really?" Roger Frossell seemed surprised. "Are you sure?"

"It's not, laddie," the Hon. Con told him, "the sort of name you're likely to forget."

"No, I suppose not. Well, you will hear it before long. Or so my uncle reckons. He says that Stepan Michailovitsch Tschitschagov will soon be as much of a household word as Solzhenitsyn or Pasternak."

These names were not exactly common currency in the Hon. Con's household, but she didn't want to make an issue of it.

"He's a novelist, you see," explained Roger Frossell, correctly interpreting the blank looks he was getting. "Stepan Michailovitsch Tschitschagov, I mean. Brilliant, everybody says. A second Tolstoy. Of course"—Roger Frossell got rather malicious—"since all his books are written in Russian, my uncle hasn't actually read any of them. And since they've never been published, nobody else much has either." He broke off to explain. "Mr. Tschitschagov is a passionate and virulent critic of the Soviet regime, so, naturally, they see to it that he doesn't get much of a hearing."

"Fancy," said the Hon. Con. She stared hard at the lumpy carrier bag, which was now lying on the bed. "So you're smuggling this chap's novels out of Russia so that your uncle can publish 'em in England?"

"Only one novel, as far as I can see." Roger Frossell poked the carrier bag. "It runs to two thousand, nine hundred and twenty-seven pages. Foolscap. Single spacing. We may"—he sighed again—"have to cut it."

Unlike the Hon. Con, Miss Jones had some respect for culture. "What's it about?" she asked politely.

The answer was brief. "God knows!"

The Hon. Con had other problems on her mind. "This sneezy fellow of yours," she began.

"Tschitschagov?"

"Won't he get it in the neck if your uncle publishes his book in England?"

"Strung up from the nearest lamppost, I shouldn't wonder." Roger Frossell seemed cheered by the prospect.

"He must be a jolly brave fellow," said the Hon. Con with grudging admiration.

"Well, Tschitschagov isn't his real name, of course. Just a nom de plume. Still, it's a dicey business."

"Does he live here in Sukhumi?" asked Miss Jones.

"No idea. My guess is he does." Roger Frossell poked the carrier bag again. "I can't see anybody carting this lot round the countryside, can you? It weighs a bloody ton. Actually, I don't know much about anything. My uncle thought it would be safer that way. I just knew that somebody would contact me here in Sukhumi and I'd get instructions about picking up the manuscript. There was even," he added mockingly, "a password."

The Hon. Con considered that she had an inalienable right to know all the details. "Who contacted you?"

"One of the waitresses at dinner last night. A couple of whispered phrases with every course. She told me that this woman with her hair in a bun and carrying a carrier bag would be sitting on the seat opposite the hotel entrance at eleven o'clock this morning. When she moved off, I was to follow her. As soon as she was satisfied it was safe and we weren't being followed, she was to hand the manuscript over to me."

"She didn't spot us!" said the Hon. Con proudly. "We were following you and she didn't spot us!"

"I just hope that's the only mistake they've made," said Roger Frossell gloomily. "I'm too young to spend the next thirty years carving chess men. Of course"—he brightened up a little—"I've got strict instructions from my uncle to abort the whole operation if anything goes wrong."

"Abort the whole operation?" repeated the Hon. Con, trying not to look shocked. She stared at the carrier bag. "How were you thinking of doing it?"

"Doing what?"

"Getting rid of that lot?"

Roger Frossell shrugged his shoulders. "Flush it down the loo, I suppose."

The Hon. Con was an expert on Russian plumbing. "It'd take you a fortnight," she said. "And how are you proposing to get it through the customs? Hide it in your luggage?"

Roger Frossell grinned sheepishly. "Well, not exactly."

The Hon. Con raised her eyebrows.

"Well, as a matter of fact, I was thinking of putting it in my mother's suitcase." He tried to talk over the gasp of horror which came from Miss Jones. "She's got one of those innocent-looking faces, you see. They never stop her in customs."

The Hon. Con excelled herself. "Ingrate!" she hissed.

Roger Frossell got up and walked over to the window. "That book may be a work of art on a level with *Hamlet* or *War and Peace* or Dante's *Inferno.* Any sacrifice would be justified."

The Hon. Con gave a disparaging sniff. "You're a young rat, that's what you are. Well, what are you going to do now?"

There was a pause before Roger Frossell, staring fixedly out the window, emitted a vague, "Eh?"

"Oh, pay attention, laddie!" expostulated the Hon. Con, marching over to join him. "Take the old finger out! I said . . ." Her voice died away. "Is that Penny Clough-Cooper?"

Roger Frossell pulled an astonishingly clean white handkerchief out of his hip pocket and mopped his brow. "She's got quite a . . . quite a body, hasn't she? You sort of notice it from up here." He cleared his throat and tried to achieve a conversational tone. "They must have come back from the beach."

The Hon. Con hadn't needed to be perched some sixty feet above Penny Clough-Cooper to appreciate her assets. It seemed that, in some things, she could still give young Frossell a head start.

"Miss Clough-Cooper?" Miss Jones lost little time in joining them at the open window. "What's she doing?"

"Sketching, I think." Roger Frossell leaned out dangerously over the sill. "Mm, she seems to be doing a sort of general view of the promenade. In charcoal. Mm, not bad." He recollected that giving the geriatrics a pat on the back was definitely not his scene. "If that sort of thing grabs you," he added quickly.

Miss Jones dismissed the artistic aspects. "I see Miss Clough-Cooper has managed to make herself the centre of attraction . . . as usual. That's quite a circle of gentlemen she's collected, isn't it?"

The Hon. Con rushed to defend Miss Clough-Cooper's honour. "It's only those blooming Abhazians, Bones!" she protested. "You know what they're like."

"Indeed I do!" retorted Miss Jones with a shudder. "Quite uninhibited. I'm merely surprised at Miss Clough-Cooper encouraging them."

"Oh, phooey!" protested the Hon. Con. "They're just naturally nosey. They'd stand round watching a pot boil, if you gave 'em half a chance."

Miss Jones had an answer for everything. "That simply makes Miss Clough-Cooper's behaviour all the more astonishing, dear. Somehow one would have thought she'd be more fastidious."

The Hon. Con stared down unhappily. "It's not her fault," she insisted, oblivious of Miss Jones's tightening face. "Anybody with half an eye can see that they're pestering the life out of her." The Hon. Con's distress made her reckless. "Think I'll nip down and give her a bit of the old moral support, eh?"

"And she could probably do with it!" Roger Frossell chipped in with an adolescent snigger. "Have you noticed? She's not wearing a bra!"

Luckily for him, the Hon. Con and Miss Jones were too busy having an eyeball-to-eyeball confrontation to pay much attention to what he was saying. The Hon. Con was determined to go down and rescue Penny Clough-Cooper, and Miss Jones was just as determined to make the sortie as embarrassing as possible.

"Oh, play the game, Bones!" pleaded the Hon. Con in a forlorn attempt to get Miss Jones to acknowledge the justice of her case. "I'm responsible for that lass's safety, you know."

"You may be responsible for protecting her from a murderer, dear," Miss Jones pointed out sweetly, "but I doubt if anybody could protect her from her own worst instincts. If Miss Clough-Cooper doesn't care for being *devoured* by all those men and their glowing eyes, all she has to do is pack up her ridiculous sketching equipment and come indoors."

Roger Frossell tried to sort things out, in spite of the fact that he hadn't the least idea of what was really going on. "Oh, you don't have to worry about the Clough-Cooper wench," he asserted with all the ripe wisdom of his tender years. "She's built like an athlete. She could brush off that bunch of flabby old potbellies with one hand, if she wanted to." He shook his head admiringly. "Why, she's got muscles on her like an Olympic weightlifter! Talk about whipcord!"

The Hon. Con dragged her eyes away from the pink-faced Miss Jones. "Muscles like whipcord?" she demanded in an ominously calm voice.

"Or finely tempered steel," agreed Roger Frossell obligingly.

The Hon. Con drew in a deep lungful of warm, magnolia-scented Sukhumi air. The picture which flashed across her mind's eye was heart-stoppingly vivid. This revolting, unlicked cub and . . . "How do you *know?*" she screamed.

And that was how young Roger Frossell returned to the Hon. Con's list of prime suspects. One could forget the penknife and the typescript of the book, but the possibility that Roger Frossell had actually handled Penny Clough-Cooper could not be overlooked.

After all these alarms and excursions, it is not surprising that the rest of the day proved to be something of an anticlimax. Lunch had, of course, been missed by a mile, but the Hon. Con consoled herself by pointing out to Miss Jones that they would have all the more meal tickets to spend at dinner.

"We'll have a real blow-out!" she promised, eyes sparkling.

Which only made it doubly disappointing when they found that they were obliged to go without their dinners as well.

"Not *another* blooming opera!" wailed the Hon. Con when the news was broken to her. "Good grief, I've seen more flaming operas in the last few days than I have in the rest of my life put together." She came to a momentous decision. "I'm blooming well not going!"

Miss Jones sighed. Although a keen devotee of art and culture, she wouldn't have minded being spared that evening's offering, but she knew from past experience that the Hon. Con was inclined to get nasty if she thought that not all the facts had been placed before her. "I'm afraid we've already paid for the tickets, dear."

The Hon. Con feigned an ignorance which sat ill on one who didn't let a ha'penny fall unnoticed. "Have we? When?"

"Back home in England, dear." Miss Jones sighed. "It seemed such a good idea at the time, you remember, what with the discount and everything. I'm afraid I hadn't quite realised how many operas were involved."

"Not your fault, Bones," rumbled the Hon. Con, which was generous of her as she was the one who was addicted to the economies of bulk buying.

"Maybe we could have a sort of high tea, dear."

"The flipping dining room doesn't open until half past seven."

Miss Jones took her courage in both hands. "I was wondering about one of the ordinary Russian restaurants, dear. I know we can't use our meal vouchers there, but . . ."

The Hon. Con knew all about ordinary Russian restaurants and the prices they charged. She ignored the suggestion. "We've still got some chocolate left, haven't we, Bones?"

TWELVE

The opera (*Boris Godunov* in what seemed like ninety-two acts) was of such a nature that it left the Hon. Con feeling jolly refreshed in the intervals. It was during one of these that she found herself marching round, shoulder to shoulder, with Desmond Withenshaw in the relentless parade that took the entire audience up and down staircases, through bars, across anterooms, and along corridors. Desmond Withenshaw, unbeknownst to the Hon. Con, had been fortifying himself during the performance with several swigs of his duty-free whisky and had now achieved that nicely mellow condition in which everybody was a friend. He was even prepared to be reasonably polite to the Hon. Con.

"Are you enjoying the performance, Miss Morrison-Burke?"

The Hon. Con took the precaution of crossing her fingers behind her back. "Super!" she declared. "Top hole! And you?"

"Oh, well"—Desmond Withenshaw grinned ruefully—"it's not, to be painfully honest, quite my line of country."

The Hon. Con nodded understandingly, as well she might. "We can't all appreciate everything," she observed with sickening sanctimoniousness. "Suppose art's more in your line, eh? Pictures and things."

Mr. Withenshaw good-humouredly agreed that this was so. "I popped into the local art gallery this afternoon," he said, "when we got back from the beach. Quite interesting."

"Good stuff, have they?" enquired the Hon. Con heartily, endeavouring to sound like one cognoscente having a bit of a chat with another.

"Not bad. Some of this Abhazian folk art is quite intriguing. Strange echoes of Navaho Indian work, actually. Of course, it's completely *different* in every possible way—materials, design, colours, function—but the *feel* reminded me strongly of some of the Navaho efforts. Not all of it, mind you."

"Quite, quite!" said the Hon. Con, searching in vain amongst the crowd of opera lovers for a life belt and not finding one. She fell back on her own resources. "You should have taken Penny Clough-Cooper along!"

Desmond Withenshaw's whole body stiffened. "Oh?" he said carefully.

"She's keen on art, too."

"Really?"

The Hon. Con's sensitive nose twitched and her voice became sharper as she abandoned the joys of social intercourse for the excitements of the chase. "Didn't you know?"

"Is there any reason why I should?"

"Well, you're a cool one and no mistake!" snorted the Hon. Con, never ceasing to be outraged at the perfidy of man. "I thought you and she were on one of these weekend courses together."

"Where did you get that idea from?"

"From Penny Clough-Cooper, of course!"

"Damn!" Desmond Withenshaw stuck his hands deep in his trouser pockets. "Blast! Well, for God's sake," he added crossly, "it's years ago now and we didn't even speak to each other. I knew I'd met her before somewhere, because I never forget a face, but it's taken me the best part of a week to remember where it was. Horwill Castle! What a dump! And what a bore those weekend courses were!" He sighed. "They paid well, though."

The Hon. Con squinted thoughtfully across at Desmond Withenshaw. "That's deuced interesting," she remarked.

"What is?"

"Do you realise that this puts you in a special category?"

Desmond Withenshaw began to sober up. "What does? Look, I wish you'd explain precisely what it is you're getting at."

The Hon. Con was delighted to oblige. "You," she said, "are the only Albatrosser who knew Penny Clough-Cooper back home in the UK. Here"—she broke off to repel a boarder in the shape of jolly Jim Lewcock, who gave her a friendly slap on the rump as he pushed past—"what the . . . ?"

"Sorry to disturb you, love"—Jim Lewcock moved his over-

familiar hand upwards and placed it on the Hon. Con's shoulder—
"but I've got to go and see if my one hope of posterity is still in
working order!" He gave her a squeeze and disappeared through a
door bearing a conventionalised figure of a man on its centre panel.

The Hon. Con drew a deep breath. "That fellow," she
announced through bared teeth, "is beyond the pale!"

Desmond Withenshaw had his own problems. "What do you
mean about me being the only one who knew Miss Clough-Cooper
back in England? I thought somebody said that the Smiths came
from the same town."

The Hon. Con had forgotten about the Smiths, but even Homer
was allowed the odd nod. "Hardly the same social class, though,"
she pointed out. "They'd heard of Penny Clough-Cooper, I don't
doubt, but you'd hardly expect her to know them."

"She didn't know me, either," said Desmond Withenshaw
impatiently.

The Hon. Con sniffed. "That's your story!"

"And it happens to be the truth. You can ask Miss Clough-
Cooper herself. She'll confirm what I say."

They paced along side by side for a few moments, unsociably
silent amidst the mob of eager chatterers. Then the Hon. Con
opened her mouth and hit, albeit unintentionally, well below the
belt. "How about your wife?" she asked.

Desmond Withenshaw took a minute or so off while he hooked
his bottom jaw back on its hinges. "My . . . my wife? What's my
wife got to do with it?"

The Hon. Con shrugged a pair of shoulders that wouldn't have
looked out of place on a heavyweight boxer. "I was just wondering
if she knew Penny Clough-Cooper, too."

"Why . . . why should she?"

You didn't need to hit the Hon. Con over the head where clues
were concerned. She stared hard at Desmond Withenshaw. "Well,
she could have been on this painting weekend with you, couldn't
she?"

"Jesus Christ!" Desmond Withenshaw confirmed some of the
Hon. Con's worst fears as he grabbed her by the arm and pulled
her into the shelter of a convenient alcove. "Look, what in God's
name are you getting at?"

"Aha!" The Hon. Con pushed Desmond Withenshaw away. "That'd be telling, wouldn't it?"

"I wondered if that blasted Clough-Cooper woman had put two and two together!" snarled Desmond Withenshaw. "Oh, damn her eyes! If Zoë ever gets wind of this, she'll have my guts for garters."

"Gets wind of what?"

Desmond Withenshaw released his hold on the Hon. Con. "As if you didn't know!" he observed reproachfully. "Women! They're always so bloody jealous!"

Nobody could say that intuition was the Hon. Con's strong point, but occasionally she could make imaginative leaps which astonished even her. "This painting weekend," she said, drawing a bow at a venture. "Were you there with somebody who wasn't your wife, eh?"

"Women always place so much bloody emphasis on *bed!*" complained Desmond Withenshaw, looking noble and aggrieved. "As if it really mattered. I mean, Helena never presented the slightest threat to my marriage. She understood it. I understood it. Why the bloody hell shouldn't Zoë understand it too?"

"I dunno," said the Hon. Con. "Suppose you tell me."

Desmond Withenshaw slumped back against the wall. "Well, Emma Jane might be one reason, I suppose."

The Hon. Con had been out of her depth for some time, but she battled bravely on. "Emma Jane? Who's Emma Jane? Another of your paramours?"

"She's our youngest kid," explained Desmond Withenshaw crossly. "God, what a sordid mind you've got! Zoë was having her that weekend. I'd have never got away with young Helena otherwise."

The Hon. Con was predictably horrified. "Do you mean that you took another woman off for a dirty weekend while your poor wife was having a baby? You rotten swine!"

Her voice was loud and Desmond Withenshaw looked round nervously. "Please," he implored, "do keep your voice down! People are staring at us." He went on to forfeit what little respect he still had in the Hon. Con's eyes. "You just wouldn't understand the deep, powerful passions that drive a man. It's something I simply can't explain. We're made differently, you see. Men are . . ."

"And what are you two up to, may one ask?" Zoë Withenshaw's voice came across to them—polite, amused, and very, very cutting. She had been circulating through the corridors with their Russian Intourist guide and had, in the course of one circumambulation, noticed her husband and the Hon. Con with their heads together. The next time round and she had no hesitation about abandoning her companion and coming over to break it up. She linked her arm possessively into Desmond Withenshaw's.

The Hon. Con went red. "Just chatting," she mumbled, quite out of her depth at being accused, however indirectly, of husband snatching. "About the—er—case."

"The case?" Zoë Withenshaw raised well-shaped, disbelieving eyebrows. "Oh—you mean Miss Clough-Cooper and her never-ending saga. Well, and what"—she let the Hon. Con have it straight between the eyes—"has a happily married man and the devoted father of three got to do with these highly ineffectual and quite improbable attacks on our heroine?"

"We can't afford to leave any stone unturned," said the Hon. Con defensively.

"I still don't see how my Des can help you. He hasn't spoken more than half a dozen words to the woman in his entire life, have you, lover-boy?"

"He may have noticed something," explained the Hon. Con. "Artists are supposed to be jolly observant, aren't they?"

"Not half as observant as artists' wives, Miss Morrison-Burke!" Zoë Withenshaw tugged gently and irresistibly at her husband. "And you don't want to believe all those old wives' tales, you know. They do say artists are highly sexed, but—take old Des here!" She sank soft fingers of pure steel into the arm under her hand. "He's got about as much temperament as an elderly sheep. Haven't you, darling?"

Unhappily the Hon. Con watched the Withenshaws as they joined and were absorbed into the throng. What was all that about? Had Mrs. Withenshaw been so intent on demonstrating that her husband had nothing to do with the murder attempts that she had overlooked her own claims to consideration? Suppose she'd found out about Desmond Withenshaw's little escapade at the painting school? Would she have . . . ? The Hon. Con shook her head. No, in that case it was Desmond Withenshaw she would have clobbered—and a blooming good thing, too. On the other hand, Desmond Withenshaw might have been trying to shut Penny Clough-Cooper's mouth before she . . .

"It's nearly time for the fourth act to begin, dear."

The Hon. Con found Miss Jones by her side. "Is it?"

"It might be a good idea to take our seats now, dear. Before the rush starts."

"Good thinking, Bones!" The Hon. Con nodded. Act four, eh? Well, with any luck, it might be the last. She was about to check with Miss Jones when another thought struck her. "Where's Penny Clough-Cooper?"

Miss Jones's perfectly straight back straightened. "She's as safe as houses, dear. I've been keeping an eye on her, in strict accordance with your very explicit instructions. She's been walking round during the interval with the Beamishes and the Frossells. It's quite extraordinary"—only someone with perfect pitch would have picked up the malice in Miss Jones's tone—"how she managed to get a man on either side of her, leaving the other two ladies to walk behind."

Somewhat surprisingly, the Albatrossers were unanimous in their opinion that Lake Ritsa was worth it. Worth, that is, the hurried breakfast, the early start from Sukhumi, and the long, dusty drive. The party sat on the verandah of the hotel, sipping a most welcome cup of coffee and gazing out across the lake to the snow-capped mountains which loomed over them on all sides.

Mrs. Beamish wasn't seduced by all this beauty into forgetting our Western values and way of life. "Of course, it's the *contrast* that makes it all look so much better," she pointed out to her husband and anybody else who couldn't shut out the sound of her voice. "I mean, there are a dozen places—in the Tyrol, for example—which are ten times as pretty as this, but one just doesn't notice them."

"It's so quiet here," sighed Miss Jones, a great lover of nature.

"No blooming Russians!" said the Hon. Con with a grunt.

Desmond Withenshaw had been trying out his Russian on the manageress of the hotel. Luckily, she spoke quite good English, so the interview wasn't entirely wasted. "The Russian tourists never get up here before lunchtime. Late rising is a national characteristic, so I'm told. The hotel directress was saying just now that, in her opinion, they miss the best part of the day."

It was left to Mrs. Frossell to kill this highly promising line of conversation stone dead. "It's quite nice coffee, isn't it?" she asked brightly and of nobody in particular. Her son buried his burning face in his hands.

Jim Lewcock, who'd been away from the table for a few minutes, came back and considerately checked his zip before resuming his place at the table. "I wonder why the hell they didn't fix up for us to stay a couple of days here?" he queried. "It's a bloody sight better than some of the dumps they've been shoving us in." Young Mrs. Smith was sitting next to him, and he gave her a friendly squeeze on the knee. "What do you think, love?"

Young Mrs. Smith glanced across at her husband from under heavily mascaraed eyelashes and giggled. "Ooh, I dunno!" she tittered, squirming ecstatically. "All these places look much of a muchness to me."

Neither of the Lewcock brothers was likely to let a remark like that pass without adding his own lascivious gloss to it, and this inspired young Mr. Smith to some saucy repartee of his own. To the casual onlooker, the Albatrossers' table was positively sparkling with bonhomie and wit as it stood in the middle of a huge and otherwise totally deserted dining room.

It must have been some five minutes later when the Hon. Con, with some relief, gave Miss Jones a nudge. "Come on, Bones!" she growled. "The boats are here!"

"The boats?" Miss Jones, not one of your Nelson breed, sighed. "Oh, yes."

The Albatrossers were to be taken on a short pleasure trip over the smooth and sparkling waters of the lake. It was going to cost them an extra couple of roubles each, but the whole scene up there in the mountains looked so inviting that not even the Hon. Con had jibbed at the additional outlay of hard cash.

Norman Beamish did the decent and assisted the ladies down the crumbling steps to the little jetty.

"Oh, isn't it exciting?" cooed Miss Jones bravely and waved a tentative hand. "So picturesque!" Reluctantly she let go of Mr. Beamish's arm. "I wonder if anyone ever goes bathing here?"

The Hon. Con was right behind. Spurning Mr. Beamish's aid, she was firmly escorting a rather boot-faced Miss Clough-Cooper down those same rickety steps. "Use the old loaf, Bones!" she advised boisterously, keeping a watchful eye on Miss Clough-Cooper's slender and descending ankles. "The guide told us back in Sukhumi. It's too dashed cold up here in the mountains. And too dangerous because it's so deep. You dive in there, old girl, and you wouldn't surface again—ever!"

With some difficulty, the Albatrossers sorted themselves out into two roughly equal groups—one for each of the pair of small sun-bleached shallow-draught motor boats which were waiting for them. When she came to think about it afterwards, the Hon. Con couldn't quite recall how it was that she and Penny Clough-Cooper got separated and finished up in different boats. However, this was a minor disappointment and, in any case, didn't affect the other members of the party. Soon everybody was thoroughly relaxed. They lounged round happily, talking away and trailing their fingers in the surprisingly chilly water.

Miss Jones, careful not to move a muscle in case she disturbed the equilibrium of the boat, smiled tentatively across at Mrs. Frossell. "Isn't it lovely?"

Mrs. Frossell happily agreed that it was. "It reminds me of the Lake District," she claimed dreamily. "The way the snow-capped mountains brood over the glassy waters of the lake." She brought her eyes back into focus. "Are you familiar with the Lake District, Miss Jones?"

Miss Jones dithered. In the end she decided that, although as a girl she had once spent a short holiday in Grassmere, she couldn't really call herself familiar with that part of the country.

Mrs. Frossell thought that this was a pity, and no doubt would have pursued the matter further if Tony Lewcock hadn't butted in and said, very rudely, that he didn't reckon that the scene before their eyes bore the slightest resemblance to the Lake District. "Switzerland, now," he suggested, "that'd be more like it. Yes"—he looked round with an air of infuriating, smug masculinity—"Switzerland! That's what it looks like."

"Rubbish!" All heads, except Miss Jones's, turned as Mr. Beamish, sitting up in the bow next to his wife, put his two pennyworth in. "It's not a bit like Switzerland. If you must make these silly comparisons, then it's Norway."

"*Norway!*" The Hon. Con's bellow polluted the environment for at least a mile in most directions. "My aunt Fanny!"

"It's exactly like the fjords!" snarled Mr. Beamish. "I happen to know Norway extremely well, and I could take you to a dozen places where the rock formation and the light values, even, are—"

"Oh, phooey!" The Hon. Con saw no point in letting people finish their sentences when they were talking such poppycock. "If you'd said the highlands of Scotland, I might have been with you. But—Norwegian fjords? No, I think not."

Mrs. Beamish was girding up her loins for entry into the battle when Miss Jones produced her olive branch. "How about North Wales?" she asked before she was howled down.

It was about three quarters of an hour later that the boats came putt-putting gently back towards the jetty in front of the hotel. In the Hon. Con's boat the controversy was still raging, though the beauties of nature had long since been left behind. The disputants had now descended unashamedly to personal abuse. Over in the other boat an awed silence reigned as everybody sat and listened.

It was Miss Jones who first became aware of this audience. She spoke like a ventriloquist through a forced smile. "Everybody's watching us, dear!"

"Let 'em!" The Hon. Con steadied herself as the boat bumped softly against the little pier. "Blooming nosey parkers!" She grabbed hold of a small upright post and, always the perfect gentleman, concentrated her efforts on maintaining an even keel as everybody else scrambled out. In the end only Mr. Beamish was left.

"After you, Miss Morrison-Burke!" He stood back gallantly.

The Hon. Con hadn't forgiven him for Norway. "On the contrary, after you, Mr. Beamish!"

Mr. Beamish had had enough argument for one day. He risked an appealing glance to the heavens and then began gingerly to edge forwards.

In the meantime, the rest of the Albatrossers were milling about on the narrow jetty like shepherdless sheep, checking their hand-bags and cardigans and generally making a nuisance of themselves. Suddenly there was a shrill scream followed by a loud splash.

Some sixth sense warned the Hon. Con what had happened. "Holy cats!" she roared, leaping somewhat injudiciously to her feet. "It's Penny Clough-Cooper!"

There were several people who would have dearly loved to see the Hon. Con proved wrong, but they were disappointed. In any case, there was no time for idle dreams. The Hon. Con plunged out of the boat and thudded onto the jetty. Some coward soul begged her to have a care.

But the Hon. Con was blind and deaf to the outside world. "Hang on, old fruit!" she bawled, and, without a thought for her personal comfort and safety, launched herself out into space.

The ensuing tidal wave proved the last straw for Mr. Beamish. He was caught with one foot in the boat, one on the jetty, and his centre of gravity hovering somewhere in between.

There was a second scream and a third splash.

Miss Jones gazed helplessly at the boiling waters. "Oh, dear," she said.

THIRTEEN

Some spark of dignity might have been salvaged from the situation if only Miss Clough-Cooper had not proved to be a far better swimmer than the Hon. Con. Still, what does it matter—as Miss Jones would keep on saying—who rescues whom as long as nobody gets drowned?

Eventually, when all the splashing, shouting, and recriminations had died down, the Albatrossers found themselves back in the hotel dining room again. This time, though, they deliberately sat with their backs to that blasted lake. And they sat for a long time.

"I simply can't see," complained Zoë Withenshaw, "how anybody can take so long to dry out perfectly ordinary clothing. I mean, they're not being asked to cope with woollen overcoats, are they?"

"We do want the things completely dry, though, don't we?" asked Miss Jones and adjusted the grey blanket round the Hon. Con's hunched shoulders. "There's nothing worse than wearing damp clothing. I think it's really better to sit round here for a few minutes extra rather than run the risk of having three cases of double pneumonia on our hands."

The Hon. Con sneezed loudly and without benefit of handkerchief.

Miss Jones regarded her anxiously. "You're not sitting in a draught, are you, dear?"

Tony Lewcock got to his feet and stumped stiffly over to the window. "Bloody hell!" he said. "What a bloody holiday! If it isn't one bloody thing, it's another."

Jim Lewcock nodded his head in solemn agreement. "You can say that again, Tone! By Christ, you can! And it's all this bloody tart's fault." He stared morosely at Penny Clough-Cooper. Not even the knowledge that she was stark naked beneath her ex-army blanket would rouse any emotion, other than that of acute exasperation, in him. Jim Lewcock had had it. Up to here!

The other Albatrossers were in much the same frame of mind, and Jim Lewcock's outburst was supported by angry mutterings about the lack of consideration some people showed for other people's comfort. In fact, to hear some of the complaints, one might be forgiven for thinking that being the target of countless murderous attacks was a social solecism in the worst possible taste.

Miss Clough-Cooper sensed that her companions were trying to tell her something. She pulled her blanket even closer and raised her chin defiantly. "I'm sorry I'm being such a trouble to you all," she said, her voice sharp but with the tears welling up in her eyes.

Guess who came galloping to the rescue!

Miss Jones sat and listened to the Hon. Con's passionate defence of her new chum and tried to console herself by recalling that loyalty is a virtue. Of course, dear Constance was overdoing things, as usual, but then judgement had rarely been her strong point.

"Just a minute, Miss Morrison-Burke!"

The Hon. Con's voice died, though her mouth remained open. She glared at Miss Clough-Cooper. "Eh?"

Miss Clough-Cooper managed a sour little smile. "It's just that I have never actually said that this was another attempt on my life."

The Hon. Con closed her mouth and blinked uncertainly. "Ah, but it was, wasn't it?" she asked persuasively. "I mean, there you were, balancing precariously on that stupid little old jetty, and somebody took advantage and shoved you in the drink."

"Hardly," said Mrs. Beamish in a very superior tone, "the most effective method of murdering anybody, I should have thought."

"Especially as Miss Clough-Cooper would appear to be an exceptionally strong and capable swimmer." Desmond Withenshaw's resentment was all but tangible. He had spent more money than he could afford on this trip to the Soviet Union and was furious at the way time was continually being wasted. For all he knew, of course, the gloomy dining room on Lake Ritsa might be infinitely preferable to what was awaiting them down on the coast at Sochi, but that was hardly the point.

The Hon. Con's face broke into a beam of triumph. "Ah," she trumpeted, "but did the murderer know that, eh? See what I'm driving at, Withenshaw? This might be a clue. Now, Miss Clough-Cooper didn't go bathing at Sukhumi—did she?—so none of us had any idea what a smashing little swimmer she is. This beastly old murderer chappie probably thought she was one of these namby-pamby duffers who can't swim a stroke and who . . ."

Zoë Withenshaw snapped her powder compact shut and stuffed it back into her handbag. "I think we've all got the picture, Miss Morrison-Burke, though frankly I don't quite see what you're getting at. If none of us knew that Miss Clough-Cooper was a strong swimmer, then any of us could be the supposed murderer. Except, possibly, you and Mr. Beamish? Right? Well"—Zoë Withenshaw pretended to hide a yawn behind her hand—"that, surely, is more or less where we were when this whole ridiculous business began. Frankly, I am getting the teeniest bit bored with the never-ending saga of Miss Clough-Cooper."

"Bored?" The Hon. Con went very red in the face. "Bored? And how do you think poor old Penny feels, eh? This is the fifth blooming time in less than a fortnight that somebody's tried to kill her, and it's for the sake of the rest of you, you know, that she hasn't gone to the police. She just doesn't want to mess up your holiday for you, and, if you ask me, it's dashed decent of her. I'd like to see how you'd behave if . . ."

Miss Clough-Cooper squirmed unhappily under her blanket. "Please!" she said, pitching her voice loud enough to penetrate the Hon. Con's habitual deafness to interruption. "*Please!* I simply slipped on the jetty and lost my balance and tumbled into the water. Nobody pushed me. I can only apologise for my clumsiness and the inconvenience that I am causing you all."

This flat statement caused some embarrassment, and there were mutters to the effect that it didn't really matter. The Hon. Con was not embarrassed, and neither was she the type to let sleeping dogs lie. "Slipped on the jetty, my foot! You? Why, you're as surefooted as a couple of mountain goats *and* you're wearing rope-soled sandals to boot!" She chuckled delightedly and slapped her thigh. "Now pull the other one!" she invited jovially.

To everybody's relief, it was at this moment that the dining-room door opened and the manageress of the hotel stalked in. She was followed by a pair of underlings, staggering under loads of clothing, which they deposited rather carelessly on one of the tables.

"Is arid," said the manageress.

This was a black lie, but nobody, not even the unfortunate owners of the clothing, was inclined to argue. Decently chaperoned and sheltered by members of their own sex, the three blanketeers (Tony Lewcock's humourous sobriquet for the Hon. Con, Mr. Beamish, and Miss Clough-Cooper) pulled on their damp and crumpled garments.

The drive to Sochi was hot and sticky, and, thanks to the countless bends and twists in the road, everybody arrived feeling very bad-tempered and slightly sick. The Intourist guide, called Maria, was waiting for them and as usual made no concessions to human frailty. "In one hour," she announced, grinning wolfishly, "I take you on your free tour of town!"

The Albatrossers were seasoned travellers by now, and they no longer wasted their breath trying to argue with Intourist guides. Meekly gathering up their hand luggage, they queued up at the reception desk to fill in their arrival cards and hand over their passports.

The Hon. Con kept her pecker up remarkably well. Of course, she was luckier than most as she was able to leave all the tedious chores like unpacking to Miss Jones. However, even the Hon. Con wasn't allowed to sit idly twiddling her thumbs.

"Bones," she said as she came out of the bathroom and got her tool kit out of the drawer into which Miss Jones had only that very second put it, "do you ever get the impression that you've been here before?"

"Frequently, dear," said Miss Jones with a martyred smile as she sank on her knees beside yet another suitcase. "Why?"

The Hon. Con selected a screwdriver and found a handy length of wire. "I wish," she remarked, heading wearily back to the bathroom, "I had a rouble for every blooming toilet I've mended on this trip. Oh, and there's no plug for the bath, either."

Miss Jones finished locking the suitcases. They were all perfectly empty, but one couldn't be too careful when travelling in foreign parts—not that Miss Jones wouldn't have locked them equally carefully back home in dear old England, and did. She just wished she had a rouble for every time she had packed and unpacked, but naturally she didn't say so. Instead she pulled herself to her feet and tried to take an intelligent interest in the Hon. Con's problems. "What's gone wrong this time, dear?"

"Cistern thing doesn't fill," said the Hon. Con shortly.

Miss Jones ventured into the bathroom. Most of the plumbing appeared to be spread out in bits on the floor.

"What," asked the Hon. Con casually, "did you think about this morning's hoo-ha up at the lake?"

Miss Jones didn't pretend not to understand. "I think it was designed as another in the series of attempts on Miss Clough-Cooper's life, dear," she said, picking her words carefully.

The Hon. Con brightened up. "You do?"

"If everybody hadn't been so cross and nasty about the whole thing," Miss Jones went on, "I'm perfectly certain that Miss Clough-Cooper would have insisted that it was indeed another attempt. In the face of all that obvious hostility, though, I don't think even she had quite the nerve."

The Hon. Con flaked some rust off the ball arm with an idle thumbnail. "You think Penny Clough-Cooper's making it all up, don't you, Bones?"

Miss Jones skirted round a direct answer. "Even you haven't been able to find any real evidence, have you, dear?"

The Hon. Con was beginning to look as though she'd had all the stuffing knocked out of her. "My investigation's been a pretty scratch affair," she admitted. "Perforce. But, drat it all, if she is making it all up, what's her motive? Oh, I know you think she just wants to be the centre of attention, Bones, but she's a jolly attractive girl. She doesn't need to go to these lengths, surely." The Hon. Con cast a lacklustre eye over the greenish hemispheres of the ball cock. "Do you think she's a nutter, Bones?"

Miss Jones, in the interests of veracity, was obliged to admit that she didn't. On the contrary, she considered that Miss Clough-Cooper was an exceptionally shrewd and calculating female.

"Somebody *could* be after her," the Hon. Con said, rather pathetically. "There's absolutely nothing to prove that she's lying."

"There's nothing to prove anything, is there, dear?"

The Hon. Con tried one improbable piece of plumbing against another. It didn't fit. "We've only got what she says," she agreed. "Mind you," she added stoutly, "I believe her!"

Miss Jones should have been a fisherman. "Of course, dear," she murmured gently.

"The thing is," said the Hon. Con, peering doubtfully into the cistern, "that all this detection and bodyguard lark is really rather putting the clappers on my holiday."

Miss Jones suppressed the joyous leaping of her heart. "You do need your rest, dear."

The Hon. Con straightened up. "I was thinking of that book I was going to write!" she pointed out sharply. "Do you realise that I haven't done half the sociological research I wanted to?"

"I know things have been very difficult for you, dear," cooed Miss Jones, managing to be both admiring and tactful. She reached across the bath for the Hon. Con's face cloth and, without really knowing what she was doing, refolded it neatly.

During the long, weary drive down from Lake Ritsa, the Hon. Con had been doing a bit of thinking. The final conclusion had been reached with astonishing ease, but the Hon. Con had had a long struggle with the problem of how to break the news to Miss Jones without a total loss of face. Now, in the bathroom at the Intourist hotel in Sochi, the Hon. Con realised that, somehow or another, she'd found the way.

She opened her eyes very wide. "I've got responsibilities to other people besides blooming old Penny Clough-Cooper."

Miss Jones thought she knew what was expected of her. "Your reading public, dear?"

"Them, too," said the Hon. Con, displaying a rather distressing tendency to whine. "Drat it all, I am supposed to be here to enjoy myself."

Miss Jones nodded sympathetically.

"Do you know, Bones," the Hon. Con went on, realising at last how hard done by she was, "I don't feel that I've had any blooming holiday at all. I seem to have spent the entire time sorting Penny Clough-Cooper out in one way or another. Well, enough's enough!"

Miss Jones agreed that it was.

"I mean, I'm not one to pass by on the other side, and if I were sure the girl really was in danger, wild horses wouldn't hold me, but . . ." The Hon. Con stuck her head back inside the cistern as the moment of unconditional surrender drew nigh. "Well, the way things are, I've decided that I'm just not going to bother my head about her anymore. It's not"—an indignant Hon. Con glared up at Miss Jones—"as though she's the least bit grateful."

Miss Jones knew that one "I told you so" from her and the Hon. Con would dive right back into the murky depths of private detection out of sheer bloody-mindedness, so she tactfully changed the subject. She looked at her watch. "I think it's time we were getting ready for our tour of the town, dear. The guide did say she hoped we wouldn't keep her waiting."

The Hon. Con was quite willing to forget about Penny Clough-Cooper for a while. She gazed, somewhat bemusedly, at all the bits and pieces spread out on the bathroom floor. "Better leave this lot for the moment," she grunted. "P'r'aps I'll have another go at it when we get back."

Miss Jones's face fell. "That's going to be a . . . that's going to be rather inconvenient, isn't it, dear?"

The Hon. Con happened to be feeling quite comfortable. "Oh, come on, Bones," she exhorted her less fortunate pal, "don't make such a fuss. You'll just have to improvise."

"Improvise?" echoed Miss Jones, going quite white.

The Hon. Con chuckled, her natural good humour quite restored. "That's right, old bean! It'll teach you to use your initiative, won't it?"

Sochi could be (and often has been) called the Blackpool of the Black Sea, but the comparison is not a good one. In spite of all its efforts in the direction of vulgar commercialism, Sochi still has a very long way to go. The largest seaside resort in the Soviet Union, greater Sochi stretches along the coast for nearly twenty miles and contains well over sixty sanatoria and rest homes in which the Soviet workers can recover their health and strength. Other entertainment is a mite thin on the ground.

The Albatrossers were duly trundled round the sights in the bus which had been placed at their disposal. The Dentrarium Botanical Gardens (Mrs. Frossell: "I always say you can't have too many trees"), the Ostrovski Museum (the Hon. Con: "Who the heck's

Ostrovski?"), the railway station (Jim Lewcock: "Anybody see a bloody bog anywhere?") and then the marble-encrusted halls of the harbour terminal building. It was left to Tony Lewcock to voice the impressions of the less articulate: "What a flaming dump!"

Maria, the Intourist guide and amateur weightlifter, was weak on the finer nuances of the English language but strong on group psychology. She sensed that her audience was less than bowled over by the charm of her native town. These accursed foreigners were always carping about something! Maria took a firmer grip on her microphone as Jim Lewcock, preceded by the pungent aroma of the last of his duty-free whisky, leaned towards her across three rows of seats.

"What is there to do here, love?"

"Greater Sochi," said Maria, sticking valiantly to her script, "can accommodate approximately one million tourists. In two years we shall—"

"I know, love! You've told us all that rubbish already. Look, what is there to do of a night, eh?"

Maria was lost. Shakespeare, Galsworthy, and the *Collected Prefaces of George Bernard Shaw* had not prepared her for the Lewcock version of the vernacular.

Jim Lewcock spoke loudly and clearly. "What do you do in your free time, girlie?"

Maria got it at last. "Here is no prostitution!" she said firmly. "Unlike countries inhabited by slaves of capitalist system." She nodded imperiously at the driver and the bus moved off.

Meanwhile, the Hon. Con had been staring fixedly at the nape of Miss Clough-Cooper's neck. Miss Clough-Cooper was sitting all by herself in one of the front seats, although up till now the Albatrossers had been quite good about not leaving her out in the cold. The incident at Lake Ritsa had, however, changed all that, and the more Penny Clough-Cooper denied that anybody had tried to kill her, the more convinced her companions became that she was lying. And it had, at long last, really come home to them that they were the ones under suspicion, a distasteful fact that, hitherto, they had known, but not really appreciated. The way things were going now, Miss Clough-Cooper would probably have done better to contract leprosy.

The Hon. Con, never keen on running with the pack, did feel a few twinges of conscience, but managed to stifle them by remembering that nobody had been made more of a mug by Penny Clough-Cooper than she had. Not only had the dratted girl completely ruined the Hon. Con's well-deserved and extremely expensive holiday, but she'd probably deprived suffering humanity of a jolly valuable book of personal observation and pregnant comment. The Hon. Con's eyes all but filled with tears as she thought of what the reading public had lost, but sterner emotions took over as she thought about what a fool the Clough-Cooper wench had made of her. The Hon. Con took her career as a private detective rather seriously, and she liked other people to do the same.

"It doesn't look very hygienic, does it, dear?"

The Hon. Con turned and blinked at Miss Jones. "What doesn't?"

"The beach, dear!"

The bus was driving slowly along the waterfront, and Maria loudly and conscientiously pointed out the sights. It was the tiny public beach which had caught Miss Jones's somewhat critical eye. It was so crowded with people that the sand was completely invisible.

"Lucky we've got a private beach at the hotel," growled the Hon. Con. "I wouldn't fancy fighting it out for lebensraum with that mob."

Miss Jones smiled sweetly. "Rank has its privileges as well as its duties, dear." This statement was intended—and taken—as a delicate compliment to the Hon. Con and her elevated social standing.

Maria, the Intourist guide, ended her conducted tour of Sochi with what she liked to think was something of a grand finale: the visit to Matsesta. It was a fairly long drive from Sochi, and the Albatrossers had recovered their curiosity by the time the coach swung round and stopped in front of a large white structure built in the style of certain Greek temples. There was some agitated rustling of guidebooks as the more erudite members of the group tried to find out what they were looking at. Jim Lewcock had been fidgeting about for some minutes. As soon as the bus came to a halt, he got to his feet and headed for the door. Maria shoved him back into his seat. She'd got her little speech all off pat in no less than six foreign languages, and nobody—but nobody!—was going to skip it.

Desmond Withenshaw stared out the window at the dozens of coaches and thousands of people all milling round. "I thought we'd already seen the bus station," he complained to his wife.

Maria seized her microphone. "We are arrived at Matsesta!" she bellowed. "The building before you is the Matsesta bath and water house, whither people come eagerly from all over the Soviet Union."

"Er—why?" asked Mrs. Frossell, taking her courage in both hands.

"For the curing," said Maria. "Matsesta is famous for its spa waters. In Cherkess, Matsesta means 'fire water.' For citizens of the Soviet Union, all curing is free." Her audience stirred uneasily as they sensed that they were about to be fed some more blooming pro-Soviet propaganda, but Maria was on the health kick this time. "Waters of Matsesta may be consumed internally or externally. Externally they cure rheumatism, arthritis, diseases of the skin, diseases of the female gender, arteriosclerosis, nervous complaints, conditions of the heart. . . ."

The Hon. Con, strong as an ox and hardy as a mountain lion, stopped listening. She found other people's ailments profoundly boring. She stared out at the crowds of the halt and the lame as they proceeded slowly and painfully in one direction or another. Oh, well—there was nothing so queer as folk. There was a gentle touch on her arm.

"We're going, dear!"

The Hon. Con and Miss Jones tagged along behind the rest of the Albatrossers as they followed Maria up the flight of shallow steps. The halt and the lame shuffled considerably out of the way.

The noise, once they were inside the building, was deafening. Every sound bounced and rebounced off the marble walls.

"What's going on?" demanded the Hon. Con, shoving a bunch of elderly patients aside as she hurried to keep up with the rest of the party.

Miss Jones, not only British but proud of it, had already taken her place in the queue. She made room for the Hon. Con. "All these poor, sick people have come for treatment, dear," she explained patiently. "Baths and things. Like Buxton or Bath, you know," she added with little conviction. She had once accompanied her dear father to Malvern, and it hadn't looked a bit like this. Still, Miss Jones wasn't the one to burden the Hon. Con with her doubts.

The Hon. Con fended off an ashen-faced woman who was trying to jump the queue. "Do you reckon this water stuff does you any good, Bones?" she asked, attempting to peer over the heads of the people in front.

"I don't imagine it would do one any harm, dear," responded Miss Jones tactfully. But the Hon. Con was no longer listening.

She had reached the head of the queue now and was staring down in amazement into a marble-lined pit. In the middle of the pit stood a huge natural boulder plentifully supplied with taps. From these taps poured never-ending streams of faintly steaming water. Round the central boulder, a dozen women in white head scarves and overalls were hard at work, rinsing glasses, filling them from the taps, and then handing them up to the people waiting in the queue. Everything was damp and the marble slabs and floor were running with water.

Under Maria's stern gaze, none of the Albatrossers felt like refusing the evil-smelling stuff, and there was a fair amount of spluttering and gagging as it went down. The Hon. Con, surprisingly, came up smiling.

"Must be good stuff," she said, trying to unscrew her mouth, "if it tastes as nasty as that." She handed her glass back to the waiting attendant.

Beside her, Mrs. Beamish also seemed to be having trouble with a shrinking palate. Eventually she managed a sour little smile. "I suppose we should really congratulate ourselves," she said.

"Huh?"

Mrs. Beamish skilfully directed the Hon. Con's attention to Penelope Clough-Cooper, who was waiting patiently in the shade of a potted palm until everybody was ready to leave. "That Miss Clough-Cooper didn't get herself poisoned, of course!" she laughed. "I must say, I was quite expecting it. Weren't you?"

FOURTEEN

It is to be hoped that Ella Beamish felt simply awful when, a mere twelve hours later, Penny Clough-Cooper came within an inch of being burned alive in her bed.

This sixth attempt to shove Miss Clough-Cooper out of this vale of tears came at a time when the Albatrossers' thoughts were beginning to turn towards home and when they were even less inclined than usual to tangle with the Soviet criminal police.

After the exertions of a day which had included both Lake Ritsa and Matsesta, they were grateful that no entertainment had been laid on for them in the evening—though there was an ugly rumour going round that they weren't going to be so lucky on the morrow. However, sufficient unto the day. They sat round the dinner table and were reasonably happy until Mr. Beamish started trying to be helpful. He had been doing some checking and, after a lengthy session with timetables and itineraries, had come to the conclusion that they would only have four hours in Moscow before they flew home.

"So what?"

Mr. Beamish was sorely tempted to bridge the generation gap with his fist, but he restrained himself and even managed to smile at young Mr. Smith. "We have to change airports, you know, and, if one can judge by past experience, they'll need the whole four hours to get us from one side of the city to the other."

"No skin offa my nose," said young Mr. Smith. "We seen Moscow once, haven't we? So, what you getting your knickers in a twist for?"

Mr. Beamish gritted his teeth. "It's simply that if anybody has any shopping to do he would be well advised to do it here in Sochi, as I doubt if there'll be time in Moscow."

Young Mr. Smith chewed his chewing gum slowly and thoughtfully. Then, without another word, he pulled himself to his feet and slouched out of the dining room.

"Insolent young pup!" snarled Mr. Beamish. He glanced down the table to where, at the far end, young Mrs. Smith was sitting. "I think even his wife's beginning to get fed up with him."

The Hon. Con was intrigued. "How'd you work that out?"

Mr. Beamish stubbed out his cigarette in his saucer. "Didn't you notice? It's the first time since we've known him that he hasn't been wrapped like a boa constrictor round that girl. It hasn't taken them long," he added grimly, "to exhaust the admittedly overrated joys of married life."

Connubial bliss was one of the few subjects on which the Hon. Con did not rate herself an expert, so she changed the subject and treated an astonished Mr. Beamish to a dissertation on the difficulties of organising matches for her women's Rugby football team. It was not long before the whole party decided to break it up and go to bed.

The Hon. Con pulled the top sheet straight. "Oh, heck," she groaned, "I've forgotten to do my flipping exercises!"

Miss Jones, who found that sheer hard work kept her weight down, smiled indulgently as she picked up the Hon. Con's hacking jacket from the floor. "It's been a long day, dear," she said.

"True. But"—the Hon. Con pummelled the well-inflated spare tyre beneath her pyjama coat—"I'm beginning to lose the battle of the bulge, you know. I miss my twenty minutes a day with the old punch-bag."

"You'll soon get back into trim when we get home, dear." Miss Jones buffed up the Hon. Con's brogues.

" 'Spect so!" The Hon. Con yawned loudly and luxuriously. "Golly gosh, but I feel absolutely whacked!" She sank majestically beneath the sheets. "Mind putting that centre light out, Bones? It's shining straight in my peepers."

Miss Jones didn't mind. What few chores she still had left to do could be accomplished perfectly well in the feeble light of the bedside lamp.

It was Miss Jones who became aware of the commotion first. She switched on her light and saw, with some resentment, that it was after four in the morning. She sat up in bed and listened. Those raised voices out in the corridor—they were English, weren't they? Miss Jones stifled an extremely mild expletive and reached for her dressing gown. This was surely where they'd come in.

Across in the other bed, the Hon. Con snorted and snuffled and thrashed round in her sleep.

Miss Jones sighed. She didn't want to wake dear Constance, who really needed all the sleep she could get, but if she didn't . . . well, Constance could be very brusque at times.

Miss Jones chose the lesser of the two evils, and the Hon. Con emerged from the arms of Morpheus with reluctance and in a filthy temper. It was some seconds before she could grasp what was going on, but when she did, her reactions were pretty much the same as Miss Jones's had been. "Oh, *no!*" she groaned. "Not *again!* I tell you, Bones"—she allowed Miss Jones to help her on with her slippers—"if somebody's tried to suffocate Penny Clough-Cooper in her bed again, I'll . . . I'll . . ." The Hon. Con searched desperately for some pungent and witty conclusion to her threat but failed to find one. "Oh, come on, Bones!" she concluded crossly.

By the time the Hon. Con and Miss Jones got out into the corridor, things had quieted down considerably. People were now merely screaming at each other, and somebody had had the sense to fling all the windows in sight wide open. Most of the smoke had been blown away, and the Russian floor maid was able to have her hysterics in comparative comfort. Or at least she would have been, had not a heavily built East German woman tourist started marching across to her with a determined air and a clenched fist.

The Hon. Con made her presence felt in the ensuing silence.

"She's in our room," Desmond Withenshaw told her, staring moodily at the black and dripping pile of bedclothes that somebody had dragged out onto the landing. "Blubbing fit to bust," he added as a disgruntled and unkind afterthought.

The Hon. Con pushed past him and surveyed the scene of the crime. The mattress was still on the bed in Miss Clough-Cooper's room. It was soaking wet and quite badly charred round the edges.

Norman Beamish, hopping unobtrusively from one bare foot to

the other, put the Hon. Con in the picture. "As far as I can understand it, it was that Russian floor maid who first spotted something was wrong. She'd been away from her post for a couple of minutes, getting herself a cup of tea, I believe, and—"

"Hold it!" The Hon. Con raised a hand in a gesture of which a long-serving metropolitan policeman would not have been ashamed. "How do you know that? 'Bout the tea, I mean."

"I was one of the first on the scene," explained Mr. Beamish. "I haven't been sleeping too well on this trip, as Mrs. Beamish will tell you. I started to get up as soon as the floor maid began screaming and shouting. I was out on the landing even before she'd got Miss Clough-Cooper's door open with her master key. I just noticed the cup of tea standing on her desk. It was still warm."

The Hon. Con swung round as ponderously as an ocean liner changing course. There was a saucer standing on the floor maid's desk, but no cup.

"I—er—snatched it up in an effort to help extinguish the fire," said Mr. Beamish, looking foolish. "That's—er—how I knew it was still hot."

The Hon. Con didn't suffer rivals gladly, and, in her considered opinion, one detective at a time was more than enough for anybody. She began to muscle Mr. Beamish back out of the act. "Just stick to the bare facts, will you, old chap? Now, have I got the sequence of events right—this maid woman gets the bedroom door open with her passkey or whatever, and you snatch up the cup of tea. That it?" The Hon. Con's eyes narrowed shrewdly. "Well, how did you know at that stage that there was anything on fire, eh?"

It was all good, penetrating stuff, but Mr. Beamish neither trembled nor grew pale. Over the years, Mrs. Beamish had done a good job on him, and he remained as polite and long-suffering as ever. "I saw the smoke, Miss Morrison-Burke. It was puffing up from underneath the door. That's how the floor maid realised there was something amiss, too."

"Oh," said the Hon. Con, unable to find any flaw in this logic.

"By the time I actually reached Miss Clough-Cooper's room, the floor maid had beaten most of the flames out with the bedside rug. I must say, I thought she kept her head extraordinarily well. It's a pity she went to pieces when the emergency was over."

"What was on fire?"

"The bedclothes."

The Hon. Con blinked. "And Penny Clough-Cooper?"

"She was lying unconscious in the middle of the flames." Without thinking, Mr. Beamish had assumed a matter-of-fact air which the Hon. Con was beginning to find very irritating. "Then some of the others arrived, and they helped with getting the last of the flames put out. Somebody very sensibly opened the windows wider, and I picked Miss Clough-Cooper up and carried her outside into the corridor. Mrs. Withenshaw said we couldn't just dump her there, so I carried her into the Withenshaws' bedroom. Mrs. Withenshaw said she would look after her."

The Hon. Con scowled. Jealousy is not a very attractive trait. "Had she regained consciousness?"

"Er—no. Not when I left."

"Drugged, I expect."

"Oh, do you think so? Well, I'm afraid I wouldn't know about that." Mr. Beamish appeared to be looking for some means of escape.

The Hon. Con caught him by the tassels of his dressing gown. "Hang on a sec, old cheese!" she implored. "Has somebody sent for the quack?"

"I beg your pardon?"

The Hon. Con, whose volatile spirits were on the rise once more, waxed jocular. "The sawbones! The medicine man! The . . ."

Norman Beamish shook his head. "No."

"No?"

"I thought we'd all agreed that we didn't want to involve the Russian authorities in our little—er—trouble."

"Holy smoke!" gasped the Hon. Con with unwitting aptness. "But—they *are* involved!" She swept a hand round to embrace the sodden bed, the charred blankets and sheets out on the landing, the circle of interested spectators. "Besides, Penny Clough-Cooper obviously needs medical attention. Look, there's supposed to be a doctor in the hotel. It says so in their booklet thing. Let's . . ."

It was Mr. Beamish's turn to raise a restraining hand. "I'm sure Mrs. Withenshaw can cope. And the other ladies are there, too. My wife holds a certificate for home nursing, you know."

The Hon. Con was far from satisfied. "But what about all this?"

she demanded, once more encompassing the surrounding devastation. "You can laugh all this . . ."

"*Smoking in bed?*"

The hotel staff had at last pulled out their collective finger and roused the hotel director. There had been some delay while this particular comrade had got washed and dressed, it not being the policy of Intourist to allow its employees to be seen with their hair down. The director had, of course, already been warned by his colleague at Lake Ritsa of what to expect, but had foolishly thought that lightning didn't strike twice.

"Smoking in bed?" The hotel director's vocabulary may have been limited, but in his well-pressed dark suit and white shirt, he looked absolutely impeccable. Of course, having a Lewcock brother on either side probably made him look a lot better.

"Smoking in bed?" The hotel director's voice rose higher with each repetition.

Jim Lewcock flashed broad winks in all directions and encircled the director's shoulders with a comradely arm. "You've got it, sonnie boy! She woke up—see?—went for a pee, and then couldn't drop off again. You know how it is. So—she fishes out the old coffin nails and ignites. Savvy?"

The hotel director, fastidiously removing Jim Lewcock's arm, crinkled his forehead as he tried to follow the explanation.

Jim Lewcock's smile was wide, bland, and reassuring in that special way much favoured by professional confidence tricksters. "Well, what happened next, mate, is anybody's guess. I reckon she just sort of dozed off and let the fag end drop on the sheet."

The director had now attracted a little circle of his staff, and they gathered round him admiringly as he poked the pile of bedclothes on the landing. Inquisitive guests looked on from a greater distance. The director was thinking, mostly about his own future. He was nobody's fool and he didn't believe this smoking-in-bed story any more than Jim Lewcock did, but one had to work out all the angles. At last he made up his mind. He turned away from the burnt sheets and snapped his fingers impatiently. Underlings promptly cleared a way through the onlookers, and he entered Miss Clough-Cooper's bedroom. Once more he plunged into deep and anxious thought while those Albatrossers not engaged in succoring Miss Clough-Cooper watched him with bated breath.

"Smoking in bed!" he said for the fourth time, making it a statement now.

"Disgusting habit," agreed Jim Lewcock smoothly, "but you know what women are like. Always needing something to steady their nerves." He dropped his voice and gave the director a nudge. "She's not married, you know."

"You were being present in the room with her?"

Jim Lewcock was delighted with this slur upon his honour and glanced round in case anybody had missed the unsolicited tribute to his virility. "Unfortunately, no!" he chuckled.

"So how you know what she is doing?"

"Eh?"

The Hon. Con always said that breeding tells. It did now. While Jim Lewcock, a working-class lout if ever there was one, was gaping like a stranded goldfish, the Hon. Con stepped forward and delivered a real whopper of a lie without turning a hair. "She told us!"

The hotel director's head swung round sharply at the sound of this new voice. "The lady is not fainted?"

The Hon. Con had no intention of spoiling the ship for a ha'porth of tar. "She recovered consciousness for a brief moment," she said. "Just long enough to tell us how the accident happened."

The director nodded and then, careful to leave unturned no stone that might later be used to clobber him, asked, "You are summoned the doctor?"

The Hon. Con realised that she was facing a worthy opponent, but she flattered herself that she was more than a match for him. "One of our party is a doctor." She saw the director's eyebrows go up as he remembered that the passports of all the Albatrossers were in his possession and thus fatally easy to check. Without a flicker of compunction, the Hon. Con smashed this bright idea clean out of sight. "Mrs. Withenshaw," she added calmly.

The director acknowledged the master stroke with a slight bow. He knew, of course, that British married women frequently travelled on their husbands' passports, and when they did, no details of their profession were required or given. Oh, you had to get up very early in the morning if you wanted to catch the Hon. Con bending!

The director was, of course, perfectly well aware that, whatever had set Miss Clough-Cooper's bed on fire, it was not a carelessly dropped cigarette. Even the most inexpert eye could see that the bed had been ignited at several points round the edges. Few people in positions of responsibility in the Soviet Union are fanatics for the truth, and the director of the Intourist hotel in Sochi was no exception. All he wanted was a quiet life, and a long one. He rubbed his hand thoughtfully over his chin. So—somebody had tried to burn this female Western tourist alive in her bed. Very uncultured. Nasty, too. And it would be even more nasty if the powers-that-be found out about it. There would be endless investigations and interrogations and all kinds of unpleasantnesses. The hotel director knew all about the ways of the Soviet police and had absolutely no desire to extend his experience in that respect. Whatever the outcome, his job wouldn't be worth a candle. No Albatrosser, therefore, was more anxious to cover up what had happened to Penny Clough-Cooper than the hotel director himself was.

The hotel director looked the Hon. Con slowly up and down, and it can be said without any equivocation that there was nothing lickerish in his glance. It was a look of purely financial speculation. Having reached a decision, the hotel director turned on the now-subdued but ashen-faced floor maid and spat a mouthful of Russian at her. She gulped, moved away, and began driving everybody back into his own room. Most of them went quite willingly, no longer interested in a scene which hadn't even got a drop of life's blood to liven it up. Soon only the Hon. Con, Miss Jones, the Lewcock brothers, and Messrs. Beamish, Withenshaw, and Frossell were left. Mrs. Beamish and Mrs. Withenshaw, ably abetted by Mrs. Frossell, were ministering to that perennial victim, Penny Clough-Cooper, while of the Smiths there was no sign at all.

The director, taking the Hon. Con as the natural leader of the group, addressed himself to her. "Some person will be required to pay for this."

The Hon. Con tried to make herself invisible.

"The damage," explained the director, indifferent to the cruel body blows he was inflicting. "In this hotel, smoke in bed is totally forbidden. Is against regulations, copy of which is in my office room and available to seekers."

With the Hon. Con attempting to fight her way through to the rear ranks, it was left to Mr. Beamish to ask the question which no self-respecting haggler should ever allow to pass his lips. "How much?"

The director pretended to calculate, though he had already done his sums. "Fifty," he said.

Nobody cared much for the sound of this.

Jim Lewcock licked dry lips. "Fifty roubles is a touch on the stiff side, isn't it, old man?"

"Not fifty roubles," said the director with a sweet smile. "Fifty pounds. English pounds."

"Jesus!" The shock went straight to Jim Lewcock's stomach. "Here, Tone"—he turned urgently to his brother—"don't let 'em start fixing anything till I get back!" He rushed off down the corridor.

The Hon. Con was sidling away, too. "Must just go and see how poor old Penny's getting on," she whispered to Mr. Beamish. "Leave you chaps to deal with all this sordid stuff, eh?" She grabbed Miss Jones by the arm. "Come on, Bones! We've got work to do!"

A few moments later Miss Jones was peering apprehensively under the Hon. Con's arm into the Withenshaws' bedroom and experiencing a twinge of remorse. Miss Clough-Cooper, stretched prone on the bed nearer the door, did look distressingly like a corpse.

"How is she?" the Hon. Con's hushed whisper roused Miss Clough-Cooper, and for a flickering moment she opened her eyes.

Zoë Withenshaw stood aside. "Why don't you come in?"

The Hon. Con and Miss Jones tiptoed into the bedroom.

"She looks a deuced odd sort of colour," observed the Hon. Con in the voice she used for talking in church. "She didn't get burned, did she?"

"No, thank God!" said Mrs. Withenshaw, who was looking pretty peaky herself. "The flames didn't actually reach her, though she must have breathed in a fair amount of smoke."

Mrs. Beamish replaced the damp face cloth on Miss Clough-Cooper's forehead while Mrs. Frossell stood by and looked sympathetic.

"Why didn't she wake up?" asked the Hon. Con. "Was she drugged?"

Zoë Withenshaw shook her head. "She'd been knocked out."

The Hon. Con's jaw dropped. "Knocked out?"

Zoë Withenshaw nodded across the bed at Mrs. Beamish. Mrs. Beamish obliged by bending over the still figure once more and removing the face cloth. Then she pushed aside a lock of Penny Clough-Cooper's hair, and the very ugly bruise was revealed in all its purpling glory.

"It's a wonder," chirped Mrs. Frossell admiringly, "that her head wasn't split right open!"

FIFTEEN

In her more unbuttoned moods, the Hon. Con was wont to claim that once she'd got the bit between her teeth, wild horses couldn't pull it out again. If Penny Clough-Cooper had a grievance, it was perhaps that it had taken six murderous attempts on her life before the Hon. Con would even admit that the bit was there.

The Hon. Con rejected this criticism with some heat and pointed out that she had been Penny Clough-Cooper's staunchest supporter right from the start. "And never wavered!" she boomed, through and above Miss Clough-Cooper's somewhat sceptical sniff. "I was just lying doggo—see? Playing possum or whatever. Pretending I thought it was all in your mind on the off chance that the murderer chappie would betray himself."

"And did he?" asked Miss Clough-Cooper with rather unnecessary sarcasm.

The Hon. Con realised that Penny Clough-Cooper had been through some dashed hair-raising experiences recently, and so she made due allowance for the old frayed nerves. "You feeling warm enough?" she enquired with a solicitude that would have had Miss Jones gasping with shock.

Miss Clough-Cooper adjusted the Hon. Con's duffle coat across her knees. "No, not really," she said.

The Hon. Con gazed round the deserted bathing beach and out across the steely-grey sea. A sudden gust of wind whipped up a generous handful of sand and dashed it across their faces. "Didn't think foreigners had weather like this," she commented gloomily. "Holy cats, we might as well be in England." She held out an enquiring hand. No, her eyes had not deceived her—it was raining.

Miss Clough-Cooper rose to her feet and handed back the

duffle coat. "There is absolutely no point in staying out here," she said.

"But we've got an unencumbered field of fire here!" wailed the Hon. Con. "We could see anybody approaching for simply miles." She struggled up out of the deck chair and scurried after her charge. "You going to sit in the hotel?" she asked.

"No." Miss Clough-Cooper forged even further ahead. "I think I shall go down into the town. I've got some shopping to do, too."

It was Hobson's choice. The Hon. Con trailed down to the shops in Miss Clough-Cooper's wake and reflected that, all in all, she'd had a jolly frustrating morning. She'd been trying to get to the bottom of this latest attack, but old Penny Clough-Cooper was being far from cooperative. No matter how many times the Hon. Con asked her, the dratted girl would keep saying that she'd been fast asleep and had neither heard nor seen anything.

"Oh, come on!" she had expostulated rather crossly. "You simply can't say that the first thing you knew was when you came round and found yourself lying on the flipping bed with Mrs. Withenshaw bending over you! You must have spotted something! You must . . ."

Miss Clough-Cooper's face had been as steely-grey as the sea. "I didn't!" she said flatly.

And, in spite of all the Hon. Con's efforts, Penny Clough-Cooper maintained this pigheaded attitude all the way on the long walk down the hill to the centre of Sochi. Indeed, if the Hon. Con hadn't had a bit of a soft spot for the girl, she might have washed her hands of the whole business there and then.

Although the seaside town of Sochi had its full quota of shops, only the handful within easy walking distance of the port area were of much interest to foreign visitors. Penny Clough-Cooper and the Hon. Con had, therefore, little difficulty in running down the rest of their party. The Hon. Con, automatically keeping a weather eye open for one-eyed lascars and sinister Chinese, strolled over to Miss Jones.

"How you getting on, eh?"

Miss Jones, to whom the tedious task of buying such presents as the Hon. Con intended to take home with her had been delegated, was in the middle of pricing some Matrushka dolls. Was five for four roubles seventy-three copecks in this shop a better bet than the seven for six roubles fifteen copecks in the other shop, when the five for four roubles seventy-three copecks had prettier faces? "Oh, quite well, thank you, dear," said Miss Jones, knowing that the Hon. Con. didn't like a grumbler. She recollected an earlier problem. "You did say you didn't want to spend more than fifty pence on your cousin, Lady Emily, didn't you, dear?"

"Didn't want to buy her a flipping present at all," admitted the Hon. Con. gloomily, "but she did bring me that potty little lace hanky from Malta. Useless thing it was, too. One blow and it was finished."

"I was wondering about one of those little clay figurines," said Miss Jones. "They're so nice and bright, aren't they? The tiniest costs well over a pound, though."

With an unerring instinct, the Hon. Con's eye fell on the least expensive item in the entire shop. She indicated a tray full of highly unattractive plastic keyrings. "Get her one of those, Bones!"

Having cut that Gordian knot, the Hon. Con strolled masterfully out of the shop. On the other side of the road, seated at a pavement cafe and consuming a large ice-cream, was another of nature's delegators—Ella Beamish. Although the weather was still cool and blowy it had stopped raining, and the Hon. Con ambled across the road to join her. Blenching slightly at the thought of what it was going to cost her, she too ordered an ice-cream. Well, she was supposed to be on holiday.

"I gave Norman a list," confided Mrs. Beamish between mouthfuls, "and told him to get on with it. I can't"—she leaned confidentially across the table—"do much standing, you know. Not with my complaint."

"Blooming boring business, anyhow," grunted the Hon. Con. "And expensive. It all adds up, you know."

"What about the Smiths?" asked Mrs. Beamish.

"What about 'em?"

"Do you know how many presents they've got to buy? Thirty-five! Think of that! *Thirty-five!* And you should have seen what they were buying, too. None of your cheap stuff for them, oh dear me no! Caviar, those silver holders for glasses of tea, enamelled spoons, and I don't know what. The money they were spending! Really, young people these days . . ."

The Hon. Con reckoned she'd got enough troubles of her own

without worrying her head over nationwide sociological problems, so she just stopped listening. When eventually she spoke again to Mrs. Beamish, her question was something of a non sequitur.

Mrs. Beamish was, happily, a shrewd and clear-headed woman, and she had no difficulty in switching onto this new track. "Well, I wouldn't say we exactly lived *near* Miss Clough-Cooper, Miss Morrison-Burke. Wattington must be a good fifteen or twenty miles away from us. By the way"—Mrs. Beamish showed that she could do the grasshopper bit too—"is she going to pay that fifty pounds?"

"Don't reckon she's got much choice," said the Hon. Con. "Fearful swindle."

"That manager's up to some fiddle, if you ask me."

"Penny was sort of dropping the odd hint that the rest of us might care to help share the burden," said the Hon. Con idly.

Mrs. Beamish was highly indignant. "Huh, I like that! Why on earth should we?"

"She said the only reason she didn't kick up a fuss and call in the cops was because she was thinking of the rest of us," explained the Hon. Con. "Still, I managed to talk her out of it. Said I didn't think it was fair on people like the Smiths, who obviously haven't got two ha'pennies to rub together." She averted her eyes from the sight of the Smiths, mari et femme, emerging from the souvenir shop opposite. Loaded down with parcels, they unconcernedly hailed a taxi to take them back to the hotel. "Jolly good ice-cream, this," said the Hon. Con quickly.

Mrs. Beamish gave the Soviet ice-cream industry her accolade. "I've tasted worse," she said.

The Smiths departed in a cloud of low-octane fumes and the Hon. Con returned to her muttons. "This latest attempt on Penny Clough-Cooper's life," she said. "What I can't fathom is how this brute manages to get into her room. This is the second time, you know. Penny says she's frightfully careful about keeping her door locked, but—well—there were no signs of a break-in, were there?"

Mrs. Beamish outglared a Russian family party who were sitting at a nearby table and gawping. Obviously they had seen nothing like this down on the collective farm. With a mixture of grotesque grimacing and overdramatic gestures, she ordered another ice-cream. The Russian family party nodded their appreciation of this performance. "I don't see your problem, I'm afraid."

The Hon. Con, ice-cream moustache and all, looked up. "You don't?"

Mrs. Beamish shrugged her shoulders. Her manner was really rather insulting, and if the Hon. Con had been at all sensitive, she might have taken exception to it. "These hotels are all the same," she said, dabbing her lips with a tissue, "wherever you go. Any key will open practically any door. It's my theory that they put the locks on the bedroom doors just for window dressing—to reassure the guests. From a security point of view, they're virtually useless."

The Hon. Con was grateful that Miss Jones wasn't here to listen to these dreadful revelations. "Are you sure?"

"Of course I'm sure! Norman and I must have put it to the test in practically every hotel we've ever stayed in."

The Hon. Con's eyes grew round. "You mean you go round opening other people's doors just to . . ."

"I mean nothing of the kind! Don't be sillier than you need be, dear! It's simply that I am often in bed and fast asleep by the time Norman decides to come to bed. You know what he's like. He'd sit up drinking and talking all night with the cat if that's all the company he could find. Well, naturally he knows better than to wake me up at all hours to unlock the door for him, and so, rather than disturb the hotel staff and get the passkey, he borrows the key of whichever layabout he happens to be with at the time. You'd be surprised how often it works." Mrs. Beamish broke off for a moment to permit herself a complacent smile. "Oh, I've got him pretty well trained over the years! There's no dropping of boots or banging of doors with my Norman! Most nights I don't even hear him come in at all, and it's only when I see him in the morning that I know for sure he's not still out on the tiles." She preened herself. "If there's one thing I will not stand, it's an inconsiderate husband. What I say is, why ask a girl to marry you if you're not prepared to . . ."

The Hon. Con, down to nearly her last lick of ice-cream, wasn't wildly interested in hints on the upbringing of husbands. "And the floor maid didn't see him because she was off getting herself that cup of tea." She looked at Mrs. Beamish with some respect. "By jove, I think you may have solved that little problem!"

"Glad to have been of help, dear." Most of Mrs. Beamish's

mind was on the feasibility of a third ice-cream. "Of course, whatever happens now, I don't think I shall ever risk another package holiday. This one was Norman's idea, of course, though I did point out at the time that you simply would never know who you'd be rubbing shoulders with. And how right I was! Of course," she added kindly, "people like you and Miss Clough-Cooper, from good families, are in quite a different category. It's those dreadful—"

"Hang on a sec!" the Hon. Con broke in. "Look, I know anybody with half an eye can see that old Penny Clough-Cooper is as blue-blooded as they come, but just for a minute there you sounded as though you *knew*."

Mrs. Beamish looked up in surprise. "Well, I do, dear. Oh, I see what you're getting at! Well, as I told you, I've never met Miss Clough-Cooper before, but, as a matter of fact, I do know her father. A perfect gentleman if ever I saw one! My own dear old daddy thought very highly of him when they were associated together on that legal case. 'Some doctors,' Daddy always says, 'are professionally and socially little better than butchers. Clough-Cooper is one of the shining exceptions!' Of course"—Mrs. Beamish picked up her spoon with a little moue of pleasure—"he was instrumental in saving Daddy a simply enormous sum of money."

"When did all this happen, for heaven's sake?" demanded the Hon. Con, feeling aggrieved.

"Oh, years ago, dear. Eight? Ten? Something like that. I don't recall all the sordid details, but Daddy was showing a prospective buyer over a house, and he—the client, that is—fell through the staircase. Dry rot, I think. Well, he—was he called Wilberforce?—finished up in the cellar. It was quite a nasty fall, I grant you, but there was nothing broken. Apart from a few bruises and a bit of shock, he was as right as rain, really. Daddy was terribly upset and drove this man all the way home in his car and even sent him half a bottle of whisky as a get-well present. You can imagine how surprised and *hurt* he was when, a day or two later, the solicitor's letter came. This Wilberforce brute was threatening to sue Daddy on the grounds that the fall had damaged his back for life. And the money he was asking for! You simply wouldn't credit the . . ."

The Hon. Con made a spunky effort to cut the cackle. "Where does Penny Clough-Cooper's father come in?"

"That's what I'm trying to tell you, dear!" Mrs. Beamish's voice had quite an edge to it. "Daddy got Dr. Clough-Cooper to examine this Wilberforce crook, and he said that there was absolutely nothing wrong with him and that he was just putting it on to extort money out of us. Well, Daddy was simply furious and . . ."

The Hon. Con's eyes glazed over as they sometimes did when she was thinking. She let Mrs. Beamish rabbit on. There were a number of questions she would have liked to have asked, such as why the Wilberforce man was suing Mrs. Beamish's father and not the owner of the house, but she let them go. There was another jigsaw puzzle that she was trying to put together in her head. Insurance claims, bad backs, Penny Clough-Cooper's father—it all added up to something somewhere.

"Would either of you ladies like a lift back to the hotel?" Roger Frossell, sent across by his mother, was rather overdoing the courtesy bit. He waved a hand, which lacked only a hat with feathers in it, to where the remaining members of the party were piling recklessly into a whole fleet of taxis. "There is, apparently, room for a couple of little ones."

In spite of this cheeky approach, neither Mrs. Beamish nor the Hon. Con was going to pass up a bargain offer lightly. Hurriedly they lapped up the last drops of their ice-creams and called for the bill. There was much muted and anxious discussion about tipping. In spite of the fact that they were nearly at the end of their holiday, neither lady had yet come up against this problem. Was tipping, they asked each other, "done" in the Soviet Union? In spite of much evidence to the contrary, they both decided it wasn't and carefully paid over the exact amounts before making a dash for it to the waiting taxis. A two-fingered gesture from the comrade waitress followed them.

"Thank heavens!" said Mrs. Withenshaw with heavy sarcasm. "I began to think you were never coming!"

The Hon. Con was delighted to discover that nobody else had wished to share the back seat in her taxi with Penny Clough-Cooper, and she flopped down happily beside her. "Get your shopping done all right?" she enquired breezily.

Penelope Clough-Cooper stared out the window. "Yes," she said stonily. If it had been possible to snub the Hon. Con, this monosyllable would have done it.

But it was not possible to snub the Hon. Con, especially when she was having a few twinges of conscience at having abandoned Penny Clough-Cooper for so long in favour of an ice-cream. From now on, she promised herself cheerfully, she would stick to the girl like the proverbial limpet. Miss Clough-Cooper's feelings on the matter were naturally not canvassed, and the fact that she would probably have preferred being murdered to having the Hon. Con tied round her neck for twenty-four hours a day did not emerge.

The Albatrossers duly had their lunch and then found themselves at something of a loose end. The weather was still far too inclement for sunbathing, and nobody fancied trailing back down to the town again. The Smiths went back to bed and everybody else lounged round and wondered if you could die of boredom. Things brightened up a trifle in the evening, though the three-hour performance of national songs and dances was just about as much as most of them could stomach. As Mrs. Frossell shyly commented, really when you'd seen one folk dance, you'd seen them all.

It was only right at bedtime that anybody could really be said to have enjoyed himself. That was when the most almighty row broke out between the Hon. Con and Penny Clough-Cooper as to where the latter was to spend the night. Miss Clough-Cooper was quite adamant that she wasn't going to share a bedroom with anybody, but she soon found that public opinion was against her. The Albatrossers, never a particularly long-suffering lot, had had enough. With their return to normal life now only a matter of hours away, the last thing they wanted was any more excitement from Penny Clough-Cooper. Tony Lewcock spoke for all of them when he commented in an aside that the Hon. Con didn't quite catch, "Well, what does it matter if old Con does turn out to be the bloody murderer? It'll clear the rest of us from suspicion, won't it?"

Penny Clough-Cooper didn't give in without a struggle, though there's not much you can do when you're outvoted eleven to one, with Miss Jones bravely abstaining. Eventually, and with a very bad grace, Miss Clough-Cooper bowed to the inevitable and was carried off in triumph by the Hon. Con. Miss Jones's face was, as they say, a picture.

It was still a picture when, just on half past seven the following morning, she came tapping on the Hon. Con's door. It was the Albatrossers' last morning in the Soviet Union, and Miss Jones, for one, was not sorry.

The Hon. Con opened the door. She was fully dressed and looking down in the mouth. If the night, as Miss Jones suspected, had been passed in unbridled revelry, the Hon. Con for one had not enjoyed it. "Oh, it's you, Bones."

Miss Jones was in no mood to make concessions, but even she had to suppress a stab of sympathy. "Did everything go off all right, dear?"

"Fine," said the Hon. Con, slouching back to sit on the end of her bed.

"I've just popped in to finish off your packing and to give Miss Clough-Cooper this head scarf. I found it under a chair in her bedroom. She must have dropped it last night when she was clearing her things out to make way for me. Er—where is she, by the way, dear?"

"In the bathroom," grunted the Hon. Con. "She seems to spend most of her time in there. She's getting dressed." The Hon. Con sighed. "She went to a day school, you see," she added, as though that explained everything.

Miss Jones looked round. "Well, I'll just leave the scarf on this chair, dear, if you'll . . ."

The Hon. Con stretched out her hand. It was, Miss Jones noted rather sadly, a little grubby. Really, if you didn't stand over Constance twenty-four hours a day . . . "I'll give it to her," said the Hon. Con.

Miss Jones dropped the head scarf into the Hon. Con's hand. It was an action that spoke louder than words, but the Hon. Con was too preoccupied with unfolding the somewhat drab coloured paisley silk square.

"Pretty!" said the Hon. Con admiringly.

Miss Jones decided to stuff the Hon. Con's packing. "We have to leave for the airport in three quarters of an hour," she said indifferently. "And you haven't had your breakfast yet."

"Be there in a jiffy," muttered the Hon. Con, staring as though mesmerised by Penny Clough-Cooper's scarf. Amongst the usual plethora of designs and patterns, one motif seemed suddenly to stand and shout. It was roughly circular in shape, maybe an inch and a half in diameter. In the centre was a red figure 1 with, superimposed, a crossed golf club and a pole bearing a small, triangular flag. Beneath was a white golf ball.

Even the Hon. Con at her most dim witted could work this out.

A thought struck her—maybe the scarf was borrowed. But, no! A Cash's name tape sewn neatly in one corner proclaimed that it was, in very truth, the property of P. Clough-Cooper.

There was a rattle from the other side of the bathroom door as the bolt was shot back. The Hon. Con jumped guiltily and then, with a warning scowl at the bewildered Miss Jones, hurriedly folded up the scarf again and placed it on the dressing table.

SIXTEEN

Not many people, even amongst the sophisticated travelling public, will have heard of Bleastead Moor Airport, and fewer will have been unlucky enough to have endured its facilities. They should count their blessings.

In 1945, after having been a totally undistinguished and highly uncomfortable bomber station during the war, Bleastead Moor sank back happily into the state of rural slumdom for which nature had always intended it. Cows grazed on the airfield and a neighbouring farmer fattened his pigs in the control tower. Then some idiot with more money than sense got the bright idea of challenging Heathrow, Stanstead, and Gatwick on their own ground. The challenge had been accepted and the gauntlet was slapped resoundingly across Bleastead Moor's blighted acres. One could have selected a more inconvenient site for a new international airport, but it would have been hard. No reputable airline would touch the place with a barge pole, and it survived, a financial miracle, on the patronage of firms like the Albatross (Glencoe) Travel Agency, which had presumably been seduced by the extravagant claims of its advertising and its near-criminal extended credit.

Albatross, in turn, made a virtue of necessity. "Why slog all the way to London?" it asked. "Fly cheaply, safely, and conveniently from Bleastead Moor—Britain's *newest* airport and your own special magic-carpet launching pad!" Nor did the lavishness stop there. Nothing was too good for Albatross customers. "Avail yourself of our *exclusive* pick-you-up-put-you-down service! We collect you *from your own home* at the start of your wonder-holiday, and return you there at the end! FREE! Ride in our *luxury* minibuses, driven by our own hand-picked, glad-to-serve-you chauffeurs! Ask yourself—WHO ELSE OFFERS YOU AS MUCH?"

Many an Albatrosser recalled these glowing promises and burning phrases as he wandered despairingly round Bleastead Moor's echoing Nissen huts. It was four o'clock in the morning, and our travellers were tired, bad-tempered, and stupid after their flight from Moscow. Inevitably, it had been one of those days, and nobody was really surprised that there was no sign of their luxury minibus or of their hand-picked, glad-to-serve-you chauffeur. There was no sign either of their Albatross courier ("We call them your smiling holiday friends") who was *guaranteed* to meet every package tour "to welcome you home, receive your appreciation, and hear your complaints (if any)." This probably saved a lynching, of course, but it was still very frustrating.

"They're crooks!" howled Jim Lewcock, in a right paddy because the customs had not only found but confiscated his packet of dirty postcards. When he thought of all the trouble he'd gone to to get them, he could have spat! You don't find pornography growing on trees in the Soviet Union, you know. "Bloody crooks!"

His brother was moving stiffly towards a row of fold-flat wooden chairs.

"You all right, Tone?" Jim Lewcock asked anxiously.

Tony Lewcock managed one of those long-suffering smiles as he lowered himself awkwardly onto the nearest chair. "Me bloody back's playing us up a bit," he allowed grimly. "Ooh"—he sank back—"but it's giving me jip!"

Though nobody else, of course, was suffering as much real pain as Tony Lewcock was, the other Albatrossers had their grievances. Most of them could be traced back to the long wait they'd had at the airport in Moscow. This was a pity because the day had begun quite well. True, there had been that dreadfully early start from Sochi, but it had been a lovely morning and they were *going* home. Only those who have themselves undergone a holiday in the Soviet Union will appreciate to the full the joy which comes flooding in when the end is in sight. Indeed, the Albatrossers were almost happy as they boarded their plane, weighed down with all their purchases that were too bulky or too fragile to pack in their suitcases. Miss Jones even accepted the alien presence of Miss

Clough-Cooper on the seat between her and the Hon. Con with a comparatively resigned heart. What did it matter, really? It was only a matter of hours now before she and dear Constance would be back in Acacia Avenue . . . alone.

They landed at Vnukovo Airport bang on time, and even then, their luck still held. Their bus was waiting for them and they were soon speeding round Moscow to the international airport, from where they were to take off for home.

Everybody checked his watch and agreed that they were going to be in good time. "If there's one thing I can't stand," they told one another comfortably, "it's being rushed."

Another of the ubiquitous Intourist guides was waiting for them at the departure terminal, and, almost as though the Soviet State couldn't wait to get rid of them, they were fed into a conveyor belt of extraordinary efficiency. The Hon. Con and Miss Jones cravenly kept as far away from young Roger Frossell as they could. If the Goddess of Luck wasn't on their side, this was where her displeasure was going to show. The boy, the Hon. Con noted miserably, was looking suspiciously fat, and she was certain that even the stupidest customs official would spot instantly that the young fool had got half that blasted manuscript strapped round his middle at the front and half round the back. "He looks like a pregnant penguin!" she had hissed at Miss Jones, and got a look of pained reproach in return. They shuffled forward in the queue.

Tickets!

Bang, bang!

Passports!

Bang, bang!

Baggage clearance!

"I hope you have enjoyed your visit to the Soviet Union. Goodbye and have a good journey!"

The Albatrossers were furious. They deposited themselves in one corner of the departure lounge and grumbled.

"They were a bit slap-dash, weren't they?" demanded Mr. Beamish indignantly. "We haven't been searched or anything. Damn it all, they didn't even go through our luggage. Well"—he pulled out his cigarettes—"if that's their idea of a security check, it damned well isn't mine!"

"I thought this was supposed to be a bloody police state!" Jim Lewcock chipped in, thoroughly incensed. "Blimey, we got ten times more of a going-over when we left bloody England!"

"It's just that they don't give two hoots."

Everybody turned to stare at young Roger Frossell, who was now grinning like a jackass with relief. He had been unable to carry out his original plan of hiding the manuscript in his mother's suitcase, and the strain of smuggling the thing through Russian customs himself had been all but overwhelming.

Desmond Withenshaw glared down his nose at the lad. "What are you talking about?"

"Simply that they don't care about hijackers or bombs or what-have-you," explained Roger Frossell, always willing to instruct his elders in the facts of life. "Not where we're concerned. We're flying on a British charter aircraft, you see, and there won't be a single Russian national on it—will there? So, the Kremlin couldn't care less what happens to it or to us. If we'd been flying on one of Aeroflot's planes, they'd have gone over us with a fine-tooth comb, don't you worry!"

"Oh, charming!" Zoë Withenshaw pulled a wry face, but she wasn't really either interested or worried. She turned to her husband. "Have I time to go to the ladies', Des?"

Mr. Withenshaw laughed. "Good heavens, yes! We've time to have lunch, if it comes to that."

The Hon. Con reacted swiftly to this thoughtless suggestion. "They'll give us lunch on the plane, won't they?"

Somebody muttered that they supposed so, but Mrs. Withenshaw's question had had an inspirational effect, and there was a bustle as coats and handbags were gathered up. Jim Lewcock led the deputation to the gentlemen's cloakroom.

The Hon. Con spotted that Penny Clough-Cooper was preparing to make a move. "You going somewhere?" she asked eagerly.

Miss Clough-Cooper swallowed down her first, thoughtless response and strove to speak more calmly. "Only to the ladies' and"—she was something of an optimist—"I don't need an escort!"

The Hon. Con was already on her feet. "No trouble, old fruit!" she trumpeted cheerfully. "It's what I'm here for! Bones, hold the fort for a couple of secs, will you?"

Miss Jones was busy looking at the inordinate number of snapshots Mrs. Beamish just happened to have brought with her. She barely had time to acknowledge the Hon. Con's request when yet another photograph was pressed into her hands.

"And that's Daddy!" said Mrs. Beamish proudly.

Miss Jones examined the thin, sour-faced man who scowled bleakly at the camera. "Very striking-looking!"

Mrs. Beamish dealt another snap. "And this is our house! Actually," she tittered coyly, "I was born there. Norman did want us to get a place of our own when we got married, but, as I said, what for? There was plenty of room for us all at 'High Tor,' and, in any case, I certainly wasn't going to leave Daddy all on his own." She sighed happily. "Isn't it a lovely house?"

Miss Jones, who had a natural affinity for stockbroker-Tudor, agreed that it was.

Gradually the afternoon wore on. The Albatrossers ate, slept, wandered around, quarrelled, and waited for the call that never came. All round, other voyagers took off for Helsinki and New York and Paris and Nairobi, and one flight even left for London, but the Albatrossers couldn't get on it.

"We have only ourselves to blame," declared Mrs. Beamish, and if the sentiment displayed true Christian resignation, the voice in which it was uttered certainly didn't. "One reads about charter flights and package holidays every time one opens one's *Daily Telegraph*. I'm only surprised that we haven't been completely abandoned long before this." She glared at her husband as though it were all his fault.

"I'll go and try to find out when we're due to take off," said Mr. Beamish with resignation. They had already made enquiries several times before, but anything was better than staying there and getting reproachful looks from his wife.

"Oh, save your energy!" Desmond Withenshaw came across to join them. "Eight hours!"

The Hon. Con had been cleaning out her ear with the tip of her little finger. She paused. "You can't mean we've got another eight hours to wait?" she said with an uncertain laugh.

" 'Fraid so. There's been some sort of hold-up at the other end, so they say, and our plane's supposed to be still on the tarmac in England."

"Jesus Christ!" said Roger Frossell. "Eight hours? What in God's name are we going to do for eight hours?" With the well-known prodigality of youth he had already exhausted all the sources of entertainment in the departure lounge.

Jim Lewcock had an answer to Roger Frossell's question. "We're going to get on one of them bloody airport buses, boyo," he said, "and hightail it back to town. God knows there's nothing much to do in that Moscow dump, but it's better than here. Come on, Tone!"

"You're wasting your time, Mr. Lewcock!" Desmond Withenshaw's mock-Oxford accent didn't make it sound any better. "I've already enquired about that and it's just not on."

"Not on?" The Hon. Con pushed herself into the centre of the group, anxious to show that her hand was still firmly clamped on the tiller.

Desmond Withenshaw backed off. "We've already gone through customs and passport control, you see."

Jim Lewcock threw up his hands angrily. "So, we can go back through 'em, can't we? Or are you trying to tell us that there's some bloody law against it?"

"It's our visas." Mr. Withenshaw remembered, a little too late, the traditional treatment meted out to bearers of bad news. "Our visas are only valid for one entry and one exit, so . . ."

"Bloody red tape!" For once, this objectionable adjective soiled the lips not of Jim Lewcock but of the Hon. Con. Even one of her impeccable breeding and upbringing could endure only so much.

Tony Lewcock turned away. "Got a fag, Jim?" he asked wearily.

His brother fished out a crumpled packet.

Tony Lewcock shook his head. "Bloody hell, haven't you got an English one?"

"No, I bloody well haven't!" Jim Lewcock's temper flared. "Have you? It's a bloody Russian one or nothing—and it has been for bloody days."

Mr. Beamish, caught with his packet of Rothman's king-size in his hand, hadn't really much choice.

The Lewcock brothers didn't need to be asked twice.

Jim Lewcock was suspicious. "How come you've got your

bloody duty-free left? You smoke three times as much as we do."

Mr. Beamish put the packet away in his pocket before it was snatched out of his hand. "My wife's ration."

"Oh. Oh well, I suppose that's one argument in favour of bloody matrimony."

In the end the Albatrossers were called upon to sit it out in that accursed departure lounge for a mere seven hours before, against all the odds, they were finally called out to board their plane. By this time Miss Jones wasn't the only one who fancied that she saw the hand of Fate in all these delays. She voiced her fears to the Hon. Con, who was already pretty irritable.

"Oh, don't be so wet, Bones! Of course we shan't crash! Why on earth should we? And"—she swung round threateningly on her chum—"if you start again on albatrosses being birds of ill omen and us being thirteen, I'll . . . I'll . . ."

Miss Jones bowed her head. "I shan't say another word, dear," she promised stiffly. "Just don't say I didn't warn you, that's all."

The Hon. Con bared her teeth and then, seeing the funny side, gave Miss Clough-Cooper, who was just ahead of her in the queue to board the plane, a conspiratorial thump between the shoulder blades. "Talk about seeing bogeymen under the bed! Old Bones is a proper dismal Desmond, isn't she?"

Miss Clough-Cooper didn't, as they say, vouchsafe an answer, but the Hon. Con took it all in good part, determined to allow nothing to mar the pleasure of going home.

The flight was uneventful, and even Miss Jones began to cheer up now that the end was in sight. They landed without incident, much to everybody's surprise and relief, and the Hon. Con leaned pleasurably across Miss Clough-Cooper to peer out the window.

"Golly gosh, wouldn't you know it!" she chuckled. "We're back in England, all rightie. It's raining."

Other passengers had noticed the weather, and there was a general outburst of murmuring as everybody scrabbled through his hand luggage in search of transparent rain hoods and telescopic umbrellas. One lady (not an Albatrosser) even produced a pair of little plastic booties which she proceeded to button on over her shoes.

The Hon. Con released the seat belt from across her tum.

"That's a jolly nice mac you've got there," she said smarmily to Penny Clough-Cooper as they taxied along the runway. "Dashed pretty colour, if you ask me."

Miss Clough-Cooper smoothed the folded dark green raincoat which she had placed in readiness across her knees. The plane swung clumsily round an invisible corner. "It's a perfectly ordinary raincoat," said Miss Clough-Cooper, trying to maintain a facade, at least, of common or garden politeness.

"It certainly is!" Miss Jones, having seen the chance to be catty, took it. "Everybody's wearing them. Mrs. Beamish has one just like it. The same colour and everything. I remember seeing it in Moscow."

"Really?" said Miss Clough-Cooper faintly.

The plane came to a stop, and at long last the Albatrossers were back in their homeland. They trooped almost gratefully into the customs hall and, with the exception of Jim Lewcock, trooped equally gratefully out of it.

But that had been an hour ago.

Where, they asked each other bitterly, was that bloody transport?

"Of course," said Mrs. Frossell, "we have arrived at a somewhat unseasonable hour."

Several voices hastened to inform her that that was no excuse.

Roger Frossell, cock-a-hoop with the success at his first smuggling venture, volunteered to go outside and see if he could find the coach that was supposed to be waiting for them. It was one way of getting away from his mother. Surrounded by their suitcases, everybody else settled down with an ill grace to wait.

"Blimey," shuddered young Mrs. Smith, "it ain't half nippy in here!" She pulled her thin fun-fur coat up round her ears.

Her equally young husband leered automatically. "I'll soon warm you up when we get home, love!"

"And if he won't, I will! I'm only waiting to be asked!" You couldn't keep Jim Lewcock down for long. Unfortunately, excitement tended to go straight to his bladder, and he pulled himself to his feet, blithely announcing to everybody that he was off to pass a pint. As had happened in Moscow, this gave everybody else ideas, and there was a mass movement in the direction of the ablutions block, an interesting if not historic edifice which had remained structurally unaltered since those halcyon days of 1940 when we stood alone and . . .

"You don't feel like paying a visit yourself?" The Hon. Con looked hopefully across the arrivals lounge towards Miss Clough-Cooper, who, this time, hadn't moved.

Miss Clough-Cooper turned a page in her magazine. "No."

The Hon. Con was near bursting. "It might be our last chance for a bit."

Miss Clough-Cooper turned another page. "Why should it be? Still, if you want to go, don't let me stop you. I shall be perfectly safe here."

But the Hon. Con knew where her duty lay. She hadn't guarded Miss Clough-Cooper all these weeks just to have the girl croak the minute they set foot on British soil. Until Penny Clough-Cooper was handed over into the care of her distinguished father, the Hon. Con had vowed not to let so much as one eyelid droop. And it was probably all in the mind, anyhow. The Hon. Con squared her shoulders, crossed her legs, and tried to think of higher things. She glowered at Miss Jones, who was placidly collecting up gloves and handbag. "Don't bother about me!" snarled the Hon. Con.

"I won't, dear." Miss Jones smiled a winsome smile.

Alone in the lounge, Miss Clough-Cooper and the Hon. Con continued to wait. After a bit Roger Frossell looked in and reported that he hadn't, as yet, even found the car park, never mind their bus. It was also still raining cats and dogs outside. "Have they got a snack bar in this dump?" he asked. "I could just do with a cup of coffee. Or a Coke." He looked round restlessly. "Think I'll go and explore." He disappeared and then, a moment later, came back again. "Oh, I almost forgot. Some little squirt said they were going to close this lounge in a couple of minutes. Put all the lights out and lock up, he said."

"And where the dickens are we supposed to sit then?" demanded the Hon. Con, outraged at the inconvenience this would cause Penny Clough-Cooper.

Roger Frossell shrugged his shoulders. "Search me," he said. "The joker did mutter something about the central concourse being available, but God knows where that is or what. You can't find anything in this crummy hole. P'r'aps that's where the others have gone. I'll go and see."

Miss Clough-Cooper shut her magazine with as much of a bang as she could manage. "I suppose we'd better make a move," she said, "before they plunge us into total darkness."

The Hon. Con gladly burdened herself with Miss Clough-Cooper's luggage in addition to her own. It was a pity about Miss Jones's modest suitcase, which had been placed neatly by her chair, but—the Hon. Con stifled a pang of conscience—old Bones should have thought about that before she cleared off. She (the Hon. Con) had, after all, only *one* pair of hands.

Bleastead Moor's passenger complex was far from being purpose-built, and what had served the Air Force reasonably well during the Battle of Britain is not necessarily ideal some thirty years on. The Hon. Con and Penny Clough-Cooper wandered up and down innumerable corridors and passages without, in the end, actually getting anywhere. They penetrated a number of offices and storerooms and even found the cafeteria. It was shut.

"Tell you what," said the Hon. Con, trying to make a joke of it as yet another promising-looking avenue turned into a dead end, "I think we're lost."

Penelope Clough-Cooper was looking anxious. "It really is too bad," she complained. "This place is like a rabbit warren. The least they could do is put up a few signs."

"Funny we haven't come across the others," said the Hon. Con. Her arms were aching, but she wasn't going to make a fuss about it. She was, rather, on the point of making some other cheerful observation about their predicament when the screaming broke out. It was loud, bloodcurdling, and coming from somewhere quite near.

Miss Clough-Cooper stopped dead in her tracks and all the blood drained out of her face. She went so white that even the Hon. Con noticed it and, dropping a suitcase, put out a supporting hand.

"Here, steady the Buffs!" advised the Hon. Con as Penelope Clough-Cooper swayed.

Miss Clough-Cooper pressed a trembling hand over the damp ivory of her forehead. "Perhaps we'd better go and see what's happened."

The Hon. Con was pawing the ground like an old war horse that hears the trumpets of war, but she hauled the overeager Miss

Clough-Cooper back. It was a good thing, she reflected, that somebody kept her head when all around were losing theirs.

Penny Clough-Cooper pulled herself free. "What on earth are you playing at?" she asked impatiently. "Somebody may be in danger out there!"

The Hon. Con generously forgave her. Well, you can't expect old heads on young shoulders, can you? "And somebody out there may be setting a trap for you, me girl!" she retorted. "Not that they'll catch an old fox like me napping, eh? Now then, we'll advance in good order—savvy? I'll go first and you stay close behind . . . whatever happens!"

SEVENTEEN

The Hon. Con had been shutting the stable door.

Mrs. Frossell was still screaming when Miss Clough-Cooper and the Hon. Con arrived on the scene, and apparently nobody in the small crowd which had collected thought of stopping her. They were all far too preoccupied with staring at the cause of Mrs. Frossell's hysterical outburst.

Huddled in a corner, half hidden by the automatic coffee-making machine, lay Mrs. Beamish. She was dead. Nobody had any doubts at all about that. There was something unmistakable in the dreadful stillness, in the awkward pose held uncomplainingly, and in the reddish-brown stain which was seeping through the full-blown roses of the head scarf.

"For Christ's sake, shut that bloody woman up!" Norman Beamish, paler if anything than the corpse, was the first to break up the tableau. He snapped angrily at young Roger Frossell, "Get your mother out of here, can't you?"

Suddenly everybody was moving and talking at once.

"I'll get a doctor," said Tony Lewcock, unable to tear his eyes away.

His brother shook his head. "It's the cops we want, Tone! Come on, let's find a phone!"

Miss Jones, a lace-edged handkerchief pressed to her lips, moved away to collapse on a bench up against the far wall. "I had a feeling something like this was going to happen," she wailed. "All day long I had a feeling!" She felt the Hon. Con's basilisk eye on her and fell silent.

Young Mr. Smith took a firmer hold on his wife. He looked sick and frightened. "Somebody ought to cover her up," he muttered crossly. "It's not decent, leaving her like that." He pulled his wife away, and they bumped into the Hon. Con, who was standing, mouth agape, right behind them. She was so taken aback by the unexpected turn events had taken that she didn't even think of rebuking the honeymooners for their clumsiness.

Young Mrs. Smith seemed to be in a complete daze. Her husband gave her another tug, and this time they knocked up against Miss Clough-Cooper. Young Mr. Smith mumbled an apology, but young Mrs. Smith drew back in horror.

"Oh, my God!" She pressed the back of her hand across her mouth. "Oh, my God!" Her eyes flicked in a panic from Penelope Clough-Cooper to the dead body and then back to Penelope Clough-Cooper again. She broke into a maniacal scream of laughter. "They've got the same bleeding coats on!" she shrieked. "Can't you see—they've got the same bleeding coats on!"

The Hon. Con was furious. She had, of course, already deduced that Mrs. Beamish had been done to death in mistake for Penny Clough-Cooper, and it was most off-putting to have a common little girl like Mrs. Smith stealing her thunder. Damn it all, who was supposed to be the blooming detective round here? Still, the Hon. Con wasn't one to blub over spilt milk (or over anything else, for that matter), and an astonishing theory was beginning to take shape in her head which, she would bet her boots, little Mrs. Loudmouth Smith wouldn't think of in a million years. Metaphorically rolling up her sleeves, the Hon. Con proceeded to take over the direction of affairs to such good effect that, when the police did finally arrive on the scene, there was really nothing much left for them to do.

The detective sergeant had different ideas, though. He waved the Hon. Con unceremoniously out of the way. "We'll get round to taking statements from you all later, missus," he assured her. "Meanwhile, if you wouldn't mind just standing to one side . . ." He grinned cheekily. "Sort of let the dog see the rabbit, eh?"

"Nobody has touched anything," said the Hon. Con, standing her ground and getting a nasty jab from a passing half-plate camera. "I saw to that. I knew you wouldn't want all the clues and fingerprints messed up. And"—she waved a piece of paper under the sergeant's nose—"here is a brief account of everybody's movements from the moment we disembarked from the plane to the moment Mrs. Frossell stumbled over the body. I think you'll find . . ."

A uniformed constable shouldered his way past. " 'Scuse us, ma!" He nodded at the sergeant. "We've got the lounge open, sarge!"

"Good!" The detective sergeant seemed to forget that the Hon. Con was there. "Well, get everybody rounded up and corralled in there, will you, Sid? And stand guard over 'em! Now, have those bloody policewomen arrived yet? And that bloody police surgeon? I thought this kind of emergency had been *planned* for. Well, we can't get very far until he's done his stuff. Fingerprints?" He turned away to deal with an importunate member of his entourage. "Well, and what do you propose to test for dabs, laddie? Now, use your brains! You know as well as me that we haven't found the murder weapon yet. I don't reckon it can be far, but . . ."

And there was nothing the Hon. Con could do about it. She was herded, just as though she were an ordinary member of the public, into the newly unlocked lounge and kept waiting there for what seemed like—and, in fact, was—hours. Her cunning ploy of demanding to be allowed out to the ladies' room was an ignominious failure, as she was escorted there and back by an apparently stone-deaf policewoman.

Miss Jones was naturally called upon to bear the brunt of the Hon. Con's frustration. "This is outrageous!" the Hon. Con had bawled when she was frog-marched back into the lounge. "It's an infringement of the liberty of the individual! I shall write to my MP about it! I shall write to the chief constable! I shall . . ."

A policeman bent down and tapped her gently on the shoulder. "No talking, ma!" he reminded her.

Even the thickest detective wouldn't have taken long to work out that the members of the Albatross package holiday were the prime suspects in the murder of Mrs. Beamish, and Detective Superintendent Mellor, who had arrived with the dawn to take over the investigation, was far from being thick. He devoted a great deal of his time to his work, as any man burdened with a wife, a mother, a mother-in-law, and five daughters is apt to do. A tall, anxious-faced man, he emerged from his car outside Bleastead Moor terminal buildings without any unduly high expectations. He quite liked murders, though. They made a bit of a change.

Superintendent Mellor's subordinates were well trained. An office, quiet and comfortable, had been commandeered for him, and the murder headquarters set up next door. The necessary staff and extra telephones and typewriters had all been installed, and somebody had even got the tea swindle going.

Superintendent Mellor was soon sitting back, warming his hands on a large, steaming cup of the stuff that cheers but does not inebriate, while his sergeant put him in the picture. The superintendent didn't believe in rushing in. Carefully and methodically he checked the murder diary, pored over the already prepared sketch plan of the scene of the crime, and ran a practised eye down the list of everybody who'd been in the vicinity when Mrs. Beamish had shuffled off this mortal coil.

"You can see that they'd hardly even got a skeleton staff on duty," said the detective sergeant. His name was Mortimer but Superintendent Mellor called him Tom. "Normally the place would be shut down completely at ten, but they had to keep open until this clapped-out old kite from Moscow staggered in. As far as I could see, the only thing the manager of this dreary dump bothers about is how much overtime his staff are clocking up. After ten o'clock last night, he was running the place on two men and a boy."

Superintendent Mellor creased his brow. "All the other passengers on that plane had cleared the airport?"

"Yes, sir. They'd left within twenty minutes of touchdown. The crew didn't hang about, either. The control-tower lot went and the customs . . ."

The superintendent scrabbled round on the desk. "Have we got a medical report yet, Tom?"

Sergeant Mortimer found it for him. "Preliminary, of course, sir. Seems we're looking for a pretty crude operator. He just ripped one of those fire axes off the wall and smacked her one across the back of the head. Well, more than one, actually. The doc reckons about six."

"Sounds like a nutter."

Sergeant Mortimer shrugged his shoulders. "Nutter or not, he wasn't daft enough to leave any fingerprints anywhere."

"Sure it's a 'he,' Tom?"

"Nope. Dr. Harvey reckons a woman could have done it, all

right. As long as she was strong enough to swing the axe, the weight of the head would more or less have done the rest."

"Oh, well"—Superintendent Mellor unbuttoned his jacket and loosened his tie—"I suppose we'd better be making a start or somebody'll be blowing his top. Any more tea in that pot, Tom?"

They'd been using teabags for donkeys' years, but Sergeant Mortimer didn't mind fostering the old boy's illusions. "I'll see if I can squeeze you another cup, sir," he promised. "What order do you want 'em in?"

"Oh—I'll see that woman who found the body first. Er—Mrs. Frossell. Then I'll take the rest in alphabetical order." He looked up. "We got any troublemakers?"

Sergeant Mortimer leaned across the desk and tapped one name with his pencil.

It was no skin off the superintendent's nose. "All right, we'll save her till the last."

Therefore, by the time the Hon. Con got her innings, Superintendent Mellor was satisfied that he'd got a pretty fair picture of the case and was even beginning to wonder about his lunch. Having examined the cafeteria kitchen during his preliminary inspection of the premises, he was not exactly sold on the idea of eating at the airport. Maybe there was a decent little pub nearby where they could get a sandwich and a decent glass of beer.

The Hon. Con's mind wasn't cluttered up with such mundane considerations. Sitting out there in the lounge, watching everybody get called out for his turn, she'd had ample time to think. And, in her experience, a rumbling stomach sharpened your wits quite considerably. So, if this policeman johnnie thought he'd taken the steam out of the Hon. Con by leaving her till last, he'd got—to coin a phrase—another think coming.

Superintendent Mellor watched impassively as the Hon. Con stumped in, took the chair that was offered her, and crossed one stout cavalry-twill–clad leg over the other. For a second or two they eyed each other curiously, and then, folding her arms, the Hon. Con took charge of the interview.

Superintendent Mellor listened with remarkable patience to the lengthy story of the Hon. Con's early life and easy times. "Very interesting," he murmured after a quarter of an hour of this rubbish. "Now, I wonder if we could perhaps get on with . . ."

The Hon. Con overdid her start of astonishment, and for a heart-stopping moment the superintendent thought that Sergeant Mortimer had done something unforgivable. The Hon. Con cleared her throat. "Don't think you've quite got the message, old chap," she rumbled.

The superintendent didn't want to be unkind. "On the contrary, Miss Morrison-Burke, I think I've got the picture quite clear, and I'm sure the assistance you were able to give the Totterbridge police was invaluable."

"Saved their bacon for 'em on two separate and distinct occasions," the Hon. Con pointed out modestly.

"So you said. However"—Superintendent Mellor opened a file and pretended to read it—"the situation we've got at the moment is somewhat different, and . . ."

"What's different about it?" demanded the Hon. Con truculently, forgetting all her good resolutions about being diplomatic. "Look, the Totterbridge constabulary co-opted me as a sort of unofficial advisor because of my expert knowledge."

"Your expert knowledge?" echoed the superintendent, trying to recall if there had been any mention of any useful accomplishment in the lengthy story of the Hon. Con's life.

"Because of my unrivalled knowledge of local affairs! I'm a storehouse of information where Totterbridge is concerned. I know the place and the people like the back of my hand, and . . ."

"But we aren't in Totterbridge," said Superintendent Mellor mildly.

The Hon. Con glared at him in exasperation. It was frightening to think how police standards were slipping. However, she took a deep breath and began to tell him all about the Albatrossers' ill-starred holiday in Russia. How no less than six attempts had been made on Penelope Clough-Cooper's life and how they had all jibbed at the idea of handing the problem over to the Russian police and how the Hon. Con, thoroughly experienced in dealing with serious crime, had been entrusted with the . . .

"Yes, yes, we've heard all this already." Sergeant Mortimer had got fed up with waiting for old Mellor to tell her to put a sock in it.

But the Hon. Con wasn't often blessed with a captive audience, and she wasn't going to be put off her stride by some snotty-nosed underling. She grinned encouragingly at Superintendent Mellor and continued with her story. Omitting nothing and concealing nothing. She frankly admitted all her initial doubts and lovingly detailed how her growing acquaintance with Miss Clough-Cooper, coupled with the cumulative effect of the attacks, had finally convinced her that the poor wee lassie's life really was in jeopardy. "From that moment on," she informed the punch-drunk policemen, "I never left her side, day or night."

Superintendent Mellor carefully avoided meeting his sergeant's eye. "We are bearing in mind, Miss Morrison-Burke, the strong possibility that Mrs. Beamish was murdered in mistake for Miss Clough-Cooper."

The Hon. Con slapped the desk in an ecstasy of delight. "Wondered if you'd spot that!" she boomed.

"We could hardly miss it," sighed Superintendent Mellor. "Every member of your package holiday pointed it out to us. They kept telling us that the two women were quite similar in build and colouring and that they were both wearing mackintoshes of pretty much the same colour and style. Then there was the lighting in that corridor. It was pretty dim. Yes"—he eased himself in his chair—"I think I'm prepared to admit that, from behind and in that light, our murderer may have mistaken one woman for the other."

"Oh, jolly dee!" said the Hon. Con, beaming her approval. "You're not as unintelligent as you look, are you? Well, I'm glad to see that you're capable of making the obvious deductions, at any rate. That's precisely what you were meant to do, of course, and it merely confirms my solution of the mystery."

Superintendent Mellor stared miserably at the Hon. Con. Women! "You're here to answer questions," he reminded her rather sulkily. "Now, where were you when you heard Mrs. Frossell scream?"

The Hon. Con took it all in very good part. "Come off it, fuzzy!" she advised. "You know where I was and that I've got a cast-iron alibi into the bargain. Penny Clough-Cooper can vouch for me—and I can vouch for her. Whoever murdered Mrs. Beamish, it certainly wasn't us." She hitched her chair nearer to the superintendent's desk. "Haven't you spotted yet what the cunning little minx was up to? She deliberately made use of me to beef up her own alibi. How's that for deviousness, eh?"

Superintendent Mellor had been pursuing his own train of

thought and now, foolishly, revealed it. The Hon. Con did tend to reduce strong men to infantilism. "Maybe you and Miss Clough-Cooper are in this together?"

The Hon. Con roared with laughter, slapped her thigh, and waggled a roguish finger. It was a blood-chilling sight. "Don't be potty, old fruit!" she bellowed. "And"—she took note of the superintendent's increasingly crestfallen mien—"do cheer up! You've nothing to worry about! I've got the whole caboodle buttoned up for you. Why"—the Hon. Con was grinning away like the Cheshire cat—"I wouldn't be surprised if you don't earn yourself a spot of the old promotion out of this little lark." She swung round and brought the full force of her personality to bear on a purple-cheeked Sergeant Mortimer. "Got your pencil sharpened, young fellow me lad? Good! Well"—she chucked the sergeant one of her more democratic grins—"sing out if I start going too fast for you. Slow but sure—that's going to be our motto!"

Sergeant Mortimer managed to keep a straight face—and men have been honoured by their king and country for less—but Superintendent Mellor had got beyond the stage of thinking that old battle-axes like the Hon. Con were just jokes. He had learned to be something of a fatalist over the years, and he also had a tendency to know when he was beaten. There were such things as irresistible forces, and unless he was much mistaken, he'd got one of 'em sitting right opposite him. He sighed. What was it Confucius had said about lying back and enjoying it?

Superintendent Mellor gave his sergeant a nod. Sergeant Mortimer picked up his pencil.

"Good show!" chortled the Hon. Con, always magnanimous in victory. "Now, Superintendent, let's start at the beginning of this pathetic little attempt to pull the wool over the peepers of yours truly."

Superintendent Mellor felt that he owed it to himself and to his sergeant to make one last effort in the cause of sanity and for the honour of the police. "It's getting rather late, Miss Morrison-Burke." He showed her his watch across the desk. "Don't you think it would be a good idea to postpone things until we've all looked after the inner man, eh?" The Hon. Con continued to look blank. "Until after lunch, that is."

"No," said the Hon. Con. "Now, exactly fourteen days ago, more or less, my close companion, amaneunsis, and dear chum, Miss Jones, and I departed from these shores for our holiday in the Soviet Union. Well"—she bethought herself in time—"when I say holiday, I don't quite mean holiday."

"No?" Superintendent Mellor disinterred his head from his hands.

"Actually, I was on a fact-finding tour," said the Hon. Con in a suitably awed voice. "For my book on social conditions behind the Iron Curtain. Going on one of these package tour things was just a blind so that those Secret Police johnnies wouldn't get wind of what I was up to."

"We've got all this preliminary stuff from the other witnesses," said Sergeant Mortimer. "They gave us very full and detailed accounts of the various attacks on Miss Clough-Cooper. I don't think we need waste your valuable time going through it all—"

The Hon. Con stopped him. "Not as full and detailed account as I am about to give you, laddie!" she boomed triumphantly.

And she was so right!

EIGHTEEN

It was one hour and thirteen minutes before the Hon. Con could be weaned away from her straight-from-the-shoulder regurgitation of her trip to the Soviet Union. She lost her audience on several occasions but got them back again by the sheer resonance and inevitability of her voice.

However, even the Hon. Con had her limitations, and when facts started getting a bit thin on the ground, she launched herself into the heady realms of speculation. Superintendent Mellor and Sergeant Mortimer exchanged glances of dismay.

"It may sound like hindsight," the Hon. Con rumbled on, "but, right from the start, I thought there was something deuced odd about those attacks on Penelope Clough-Cooper." She answered the query on Superintendent Mellor's long-suffering face. "For one thing, I couldn't believe that any potential murderer could be so jolly inefficient. Six blooming shots at it and, apart from that last bash on the head, not so much as a scratch on her. Made you think he wasn't really trying, eh?"

"Why didn't you say something, then?" asked Superintendent Mellor rather peevishly. "The rest of your party said you took the whole thing perfectly seriously. You appointed yourself investigator-in-chief, didn't you?"

"Only in response to popular demand!" snarled the Hon. Con. "And naturally I didn't care to share my suspicions with every Tom, Dick, and Harry. Besides, at that time I hadn't worked out what was going on."

"But now you have?" Superintendent Mellor's feeble attempt at sarcasm fell flat on its face.

"Came to me in a flash!" the Hon. Con explained cheerfully.

"As soon as I clapped eyes on Mrs. Beamish lying there in her gore, something went click inside the old brain-box. All the little doubts and suspicions and tentative theories slotted neatly into place. It was," she concluded demurely, "like a miracle."

Sergeant Mortimer ran a limp hand over his face. He could do with a shave. "Who did murder Mrs. Beamish, then?" he asked.

To everybody's astonishment, the Hon. Con came out with a straight, unequivocal answer. "Her husband, of course!"

There was a faint whiff of disappointment. The two policemen had expected something better than this from the Hon. Con. "Husbands are the automatic chief suspects in any cases of murder," Superintendent Mellor pointed out.

"You don't have to tell me that!" retorted the Hon. Con. "And you don't have to tell Beamish, either. Why else do you think he went to all this trouble trying to confuse the issue? That's what all these silly-billy games in Russia were about."

Superintendent Mellor frowned. "You mean that Mr. Beamish was responsible for all those attacks on Miss Clough-Cooper?"

"Not exactly. Because there weren't, properly speaking, any attacks on Miss Clough-Cooper. That girl"—the Hon. Con sighed over the joys that might have been—"is in this up to her back teeth."

The frown on Superintendent Mellor's face deepened. "But she was quite badly hurt in that last assault, wasn't she? She showed us quite a nasty-looking bruise, at any rate."

" 'Fraid she did that herself. She realised I was beginning to have my doubts and made one last desperate attempt to convince me." The Hon. Con changed legs and her chair creaked in sympathy. "It was all so crystal-clear, really. My preliminary investigations showed that." The Hon. Con was rarely averse to gilding the lily of her own genius. "I worked it out like this—an analysis of two or three attempts, never mind six, should have enabled us to isolate the attacker. Follow me? After all, we only had ten suspects." She saw the superintendent's head come up. "I exempted myself and Miss Jones from suspicion, of course. I mean, the more you looked into things, the more the whole bag of tricks just didn't add up."

Sergeant Mortimer suddenly had one of his brighter ideas. "Er—would you like a cup of tea, Miss Morrison-Burke?"

Miss Morrison-Burke would have given her eye teeth for a cup of tea, but she could recognise a red herring when she was offered one. She shook her head and sportingly refrained from making some cutting remarks about the lack of stamina in the present-day police force. There was no point in making enemies unnecessarily. She picked up the thread of her argument again. "So, under cover of professing friendship for the girl, I watched Penny Clough-Cooper pretty closely. As I said, I knew there was something screwy somewhere, but I couldn't for the life of me fathom out what it was. It was only with the murder of Mrs. Beamish that I found out for sure."

Sergeant Mortimer scratched aimlessly in his notebook while his superintendent scowled unhappily at the Hon. Con. "Are you accusing Beamish and Miss Clough-Cooper of being accomplices, miss?"

"I am!"

Superintendent Mellor took over again. "Have you any evidence?"

"Tons!" declared the Hon. Con roundly. "Take the cigarette smoke!"

"The cigarette smoke?"

"Penny Clough-Cooper is a nonsmoker. Right? So why did she buy her ration of duty-free cigarettes on entering the Soviet Union?"

"I can think," said Superintendent Mellor wearily, "of a thousand reasons."

The Hon. Con flung down the gauntlet. "Name one!"

"As a present for somebody."

"Precisely!" The Hon. Con's yelp of triumph cut straight through Superintendent Mellor's head. "And somebody is Mr. Norman Beamish, Esquire! He's the recipient! Smokes like a chimney. At least forty a day, on my caluclation. Now"—she saw the superintendent's mouth open and hurried on—"work it out for yourself. The duty-free ration is two hundred cigarettes—right? So his carton lasts him five days. His wife was a nonsmoker and her ration would last him another five days. Follow me? Making a total of ten days, after which Norman Puff-Puff Beamish should have been smoking Russian cigarettes, but he wasn't. When we were hanging round Moscow airport yesterday, Beamish was smoking

English cigarettes. Everybody else in our party who smokes has been on Russian cigarettes for days."

"Oh, blimey!" groaned Superintendent Mellor, gripping his hands until the knuckles went white. "Look, even if your hypothesis is correct—and there's no proof that it is—it still doesn't make Miss Clough-Cooper an accessory to murder. She could have given those blasted cigarettes to Beamish for a dozen perfectly innocent reasons."

The Hon. Con chuckled. Really, this chap didn't half walk right into it! "Name one!" she invited him again, joking this time. "No, never mind, because I agree with you. The duty-free cigarettes are little more than a straw in the wind. There is also the matter of the smell of cigarette smoke in Penny Clough-Cooper's hotel bedroom."

Superintendent Mellor looked for help to the heavens, but none came.

"My chum, Miss Jones, spotted it one day when she called unexpectedly on Penny Clough-Cooper. In Bukhara, it was. Somebody had been smoking in her bedroom. Now, who else could that have been except Norman Beamish? He can't go five minutes without lighting up, as we have all had ample opportunity to observe over the last fortnight. Another straw in the wind, you will say. I agree, but it still puts Beamish in Penny Clough-Cooper's bedroom on at least one occasion—and we all know what *that* means."

"Maybe they're old friends," said the superintendent, just to remind himself and everybody else that he was still there.

"Oh, I don't doubt that for one minute!" snorted the Hon. Con. "But they did their best to hide that particular fact, didn't they? And what about the golf?"

Superintendent Mellor swallowed his better feelings. Much better let the old girl get it all off her chest, he supposed. "What about the golf?"

"You may well ask!" blustered the Hon. Con. "Norman Beamish is a golf fanatic. His wife complained about it on several occasions. Said he spent more time on the golf course than he did in his office—you know the sort of thing. Now, on one occasion somebody—one of the Intourist guides, I think—asked Penny

Clough-Cooper if she played golf. She got curiously hot under the old collar and said, quite definitely, no—she didn't. It was a black lie!"

"You don't say!"

"Just before we set off for home, I happened to come across one of those silk head scarves. It belonged to Penny Clough-Cooper. No doubt about that at all, because I handed it over to her with my own paws. Funny-looking thing. It was a kind of paisley pattern, but when you examined it closely, you saw it wasn't at all the usual sort. Having played a bit of golf myself, I recognised it at once, you know. It was a special scarf for those lucky dogs who've done a hole in one, and so, naturally, it's a pretty rare old item. Actually, I've only ever come across one other woman who was entitled to wear one."

"But what about her brother or her father or a boyfriend? They might have won it, mightn't they? Couldn't they have given it to her, perhaps? Some men do hand their trophies over."

The Hon. Con. threw this suggestion right out the window. "Men get *ties,* not silk head scarves, laddie! No, Penny Clough-Cooper is a golfer all right and, by all appearances, a pretty keen one. Why deny it?"

"Because it might link her with Beamish?" Superintendent Mellor was mildly interested in spite of himself. "It's still frightfully thin."

"Let's move on to a consideration of Mrs. Beamish, then," said the Hon. Con, used to being surrounded by doubting Thomases. "Was she the sort of woman a husband would want to murder? Well, she was an inveterate grumbler, and she nagged Beamish day and night without cease. She was also ten years older than he, and he obviously couldn't stand the sight of her."

Superintendent Mellor shook his head. "Those are grounds for divorce these days, Miss Morrison-Burke, not murder."

"Money!"

"Money?" Superintendent Mellor leaned back in his chair. "She held the purse strings, did she?"

"Tightly," said the Hon. Con. "The Beamishes lived pretty well, you could see that. But she was footing all the bills—or her father was, which comes to the same thing. If Norman Beamish had got a divorce, he would have lost all that—and his job, too. The partnership in his father-in-law's firm was a wedding present. If Mrs. Beamish died, though . . ."

Superintendent Mellor beat a ruminative tattoo on his teeth with a pencil. "I wonder if they made wills leaving everything to the other? Lots of married couples do. Still"—he shook his head—"it's not what you might call evidence, is it?"

"Miss Clough-Cooper didn't look to me like a girl who'd be satisfied with love in a cottage, sir." Sergeant Mortimer's specialty was the female psyche, and he pushed his instant analysis even further. "Or that she'd go much on being the other woman in some mucky little divorce case." He noticed the look on Superintendent Mellor's face. "It's just the sort of impression she gave me, sir."

The Hon. Con. nodded in agreement. "And Mrs. Beamish would have kicked up a real stink," she pointed out. "Dirty washing and everything. The newspapers would have had a field day."

Superintendent Mellor stood firm. "This is still all theory."

"It's jolly well not theory that Penny Clough-Cooper went out of her way to look as much like Mrs. Beamish as she could," objected the Hon. Con. hotly. "Her clothes and everything. People were always mistaking them for each other, and that green raincoat was just the most obvious example. She changed her hair style, too, so that she would look exactly like her victim."

"Oh, come on!" interrupted the superintendent sceptically. "How on earth could you possibly know that? You told me you'd never met Miss Clough-Cooper before."

"Saw her passport picture!" retorted the Hon. Con. "She used to have her hair quite long. You check it! Bet you'll find she only switched to this short, wavy style just before coming on this holiday."

Behind the Hon. Con.'s broad back, Sergeant Mortimer held up his watch and tapped it. Superintendent Mellor took the hint. He put his pencil away in his waistcoat pocket. "Anything else?" he asked briskly.

"Holy cats!" exploded the Hon. Con. "What more do you want? Jam on it? Look, I'll spell it out again for you. Beamish and Penny Clough-Cooper were jolly good friends long before they came on this package holiday. It's my guess that they probably met playing golf, but however it came about, they know each other well enough for her to help him out with cigarettes and for him to visit her in her bedroom. Now, Mrs. Beamish obviously didn't know what was going on, and the only way Norman Beamish and his paramour could spend the rest of their lives together and still eat was to murder Mrs. B." A thought struck the Hon. Con. "A pound to a penny," she said, "that Mrs. Beamish was heavily insured and that her husband stands to collar the lot. You'd better check that, too. Now, where was I?"

"Was it Mr. Beamish's idea to go to Russia?" asked Superintendent Mellor.

The Hon. Con couldn't remember. "Of course it was!" she said firmly. "They wanted an environment where it seemed sensible *not* to report these murderous attacks to the police. Then they could build up the idea that Penny Clough-Cooper's life was in danger. Where better for a lark like that than the Soviet Union?"

"They were lucky to find you in their party," said Sergeant Mortimer with a grin. "In a way," he amended quickly as he caught sight of the look on the Hon. Con's face.

"In what way?" demanded the Hon. Con through a stiffening jaw.

"Only that you salved everybody's conscience by promising to carry out a proper, police-type investigation," said Sergeant Mortimer, trusting that the sky wouldn't come crashing down on his head. "With your experience as a—er—private eye, you see. Otherwise somebody might have insisted on going to the police."

"True," said the Hon. Con.

"I expect Beamish and Miss Clough-Cooper were thrilled to bits," Sergeant Mortimer went on, warming to his fantasies. "They probably thought they could fool you as easy as pie, so that, when Mrs. Beamish was finally killed, you'd conclude that it was in mistake for Miss Clough-Cooper."

Superintendent Mellor might have been a bit weak with the Hon. Con, but he had no intention of extending this indulgence to his sergeant. "That'll do, Tom!" he said heavily. "It's not our job to go round jumping to unfounded conclusions."

Sergeant Mortimer accepted the rebuke. "Sorry, sir."

Superintendent Mellor stared at the Hon. Con. "If," he said, "Beamish and Miss Clough-Cooper were really plotting to murder

Mrs. Beamish, why didn't they do it in Russia? I should have thought they stood a better chance of getting away with it over there. Once they were back in England, they must have realised that they'd have a full-scale murder investigation on their hands and that there was a fair chance it would uncover their illicit relationship, if any. I mean, once that's been established, we're home and dry, aren't we?"

"Oh, I think the reluctance to let the Russian cops get in on the act was quite genuine, don't you?" asked the Hon. Con. "Innocent or guilty, none of us wanted to get involved with that lot. That's why the murder really had to take place here at the airport—and while we were all still together, of course. That was very important. If they'd waited any longer, we should have all dispersed to our homes and this elaborate scheme they'd dreamed up would just have collapsed."

Superintendent Mellor was becoming painfully conscious of time's winged chariot. The pubs would be shut soon, and if he didn't get rid of this . . . He scraped his chair back and stood up. "Well, thank you very much for your help and cooperation, Miss Morrison-Burke!" The sincerity rang in his voice like a cracked cup. "I'm sure you've given us a great deal of food for thought, and I can assure you that we shan't forget you and your invaluable assistance."

The Hon. Con had risen to her feet too. Her disappointment was obvious. "I thought I might sort of work alongside you," she said.

Superintendent Mellor flashed her a frank, open smile. "But you've already done all the work for us!" he told her heartily. "All that's left is for us to do a few dull, routine checks. Not your line of country at all. Far too tedious and . . ."

"Checks?" The Hon. Con's frown was horrible to behold as the worm of suspicion began to gnaw. "What I've given you is the plain, unvarnished truth."

"We can't afford to leave any avenue unexplored or stone unturned," said the superintendent lamely.

"Ah, now I get it!" The Hon. Con grinned as comprehension dawned, and she sat down again. "You're worrying about the other chaps in our party! Well, I suppose they count as suspects of a sort, but you really don't have to go bothering your head about them."

"I don't?"

"Good grief, no!" The Hon. Con's grin became complacent. "I ran the old slide-rule over 'em ages ago. I've cleared them all."

"You—er—have?"

"Oh, not that I didn't have my doubts earlier on," admitted the Hon. Con, settling back in her chair, prepared to make a day of it. "That Frossell boy and his mother, for example. Now, he behaved in a most suspicious manner, but eventually I managed to root out what the trouble was. He was attempting to smuggle one of those illicit manuscript things out of Russia so that his uncle or somebody could publish it in the West. Frankly"—the Hon. Con was a bit of a Philistine, and occasionally it showed—"I dunno why they bother. Still, it wouldn't do for us all to be the same, would it? I did wonder, you see, if Penny Clough-Cooper had somehow latched onto what the lad was up to and threatened to blow the gaff on him, but it all began to look a trifle farfetched. Then there was Mr. Withenshaw, the artist. Did you know he was the only person who admitted to having known Penny Clough-Cooper before?"

"Yes," said Superintendent Mellor hurriedly. "As a matter of fact, we did. He told us all about it and . . ."

"My goodness, I kept an eye on him, all right!" chuckled the Hon. Con. "You see, on this weekend painting course where he was a teacher and Penny Clough-Cooper was a pupil, the lady he was with was not his wife! Get it? And you've seen Mrs. Withenshaw. She'd make mincemeat of him if she ever found out what he'd been up to. I did toy with the idea that he might have tried to kill Penny Clough-Cooper to stop her spilling the old beans, but somehow I couldn't quite make the whole thing jell. You know how it is. For one thing, you see, Penny Clough-Cooper didn't seem to know anything about the presence of this Other Woman, so she could hardly let that pussy-cat out of the bag, could she?"

"No," said Superintendent Mellor, looking haggard. "Well, thank you . . ."

"The Lewcock brothers were next on my list," rumbled the Hon. Con, rather pleased with the way her vague and muddled speculations were coming out in such an orderly and scientific manner. She hoped her two listeners were being suitably impressed. "Now, there's a couple of low-class crooks you bobbies ought to be keeping under surveillance. Do you know what they're up to?"

Superintendent Mellor consoled himself with the thought that, at least, he knew a lost cause when he saw one. He shook his head, secure in the knowledge that the Hon. Con would have enlightened him whatever response he had made.

"They are engaged in an insurance swindle," she said, her eyes growing round at the thought of all that money getting into the wrong hands. "The younger lout apparently twisted his back at work, and their trade union is going to sue his employers for thousands and thousands. There's not a dashed thing wrong with him, of course."

Superintendent Mellor smiled weakly. "I don't quite see . . ."

"Penny Clough-Cooper's father is an orthopaedic surgeon," explained the Hon. Con proudly. "I made a few discreet enquiries and found out that, from time to time, he undertook work in connection with insurance claims. Well, you can see how the old brain-box was working, can't you? Just suppose he was the medical expert called in by the insurance company used by the Lewcock fellow's employers to examine his reputedly crocked back. And suppose that, on her return from Russia, Penny Clough-Cooper told her pater all about her holiday and the people she travelled with." The Hon. Con glowered resentfully at the fidgetting superintendent. "Be perfectly natural, wouldn't it?"

"Er—yes—I suppose so."

"Well," said the Hon. Con blandly, "it wouldn't take an intelligent man long to put two and two together, and Lewcock's not all that common a name. Penny Clough-Cooper's father would have realised that this working class miscreant who had been bounding about up and down the length of the Soviet Union had absolutely nothing wrong with his blooming back or anything else. And he would have gone into the witness box and given expert evidence to that effect." The Hon. Con grinned cheerfully. "And the Lewcocks could have kissed goodbye to that garage then, couldn't they?"

Superintendent Mellor clasped his hands tightly round the back of his neck and pulled. Maybe that would relieve the tension. "What garage?"

"Oh, never mind the garage!" said the Hon. Con breezily. "I've cleared the Lewcocks of any involvement in the murder. Once I discovered that Mrs. Beamish was the real victim—and always had been—I crossed the Lewcocks off my list. Mind you, I still think you ought to get 'em on conspiracy to defraud, but I don't want to teach you chaps your job, eh? Anyhow, we can go into all that later. So"—she rubbed her hands—"that's the state of play as of this moment. I have examined all the other possible suspects and eliminated 'em."

"What about the Smiths?"

"Eh?" The Hon. Con swung round to glare at the author of this impertinence. "The who?"

"The Smiths," said Sergeant Mortimer, wishing he'd kept his mouth shut. "You didn't mention them." He checked his list again as though to prove he wasn't inventing the Smiths out of his own feverish imagination. "They were members of your holiday group."

"I know who they were!" snarled the Hon. Con, who did—now.

"I just wondered if you'd cleared them from suspicion."

The Hon. Con regarded Sergeant Mortimer through narrowed eyes. Was this unlicked cub trying to take the mickey? "I did not," she said, very slowly and deliberately, "clear the Smiths of suspicion because . . ."

Sergeant Mortimer waited with his pencil poised in midair.

". . . because I was never stupid enough to suspect 'em in the first place!" The Hon. Con's whoop of triumph echoed round the room several times.

Superintendent Mellor steeled himself to be ruthless. "Well, thank you very much indeed, Miss Morrison-Burke! Now, I'm afraid I'm going to have to ask you to excuse Sergeant Mortimer and me now. We've got some work to do. We don't want to haul Beamish and Miss Clough-Cooper up before a judge and jury and then have the case slung out for lack of foolproof legal evidence, do we?"

"We jolly well don't!" agreed the Hon. Con. In her eagerness to help the cause of justice she allowed Superintendent Mellor to place an assisting hand under her elbow. Under his firm guidance she rose from her chair, and Sergeant Mortimer leapt forward to get the door open.

Superintendent Mellor lowered his voice. "I wonder, Miss Morrison-Burke, if I could prevail on you to keep all this business quiet for the moment. Under your hat, eh?"

"Mum's the word!" hissed the Hon. Con. She held up two fingers. "Scouts' honour!"

They were over by the door. Superintendent Mellor clasped the Hon. Con's hand and shook it fervently. "Thank you so much—and goodbye!"

Sergeant Mortimer took his cue and the Hon. Con was through the door before she realised what was happening. The sergeant was quite ruthless. He bundled the Hon. Con down corridors and through halls and into a waiting police car before you could say Sir Robert Peel. No expense was to be spared and the police car was ordered to drive the Hon. Con home.

Back in the temporary police headquarters office, Superintendent Mellor was dragging his coat on when Sergeant Mortimer returned. "Move it, Tom!" he exhorted his sergeant. "We might just make it before they put the towel over the pumps."

Sergeant Mortimer snatched up his own raincoat. "I'm right behind you, sir! I reckoned we've earned ourselves a drink."

They walked quickly to the main gates of the airport.

"She was a real old cow, wasn't she, sir?"

"You can say that again, Tom! I dunno, I always seem to get 'em. There must be something about me that brings out the worst in middle-aged unmarried ladies."

"Somebody ought to certify her."

The superintendent grunted his concurrence with this uncharitable remark.

"You don't think," Sergeant Mortimer went on, shooting a doubtful glance at his boss, "that there's anything in what she said, do you?"

" 'Course not! It was a load of old rubbish from beginning to end." Superintendent Mellor had no wish to be the laughing stock of the entire police force. "Still"—they had reached the pub which stood just outside the main gates—"it mightn't do any harm to make a few enquiries."

"What sort of enquiries?"

"Well"—the superintendent shouldered his way into the Select —"we might as well see if there is anything in this idea that Beamish and Miss Clough-Cooper knew each other before. I mean, he's the natural suspect and if we could fit him up with a motive . . ."

"I'll ask around at Beamish's golf course, shall I?"

"That seems as good a place as any to make a start. Ah!" Superintendent Mellor greeted the barmaid like a long-lost daughter. "Two halves, please, miss!"

"Well, if there is anything between them, that's where it'll show up, I reckon." Sergeant Mortimer watched with longing as the two tankards filled up. He reached for his. "Cheers, sir!"

"Down the hatch," said Superintendent Mellor. He drank thirstily. "Ah, that's better!" He wiped his mouth. "Not, Tom, that I think there's anything in it for one moment, but it would just put my mind at rest."

"It's no skin off my nose," said Sergeant Mortimer amiably. "I'll get on with it right after lunch."

Superintendent Mellor is now in line for accelerated promotion, and the Hon. Con is going to have a shot at writing a detective story. She's just waiting for Miss Jones to learn shorthand before she makes a start.

Oh, and both Norman Beamish and Penelope Clough-Cooper got life.